T0095188

Gestapo 33

CLYDE DOYAL

iUniverse, Inc.
New York Bloomington

Gestapo 33

iUniverse books may be ordered through booksellers or by contacting:

iUniverse
1663 Liberty Drive
Bloomington, IN 47403
www.iuniverse.com
1-800-Authors (1-800-288-4677)

ISBN: 978-1-4401-8631-8 (pbk)
ISBN: 978-1-4401-8632-5 (ebk)

Printed in the United States of America

iUniverse rev. date: 10/28/2009

Author's Note

After World War I ended with Germany's defeat, several new political parties came to life in that country. Among them was the National Socialist German Workers Party, more commonly known as the Nazi Party. The Weimar Republic, the ruling government, was unable to halt a downward spiral in economic conditions in the 1920s and early 1930s. The government's failure led to a demand for change. The change came in the form of a dictatorship that would eventually incite World War II. In 1933, Adolph Hitler, leader of the Nazi Party, was appointed chancellor of Germany by President Paul von Hindenburg. Shortly thereafter, the most powerful secret police agency the world has ever known was created, the Geheime Staatspolizei, better known as the Gestapo.

Chapter One

In the fall of 1930, Major Konrad Becker, the military attaché at the German embassy in Washington, was enjoying the good life in America. He was engaged to a pretty young federal government secretary, who also happened to be the daughter of a U.S. congressman. In January 1931, Major Becker received orders from the German Army Command to report for duty at the defense ministry in Berlin the following October. This was devastating news for Becker as his fiancée had previously informed him that she would never leave the United States to live in another country. Major Becker had promised that he would not go back to Germany without her so he had to promptly confront the problem and seek a solution. . .

After conversations with the congressman and a state department official, Becker and his fiancée decided that it would be in their best interest for the major to apply for asylum in the United States and give up his commission as a German officer.

1

The State Department official involved in the case came up with what he thought was a brilliant idea: Why not substitute an American for Major Becker, returning that person to Germany as an undercover agent for the United States? After all, spying on other countries was almost a standard practice among civilized nations, whether friendly or otherwise. The men bounced around the idea, finally taking it to the secretary of state. The secretary of state took the idea to the secretary of war, and when he approved, officials in each department formed a joint task force to work out the details for the switch.

The main part of the puzzle would be to find a perfect match for the substitution. The first requirement was, of course, finding a person with similar physical attributes to Major Becker. Secondly, the man had to be fluent in German. From there, with plastic surgery, the transformation would be complete. The plastic surgery would be done by physicians at Johns Hopkins Hospital in nearby Baltimore.

The doctors examined Major Becker to determine the exact physical specifications that would be required for his substitute. The specifications showed the ideal candidate to be a white male, six feet tall and weigh180 to 185 pounds, athletic frame, sandy colored hair and brown eyes.

The officials searched exhaustively through military records and then colleges and universities to find their needle in a haystack. Among thousands of prospects, one man stood out. His name was Abraham Guttman.

Abraham Guttman had been born in Berlin in 1899. He migrated from Germany with his parents and landed at Ellis Island in 1912. He attended New York public schools, where he learned English. Upon graduation from high school, Guttman attended City College, where he earned his degree. He was later hired at that college as an assistant professor teaching German. The background check did reveal a potential problem. Young

Guttman had a reputation for being a tough guy, and did not seem to be ashamed of it or regret it. The officials decided that this problem might actually be a plus for the role Guttman would play if selected.

The next step was Guttman's interview with State Department official William Hopson and War Department Colonel Pete Burns. The plastic surgeon also attended. Colonel Burns initiated the conversation. "Mr. Guttman, the position we are seeking to fill involves government service and would require our selected candidate to work and live in a foreign country. We have purposely not given any details as to the duties or location because of the nature of the assignment. It involves covert action and secrecy; therefore the secrecy is extremely important not only to protect our country from exposure but to protect the safety of the person that is selected for this mission. Do you understand that?"

"Yes, sir," Guttman replied. "I have been told that there would be personal risks and that the work would be performed in a foreign country. I pretty much concluded from what I have been told that the job would involve, well, to put it bluntly, spying."

"Your conclusion is entirely correct, Mr. Guttman," said Hopson. "Pending the outcome of this interview, we are prepared to offer you a position with the U.S. government, providing, of course, that you are willing to abide by the necessary requirements. Are we clear on that, sir?" Hopson asked.

"Yes, sir, quite clear," Guttman responded.

"Mr. Guttman, I see from your application that you were born in Berlin in 1899 and left that country in 1912," Hopson said.

"Yes, sir, my parents decided to seek a better life for our family in America," Guttman replied. "My father was a watchmaker and fortunately was able to get a job and provide us with a decent living in New York City."

"Your name is Guttman, is that Jewish?" Hopson inquired.

"Yes sir, it is a Jewish name. My parents are Jewish."

"But you don't look Jewish," Hopson said.

"Neither do you, Mr. Hopson," Guttman said with a chuckle.

"Since I am not Jewish, your point is well taken, Mr. Guttman. You have a sense of humor I see," Hopson replied.

The meeting lasted a little more than four hours. The officials observed Guttman's mannerisms, attitude and personality. They listened to his German and asked about his willingness to agree to whatever assignment he was given, as well as his consent to have his facial features altered. The latter bothered Guttman somewhat, but he changed his mind when he saw a photo of the face he would wind up with. There was no question that Becker was an extremely good looking man. The plastic surgeon examined Guttman and assured the group that the plastic surgery would be easy. At the end of the meeting, Hopson looked at his fellow officials for a sign of approval.

After receiving a nod from Burns, Hopson asked, "Will you accept our offer, Mr. Guttman? If you would like to think it over, please feel free to do so. We only require that you speak to no one about this matter. Do you have any questions for us?"

"No, sir, not at this time," Guttman replied. "I think I know enough and, having thought about this from the beginning, I am prepared to accept your offer. I promise to faithfully carry out my assignment. As a foreign-born, naturalized American citizen, I would consider it a great honor to serve my adopted country."

Everyone stood, and Hopson extended his hand to welcome Abraham Guttman aboard. After the hand-shaking was over, Hopson asked when Guttman would be available to start his new job as a foreign agent for the United States.

"I will immediately tender my resignation to the college and give the customary two week notice," Guttman said. "I will report for duty in two weeks, so all I need to know is where and to who do I report to."

"Good question, Guttman," replied Hopson. "You will report to Colonel Burns at his office."

"Thank you, sir," Guttman replied. "And now I have a question to which I think I know the answer: To what country will I be assigned?"

"Germany," Burns answered.

"That is what I thought," replied Guttman, "and I am pleased that it is a country that I am somewhat familiar with. It should make my task much easier."

For the next step, Hopkins contacted Becker and scheduled a meeting. If there was no hitch there, then plastic surgery would be scheduled.

Chapter Two

Becker and Guttman met in a Washington Hotel room. Hopkins thought that the two should never meet in public as a precaution. Becker and Guttman spoke mostly in German and were compatible. The major told Guttman about his background and his duties at the embassy and as an officer in the German army. This meeting would be one of many in order for Becker to indoctrinate Guttman on German military policy and procedures. The meetings would also afford Guttman with the opportunity to familiarize himself with Becker's mannerisms and speech patterns. Guttman clearly had much work to do in this area to avoid the suspicions of Becker's acquaintances. The small group of American officials that was involved had a great deal of optimism that placing a spy in German Military Intelligence would be of great benefit to the United States.

The next step was to transform the appearance of the new Becker to that of the real Becker. At the end of April, Guttman entered Johns Hopkins Hospital for plastic surgery. A team of surgeons headed by Dr. Alfred Connell would be doing the surgery. In addition to facial change, it would include body marks such as a scar on Becker's lower back from the wounds he incurred as a young soldier in World War I. Becker would be there for the surgery, which lasted more than nine hours, so that doctors could make a close comparison and observe detail.

Several days after the operation, nurses removed Guttman's bandages. Dr. Connell declared the operation a total success. Looking in the mirror, Guttman could hardly believe that he was looking at himself. The person he saw in the mirror was Konrad Becker.

Now Guttman could resume the task of filling in the details of Konrad Becker's life. All of this had to be done before Becker was required to return to Berlin for duty. From this day forward, Abraham Guttman would be Major Konrad Becker of the German army.

The original Becker would later receive a new name and be placed in an undisclosed location with his fiancée.

After Guttman's release from the hospital, all the meetings between the old and the new Becker took place in hotel rooms and private homes around Washington. This ensured privacy and helped avoid suspicion from the German Embassy and others that might pose a threat to the program. The two men met daily, sometimes during the day and other times in the evening. They scheduled the meetings around Becker's work at the embassy. The meetings covered many topics, including background information on Becker.

Guttman learned that Konrad Becker was born June 19, 1898, in Munich. He was the first and only child of Otto Becker, then an army lieutenant, and Gertrude Becker. Otto later rose to the rank of general.

Young Konrad had attended *Grundschule,* or elementary

school, until the age of ten and then he attended Grand Gymnasium until he graduated in 1916. Upon graduation from Grand, Becker entered the military academy in Berlin. Then he was commissioned lieutenant and sent to the Western front. He was wounded and returned to Berlin for his recuperation.

Having served in intelligence, Becker was familiar with most Nazi leaders because the Weimar government had dealt with them, mostly under adverse conditions. Becker knew about Goring, Himmler, Goebbels, Rohm and other prominent party hacks. He shared all the information he had with Guttman. Having information on incidents that involved Goring would open the door for the new agent to establish a relationship with him. Infiltrating the Nazi hierarchy was one of the main goals of the plan.

In August, the time came for the new Becker's first real test. He made his first appearance at the embassy in place of the original Becker. Guttman started at a half day. Surprisingly, he did not feel nervous that first day, and no one seemed to notice the difference. This was a great confidence builder.

After a few half-day trial runs at the embassy, Guttman began staying for full days. He occasionally did not recognize people, but mostly the appearances went smoothly. Becker's coworkers assumed the lapses were because of lack of concentration or being preoccupied by the upcoming return home. Finally the agent was as ready as he was ever going to be, and time was fast approaching for his return to Germany. Becker announced to the embassy staff that he had broken off his engagement to his fiancée because of her refusal to leave America.

Chapter Three

In October of 1931, the new Major Konrad Becker prepared for the flight to Berlin. He was to report to Colonel Leon Richter for duty on the staff of General Kurt Von Schleicher at the Ministry of Defense. This assignment would place him in the military police unit of the Ministry of Defense.

On a cold, wet day in early October, Major Becker boarded the Graf Zeppelin for a flight from Lakehurst, New Jersey, to the Zeppelin Base at Friedrichshafen, Germany, to enter an exciting and dangerous new life. One mistake could result in the loss of his life and a failed mission. Among his instructions were to ingratiate himself with important Nazi leaders. Despite the many information sessions with the real Becker his efforts to share even the most minute details, it remained likely that something or someone had been overlooked. Though the new major had studied photographs and facts about Becker's former associates, there would be occasions when future recognition would be difficult. In such cases, he would have to work his way through the situation. His only contact with American authorities would be through a man named James Fritsch, an employee at Deutsche Bank. Fritsch was also an undercover agent. He worked for the British government. The code word for Becker's meeting with Fritsch would be "'The Kaiser must be turning in his grave.' They would speak only to establish their initial meeting and any future contact, when information was to be transmitted. As in the meetings between the two men, utmost discretion must be used to avoid detection by the Germans. The new Becker was provided $2,000 for his journey. This was a substantial amount of money, but not enough to raise suspicion or questions about where it had come from. He would later deposit the money in the Deutsche Bank, where he would have the opportunity to meet banker Fritsch. Becker's compensation for employment would be $225 per month, which would be deposited in a trust account in his name in a bank in Washington.

As the flight ascended over Lakehurst, Becker thought about what the future might hold. He looked down and wondered if he would ever see America again. But his thoughts quickly turned to what he was going to do when he reached his destination. Where was he going to live? He knew he did not want to live on a military base. U.S. officials had given Becker locations of apartments that might be of interest, and he would just have to check them out when he arrived in Berlin. His thoughts from now on would have to be the thoughts of Major Konrad Becker. Abraham Guttman no longer existed.

Becker wondered how he would go about his assignment once he reported for duty. He knew that he would be working in the military police security unit in the Ministry of Defense. This position would allow him to meet the right people in the Nazi Party without arousing suspicion. Of all the people he had been encouraged to get to know, he decided his first effort would be

Hermann Goring. Goring was close to Hitler and appeared to be the most powerful among those surrounding Hitler. If Becker was unable to cultivate a relationship with Goring, then he would be forced to try one of the other names that he had been given.

After what seemed an eternity, the large aircraft made the final approach to land at Friedrichshafen airfield. On the ground, Becker's first test awaited him. The driver who was to pick him up had seen photographs of Becker, so there should not be a recognition problem. The real recognition test would come when Becker reported to his new office for duty. Fortunately the original Becker had been away for four years, so that should dim people's memories. Sooner or later, the new Becker would certainly meet people he was supposed to know, but he would have to wait for that scenario to play itself out. The giant airship landed softly. As Becker set foot on the ground, he noticed that the weather was similar to what he had left behind in New Jersey: in the forties and windy. As he entered the terminal, he saw an army sergeant headed in his direction.

"Major Becker?" the man asked.

"Yes sergeant?" Becker answered.

"Sir, I am Sergeant Gerhard Heinz, your driver."

After the two exchanged introductory greetings, Heinz directed Becker to a waiting car, loaded the major's baggage and headed for Berlin.

"How was your flight, major?" Heinz asked.

"The flight was amazing, sergeant. The views from up there are incredible," Becker replied. He told Sergeant Heinz to take him to the *Tiergarten* Hotel, where he had reserved accommodations. These would be temporary living quarters until he found permanent, more affordable housing.

On the long drive to Berlin, Becker engaged the driver in conversation on a number of topics, including small talk and a lot of questions. Becker asked about Heinz's family, the weather and current events. Becker was eager to soak up as much information as he could, knowing that it was important for him to be familiar with things that German citizens would take for granted.

After arriving at the hotel and checking in, the major instructed Heinz to pick him up the next morning to take him to his new office, located at Prinz Albrecht Strasse 8. Becker unpacked and then decided to take a stroll to see some of the sights. He was in a city that he had not seen since he was a young boy. The temperature had dropped into the thirties, but the wind had subsided, and he felt quite comfortable. There were fewer automobiles than he was used to in Washington and consequently much less noise to interfere with his enjoyment of the city.

Becker was taken aback by the beauty and the majesty of what he saw as he strolled down Unter den Linden. It brought back memories of his childhood. In spite of having been born in Germany and all the cramming he had done, he realized that he knew little about Berlin and practically nothing about Germany as a whole. He spent the next two hours walking and taking in the sights.

There was the Reichstag, where the parliament and other government offices were housed, and the famous Brandenberg Gate. Becker had vague memories of both but nevertheless stood in awe as he took it all in. He marveled at the site of the huge, domed Reichstag building. He was struck by the beauty of the Brandenberg Gate, with its twelve columns and the chariot sitting on top of the structure. Deciding that he had seen enough for the evening, he returned to the hotel, went to his quarters and retired for the evening.

Chapter Four

Upon arrival at the office the following day, Becker was introduced to his immediate staff, consisting of a secretary and an aide, in addition to his driver, Sergeant Heinz. The secretary was Berta Stecht, a slightly overweight blond woman in her mid-thirties. Becker's first impression was that Stecht was pleasant and appeared to be competent. Taking an all-business approach, Becker was glad that there were no flappers or beauty queens in the office. They would only be a distraction. His office was situated to the left of the main reception area. It was not very large but did have a good view looking over the city, and the furnishings were adequate.

The aide was Captain Kurt Schwarz. Schwarz was a blond German who was thirty-five years of age. He was six feet tall and of medium build, and he looked like the typical Prussian officer. Schwarz's office was to the right of the reception area. Becker spent most of the morning being briefed by Captain Schwarz on the duties and routine of his new position.

That afternoon, Becker met his immediate superior, Colonel Leon Richter. Richter was a jovial, aristocratic person, and Becker felt quite comfortable with him. Richter was fifty and slightly balding. He delighted in telling his war stories and provided Becker with a great deal of information on what had been taking place in Germany while Becker was away. It became apparent that Becker would have little contact with the minister, General Wilhelm Groener and General von Schleicher, and that suited him just fine.

"Major, if you like, we will go over to the ministry office and meet some of the people you will be working with," Richter said.

"Yes, thank you, colonel. I would like that," Becker said.

They walked over to the ministry office, which was just a short distance from their building, to meet the general and his staff. Upon entering the general's waiting room, Richter introduced Becker to a young woman in her early twenties named Sara Klein. Sara was a five-feet-five-inch, 110-pound blonde with a flawless olive complexion. She had the attributes of a beauty queen, with ice-blue eyes and a smile that took Becker's breath away. Sara had an hourglass figure but was not overly endowed. She was friendly, and her demeanor seemed to suggest a connection that offered the possibility of something more than a casual introduction. The new Becker was somewhat reserved in first-time meetings with members of the opposite sex, but he was quite taken with Sara and thought she picked up on that right away. She was everything a man would wish for in a woman except she was married and therefore unavailable.

After a few minutes of chit chat, Sara ushered the men into General von Schleicher's office. He was bald, sixty years old and amiable. During the course of his conversation with the visitors, the general made it clear that he did not like Hitler. Von Schleicher was quite informative on the political situation.

"I can't stand the little bastard," the general said, "or the rest of the damn Nazi movement."

"What about Hermann Goring?" Becker asked.

"I don't have any use for that fat son of a bitch either," the general said.

After an hour of conversation, the major thanked the general for his generous hospitality and excused himself.

Becker spent a couple of hours with Colonel Richter and received instructions and a briefing on what his duties were. Then he guided the conversation back to Goring. "Colonel, I need to know as much about the Nazi movement as possible, since we may be looking into their activities," Becker said.

"We are headed for big trouble with the Nazis, and you are right, you should know as much about them as you can. I know you have been away for the last four years, and much has changed. They are not only a threat, but I predict that before too much longer, they are going to take over this country. Mark my words." Richter said with a look of worry.

Becker was focused on finding ways to gather information that would be useful for his mission. Richter told Becker what he knew about Goring and other Nazis. It turned out not to be as much as Becker would have liked.

"I do know of an individual who is associated with Goring," Richter volunteered. "His name is Karl Braun, and perhaps we should make an effort for you to meet him."

"Yes, Colonel Richter, that is an excellent idea," Becker replied.

Richter said he hoped a meeting with Braun would lead to an opportunity for Becker to meet Goring.

"If you can arrange such a meeting," Becker said, "it will give us the chance to make inroads into what these people are thinking and doing. Perhaps we should also keep this conversation we are having go no further in order to protect our involvement with such an investigation."

"Braun and a number of Nazi bigwigs frequently hang out at Gus beer hall only a few blocks from the office," Richter said. "I suggest we drop by the beer hall occasionally in hopes of running into Braun."

"Good idea, colonel. Let's start today," Becker said. They agreed to start the plan that very day. "I must take care of some business at Deutsche Bank, colonel, so if it is convenient for you, I will meet you at Gus' at six. My driver will know where to drop me off."

"Six it is," Richter agreed.

Major Becker left the office and had Heinz drive him to the bank. When they arrived, Becker asked the receptionist for James Fritsch. She called him to the lobby. In two minutes, a tall, thin gentleman in his fifties with a handlebar mustache appeared.

"Good afternoon, I am James Fritsch," the man said. "May I be of service to you?"

"Yes, how do you do, Herr Fritsch?" replied Becker as he whispered the code."The Kaiser must be turning in his grave."

"Welcome to Germany, major," Fritsch said. "I have been expecting you. I hope your trip was pleasurable and that we can help with your banking needs. Please, if you will, let's step outside for a moment while I have a cigarette Our president does not like for us to smoke in the building.

The two found a bench in the atrium. Fritsch warned Becker that they must be careful in their meeting so they would not attract attention. "There are members of the Nazi party that have infiltrated our bank, and they are watching everything and everybody," Fritsch said.

"I understand. I just wanted to make this initial contact to be sure everything is in place," Becker replied.

"Yes, as you know, we do not have much of an operation here at this time. I have warned my superiors that things are becoming increasingly dangerous in Berlin. I am afraid the Weimar Republic will fall at any time, and that bloody rascal Hitler will take over the country. It is quite serious indeed," Fritsch said.

"I understand," Becker said. "I will try to make contact with Hermann Goring as soon as possible. I feel he is our best bet to get inside their heads and establish some sort of relationship."

"Splendid idea, but do watch your step," Fritsch warned. "They are a ruthless lot."

"Yes, I know," Becker replied. "I must get back to my office. I will only contact you when it is necessary. If you need to get in touch with me, you may reach me at this number." Becker handed the agent a number. "Now I will bid you good day, and I will open an account in the bank, if you will direct me."

"Certainly, I will be happy to assist you." Fritsch summoned a clerk to handle opening the account so that Becker could make a deposit. Now Becker had a bank account with enough money to spend and a contact that would assist him in carrying out the assignment.

Becker arrived at the beer hall at six o'clock and saw Richter sitting in the corner with a civilian. He went over, and both men stood. Richter introduced Becker to Braun. "Braun, Major Becker has just returned from America and is now with the intelligence division of the military police" Richter said. "I am pleased to meet you Major Becker" Braun said "We could use a friend in that position" he quickly added. "Who do you mean by 'we'?" Becker asked. "The Nazi party sir" Braun replied. Becker ordered a drink, and they discussed mundane matters to break the ice. Braun was anxious to let them know that he had lots of connections and was an important man. He mentioned that he made a living as a political consultant and public relations agent. He was short, only five and a half feet tall, and middle-aged. Braun walked with a slight limp, which he explained in great detail was due to war injuries.

After about thirty minutes of small talk, Richter excused himself and left for home. It became obvious that Braun was quite interested in Becker's background and new assignment.

"I have some important people that you should get to know," Braun suggested.

"I am open to meeting important people," Becker answered.

Becker, a keen judge of character, knew where the man was coming from. The Nazis were always interested in someone who could help their cause. The Nazi movement was growing more powerful and gaining in popularity each passing day. Without showing too much enthusiasm, Becker indicated that he was approachable and might be willing to do business. The pair had several drinks and, after a couple of hours, Becker decided it was time to go.

"There's a very important associate of mine that you should get to know," Braun said. "He is going to be at the top of government when we take over Germany."

"All right, let's cut to the chase," Becker said. "This all sounds good, but I don't have time to waste on second-rate hustlers. I don't want to talk to people who don't have any authority."

"Oh, no, it's nothing like that," Braun said. "I'm talking about one of the highest-ranking officials in the Nazi party."

When Becker gave him a look of interest, Braun went on, "The associate that I am talking about is the number two man in the party, Hermann Goring. You can get no higher than that except Hitler, and I don't have that kind of clout."

"I know of Goring and his position in the party," Becker said. "He is a person I could deal with. He has the reputation of being trustworthy. I would be most happy to meet Herr Goring under the right conditions, but no one is to know about the meeting except you and Goring. Now get this," Becker continued with a stare, "I don't like being played. If you try to pull something over on me, it will be the last thing you ever do. Understood?"

"Absolutely, major," Braun said. "You can trust me. I will contact you with a time and place for a meeting. Please be assured that it will be discreet and under protected circumstances appropriate to your and Goring's statuses."

It suddenly dawned on Becker that it was not necessarily in the best interest of a young German army officer to be cavorting with one of the Nazi party's most prominent individuals like Goring even though at the time Goring was a member of the Reichstag. "Braun, the hour is getting late so I will bid you a good evening and expect to hear from you soon" Becker said as he got up to leave. "Yes sir, Major Becker, I will be in touch as soon as I can make the arrangements" Braun replied.

As Becker returned to his quarters that evening, he wondered whether he could trust Braun in having enough influence to do what he said he could do. The answer, of course, was no, but it made no difference because his real mission was to get Nazi's to trust him. He went to bed thinking about what would happen next.

The next morning, Richter dropped by Becker's office and asked how things had gone with Braun.

"It went well," Becker said. "The meeting was enlightening and beneficial I think" he added."

"Good. Incidentally, you made a favorable impression at the ministry office yesterday, particularly with the ladies, and specifically with Sara Klein. Sara is our trophy sweetheart and, as you no doubt noticed, quite a looker. Everybody that sees her becomes enamored of her. I must say, though, this is the first time I have seen her so animated with a man. She is normally a friendly person, but not to the extent that I saw yesterday. I must warn you, though, she is married to some little shit over at the chancellery, and he is very jealous. He has made it pretty obvious that he would not take kindly to anybody that expressed an interest in Sara. That hasn't stopped admirers from trying to make it with her, although you are the first man that I have seen that has lit a spark in her pretty little face. I still can't get over the way she acted after you left. She was beside herself. What is your secret?"

"That is flattering, but I have no interest in cultivating relationships with women that I work with," Becker said. "I will say, though, that she did not go unnoticed. My question is, how come a woman that good-looking is working in a government office?" As good as Sara looked, he felt like he should pass on her, at least for the time being.

The major realized that the conversation had strayed from the main subject matter, the conversation with Braun. "Colonel, getting back to business, Braun was eager to set up something with Goring. He said he would contact me with the details of a meeting. I anticipate that it will take place soon."

"Very good," Richter said, "sounds like our plan is in motion. This operation will remain covert, at least for the time being. And by the way, this conversation is for your ears only."

"Certainly," Becker said, "and I appreciate the confidence that you have placed in me. I will keep you abreast of my dealings with Herr Goring."

"Thank you, and do be careful of Sara's husband, Karl Klein. He is a nasty little bastard, and if he finds out about you, and knowing Sara, he probably will, he will likely try and cause you some problems. I don't really know what he does over at the chancellery, but he seems to think that he is a power to be reckoned with," Richter added.

"Thanks for the warning," Becker said. "I will tread lightly, but if he does try to cause me a problem, he will regret it. And be sure and thank the staff members at the ministry for their gracious welcome. I look forward to a long and happy relationship with all of you."

The next morning, Major Becker called in his aide, Captain Schwarz for a meeting. The major's first impression of the captain was that he was likable and would be useful. The captain also had heard that the major was a big hit with the ladies at the ministry. He also was very high on Sara Klein and warned Becker that she could be trouble with a capital T. "Thanks captain, but I have already been warned about the Kleins" Becker replied.

Since they were primarily involved in security and intelligence, it was not only quite proper for them to take an interest in the Nazi party and its members, but it was expected that they should do so.

"Sara was quite vocal in her praise of you," Schwarz said. "Her husband must be neglecting her. I'd give my right arm for her to give that kind of attention to me."

"Settle down," Becker said. "It's my understanding that she is a happily married woman. Anyway, you are welcome to her. I've got more important things to do than to get hooked up with some crazy woman that has a crazy husband."

"Guess you are right," Schwarz replied, "and you are absolutely right about that little asshole of a husband of hers. They say he watches her like a hawk, but then he goes around trying to bed every woman he runs into. She would make a good contact over there for us, though. You might think about that angle."

"Don't worry, I'll be nice to her," Becker said. "Like you said, she could be useful to us."

It didn't take long for Braun to resurface. Obviously the Nazis' interest was high. Braun called Becker two days later to set up a meeting with Goring at 8 PM the next day at Braun's residence on Primrosestrasse (street). Becker did not want his driver to know about the meeting so Braun arranged for a car to pick Becker up at the *Tiergarten* at 7:30 PM.

When Becker arrived at Braun's house, he was greeted by Braun and a storm trooper and promptly escorted to the parlor, where Hermann Goring was seated. Goring stood and extended his large hand to Becker. After a firm handshake, the two sat down and began their meeting. As Becker had expected from previous descriptions, Goring was a large man and was courteous and friendly. Goring's attitude wasn't a surprise, since Becker knew that the Nazis wanted to establish a relationship that would benefit their cause.

"Major, it is a great honor to meet you," Goring said. "We have looked into your background, and we are impressed with your war record and military credentials." "Thank you, Herr Goring," Becker replied.

"Just call me Hermann. Let's drop the formality."

Ignoring the invitation for intimacy, Becker replied, "I know you are a busy man, sir, so I'll cut to the chase. I have heard a great deal about you, and I have nothing but admiration for you," Becker lied. "I think we both have something to offer. As for me, I am willing to offer my service and loyalty to you. In return, I would expect you do likewise.

"That is quite generous of you major, and I will be most happy to return the favor," Goring said. "You may rest assured that in the not-too-distant future, our party will take control of the government. I assure you that you will be properly rewarded for your service. We desperately need military men of your stature. Our Storm Troopers are a ragtag outfit and offer nothing in the way of military strength. They will be discarded after we take control of the country. We are going to need the army, and this is where you can help us."

Goring was confident in his presentation. Becker beginning to conclude that Goring was right: It was just a matter of time before the Nazis would succeed. Based on what Becker was hearing it was inevitable that Adolph Hitler would be elected the head of the new government.

Becker agreed to provide information to Goring and exert influence on local police in cases where members of the party were arrested for alleged crimes against the state. The meeting lasted well past midnight, and Major Becker could tell he had made a good impression on Goring. Goring was affable and commented that he was pleased with their meeting and that Becker had exceeded his expectations. The two decided that Becker would deal directly with Goring, and that Braun would no longer act as a go-between.

During his daily briefing, Becker informed Richter about making contact with Goring and said the meeting had been pleasant. However, he did not reveal the details of the meeting, nor did he discuss the pact he made with Goring. Revealing that could create problems for Becker and his mission.

This was the first part of 1932. With spring elections around the corner, the political maneuvering had begun.

"Major, I am concerned about the upcoming elections," Richter said during their meeting. "It does not look good for the country."

"I quite agree with you, but you seemed to be bothered by something else. Do you mind telling me what it is?" Becker asked.

"I try to stay out of politics, but von Schleicher is undercutting the minister and the chancellor. He seems to be throwing in with Hitler. I know he is doing it for personal ambition, but I think the military should not engage in politics," Richter said.

"You are right. This is somewhat of a surprise to me," Becker answered. "I recall the general speaking harshly of Hitler and Goring.

"I am glad your meeting with Goring went well, Major Becker, but I must get back to my office for an appointment," Richter said.

"Thanks again for the information and I will be in touch," Becker answered as the colonel left the office.

In spite of his heavy cramming on events and people in Germany, Becker found himself almost overwhelmed by trying to absorb all of the things with which he should be familiar. On more than one occasion since he had returned to Germany, he had found himself in awkward situations that he had to bluff his way out of regarding things that he should know. The pressure was great but not unexpected. Becker knew that those situations were going to arise, and he would just have to keep dealing with them as they came up. One of his fears was that he would run into someone who knew him but whom he would fail to recognize.

Becker spent every minute of the day that he was not on duty studying and reading about Germany. He had little time or occasion to attend social functions. He thought he could use a night out to relieve the stress. He had turned down several invitations from Captain Schwarz to go out for drinks or to parties for fear of being compromised. But after his first meeting with Goring, Becker agreed to attend a cocktail party with Schwarz. The party was honoring a retiring general at the ministry. The ladies at the ministry, particularly Sara Klein, had insisted that the captain bring Becker.

Chapter Five

At the reception, Schwarz and Becker made the rounds so that they could meet and fraternize with as many notables as possible. While Becker was talking to one of the officers and his wife, someone came up behind Becker and placed their hands over his eyes. A sultry voice asked, "Guess who?" Becker turned around to find none other than Sara Klein.

"Hello, Sara, what a pleasant surprise to see you here," he said.

"Oh, major, it is so good of you to come," she said as she held out a delicate hand.

The woman looked fantastic. Her skin was as smooth and flawless as a baby's. "I don't know what kind of perfume you have on, my dear, but it is captivating," Becker said.

"Thank you, sir. This fragrance is especially for you" she replied.

Self-preservation took over, and Becker contained his

exuberance. He thanked Sara for her gracious welcome. At that moment, a gentleman approached the couple.

"Major, I would like for you to meet my husband, Karl Klein," Sara blurted. "Karl, this is Major Konrad Becker, our new intelligence officer with the military police."

As Becker reached out to shake Klein's hand, he sized him up as an upper class snot bag. Klein reluctantly shook Becker's hand and contemptuously mumbled a half-assed greeting. Becker's first impression was proving to be accurate. "Pleased to meet you, Klein," he said as he finished the handshake. "You have a beautiful wife. I suggest you take good care of her, or else someone might come along and steal her away."

"Thank you, sir, but she is well taken care of, and I have no fear of someone stealing her away," Klein said with a sneer.

"Good," Becker said. "Now if you two will excuse me, I am being summoned by my aide to meet some of the other guests. It was a pleasure meeting you Klein. And Sara, I will see you later." He turned and walked away, satisfied, thinking that he had just planted a seed of doubt in the Karl Klein's mind.

As Becker turned to meet some of the other guests, he could hear the irate Klein complaining to Sara about her lack of attention to him and her flitting around the party like she was available. Klein was a decent-looking fellow, but the major thought to himself how easy it would be to kick the guy's ass over his shoulder. In fact, Becker envisaged the pleasure he would get from doing just that. He smiled. This was neither the time nor place to get physical. His next thought was a feeling of compassion for Sara for being saddled with such a nincompoop.

Becker spotted Schwarz at a table, conferring with a couple of attractive young women. "Major, would you care to join us?" Schwarz asked.

"Thank you, I would be pleased to join you and these lovely ladies," Becker answered as he pulled up a chair. After the introductions were made, the major had a drink and joined the conversation. But his mind kept wandering back to Sara. One of the women at the table suggested that they all leave the party and go to her place for some more drinking and ... whatever. Although the women were both quite attractive, the major begged off. It was too early to leave the reception, he said, but perhaps another time. The ladies expressed their disappointment but extracted a promise from the major that "another time" would not be too far in the future. The entire time he was with the young women, Becker felt frequent glances coming from Sara Klein. But reality reared its ugly head, and Becker reminded himself he had to stay focused on his mission. Now was not the time to get sidetracked and involved in extracurricular activities. He did not realize that his coolness was fanning the flames of desire in Sara Klein.

When Becker got to the office the next day, Berta said that a Mr. Braun was trying to reach him and that Becker should contact him as soon as possible. When Becker reached him, Braun said, "Herr Goring needs to see you as soon as possible. We have a problem."

"Where is he?" Becker asked.

"He is at the Reichstag and would like to meet you at Tiergarten Park by the park entrance. He will be waiting in his black Mercedes. Would you like for me to pick you up, sir?" Braun asked.

"No, that will not be necessary," Becker said. "I'll grab a taxi and should be there in twenty minutes."

"Thank you, sir. Goring will be there," Braun replied.

Goring was waiting when Becker got there and seemed to be on edge. Becker had heard that Goring dabbled in drugs. He figured that was why the man was edgy. But it turned out that Goring was concerned about some of his men that had been arrested the night before in an altercation at one of the beer halls.

"One of the accused is a close aide of mine, and I don't want this matter to get out of hand," Goring pleaded.

"Give me the names of those involved, and I will take care of it," Becker assured him.

Goring gave Becker the names and expressed his appreciation. "I am most grateful. You will be remembered. I have been hearing good things about you.

"Thank you, Herr Goring. I will be in touch," Becker said as he left the car.

He returned to the office. Becker was pleased that he was gaining Goring's confidence.

When Becker returned to the office, he had Sergeant Heinz drive him to police headquarters. They met with one of the senior police officials and worked out a release for the three men. They had been in more than an altercation. One person was killed and two others badly beaten. Becker told the police officer that the men were under surveillance, and he did not want anything to interfere with his investigation. With the Nazis growing in strength, the police officer did not resist. He readily accepted the explanation. The officer told Becker that some of the detectives were investigating illegal activities on the part of Goring, Rohm, and Himmler. There were photos showing Rohm and several unidentified male companions in compromising positions. Becker instructed the officer to bring the photos and other evidence to him at Gestapo(secret state police) headquarters.

Arriving back at the office, Becker told Berta to summon Captain Schwarz to his office. As Schwarz entered the room, Berta announced: "There are two police detectives in the outer office." "Captain, they have information on criminal activities that may involve certain Nazi party officials, so bring them in and let's see what they have" Becker said."

"Yes, sir," Schwarz said. He stepped into the other office and then returned with the two men.

"Detectives, have a seat and let's see the files," Becker said.

"Yes sir. I am Detective Garrard, and this is my partner, Detective Ansbach," one of the men said.

"Here are the files and the photos, sir," Ansbach said.

The photos were quite compelling, showing two unidentified naked males with Ernst Rohm in compromising positions. Ernst Rohm was chief of staff of the storm troopers, a large paramilitary organization of the Nazi party. Revelations of such conduct would be a devastating blow to the careers of any high-ranking members of the Nazi party. Immediate exposure would be warranted, but Becker felt that the material would be invaluable to him in pursuing his agenda to gain Goring's confidence.

Becker addressed the detectives, "There was mention of Hermann Goring. He is not in any of these photographs, so how does he fit into your investigation?"

The detective replied that the major would find references to both Goring and Himmler in the files. They had engaged in illegal activities, such as secreting away arms that had been outlawed by the Weimar Republic. Witnesses claimed they had observed the two men using illegal drugs with two unidentified females. "All of the information is in the files" Detective Garrard said.

"Thank you detectives," Becker said. "Now we will take control of these files, and you are not to discuss this matter with anyone other than me or Captain Schwarz. Is that clear?"

"Yes sir, colonel. To tell the truth, we are glad to be taken off of this investigation. If you need anything further, please contact us at police headquarters" Detective Garrard said.

"Thank you Garrard and a good job by both of you. Captain, will you show these gentlemen out?" Becker said. The captain escorted the two detectives out of the office.

With the turmoil in Germany, Becker understood that these

men were eager to curry favor with army intelligence and to be removed from an explosive situation. Becker discussed the danger of possessing such damaging information with Schwarz and ordered him to discreetly have copies of the originals made.

Becker planned to divulge this damaging information only to Goring. If Goring chose to share the information with the others, that would be his decision. Becker felt that this evidence might give him some additional protection if something went wrong with his mission. It most assuredly would afford him a great deal of leverage in dealing with the Nazis. Having information like this on those bastards was a stroke of good luck. This was a big break for him, and he intended to take full advantage of it.

"Major Becker, Sara Klein is on the phone" Berta interrupted. "Thank you Berta" he said as he picked up the phone. "Hello, this is Major Becker" he said. "Hello Major Becker, this is Sara. I just wanted to call and apologize for my husband's rudeness at the reception.

"I hope it did not diminish any personal interest that you may have in me." she said. "Of course not Sara, you must not worry about such nonsense," he answered. I'm sure your husband was only being protective and I paid no attention to his behavior.

Becker's attempts to discourage Sara's overtures apparently only wetted her appetite. She seemed to interpret his rebuffs as playing hard to get. She came right out and asked, "When will I see you again, major?"

Not wanting to completely alienate her, as she might prove to be useful because of her position at the minister's office, Becker told her, "Probably the next time I am in the ministry office, unless we meet for lunch one day."

"That would be nice. You can call me anytime," Sara said, sounding as though her hopes had been raised.

Becker told her that he had a meeting to attend and politely said goodbye.

Over the next several weeks, Becker spent more and more time with Goring. The Nazi leader had been pleased with the way Becker handled the incident involving his aide. Goring became more comfortable with the major and more candid with him about the Nazis' activities and plans for the future of Germany. He occasionally introduced Becker to higher-ranking members of the Nazi party. Some of the men Goring hung out with were reputed woman-chasers. Becker suspected that they had participated in a great deal of debauchery and lewd behavior, but it did not matter to him. Becker turned down several invitations to join them in their peccadilloes. He always declined such invitations. While Becker did not approve of their conduct, he kept his feelings to himself, as doing otherwise would have been foolish.

Becker and Goring had developed such a good working relationship that Goring had become quite dependent on him. This was the right time to drop the little matter of the investigation on him. "Herr Minister," Becker said, "I have uncovered a problem that could having an adverse effect on prominent members of the Nazi party." Becker told Goring all the gory details about the evidence. The most incriminating part, of course, was the photos. "Don't worry about the photos," Becker said. "They are not of you. Only Rohm is in the photos."

"That is a relief. What do they have on me?" Goring asked.

"The evidence about you and Himmler shows prohibited weapons, secretly rearming the SS(Shutzstaffel, an elite paramilitary unit of the Nazi Party) and the SA(Storm Troopers, a much larger paramilitary organization of the Nazi Party) and illegal drug activity.

"I assure you that I have never done drugs," Goring said.

Becker knew Goring was lying but played along. "Of course not. Don't worry Herr Goring, I have taken jurisdiction over the case, and it is under my control. You can do what you wish with the Rohm photos. The information is in my hands and safe from discovery." Becker handed Goring the photos.

Goring's face lit up like a Christmas tree. "Perfect. Major, you may have made our case against Rohm. Himmler and I are both concerned about his arrogance and his ambition to take over the party. The fuhrer is also aware of that but has been reluctant to act against him. This may just be what the *fuhrer* has been looking for. This will bury that son of a bitch Rohm. Just look at that bastard. I told you that he was crazy. And letting himself get photographed in those compromising circumstances is just unbelievable. I don't think he really gives a shit what he does. He has been flaunting his illicit behavior for years. Are there any other copies?"

"Yes, I have a set, but they are in a secure place," Becker said.

"How can I ever thank you enough for watching my back?" Goring said. "You have truly earned your place in the Third Reich. You can rest assured that when the fuhrer is made aware of these photos, he too will be appreciative of your work. But for the time being, I am going to sit on this. We will spring it at the right time."

"Thank you for the confidence you have placed in me," Becker replied. "The information you have in your hands will not be used by anyone but you. I am sure you will take good care of me and my people when the time comes."

Goring again profusely thanked Becker and vowed that he would be properly rewarded. Goring's promise would soon pay off. In January 1933, Adolph Hitler was named Chancellor of Germany.

Chapter Six

Once Hitler was named chancellor, the wheels really began to turn for Becker. Hermann. Goring was appointed minister of the interior of Prussia, giving him control over most of the police in Germany. He purged the department of most of the politically unreliable officers and had hundreds of the party faithful sworn in as police auxiliaries with the power to make arrests. They would take full advantage of their authority. The Storm Troopers also started their reign of terror. A decree was issued by the fuhrer with a new doctrine called "protective custody." In April of 1933, Goring founded the Geheime Staatspolizei (the German state secret police force), or the Gestapo, as it was later called.

A week later Becker was meeting with Colonel Richter when Berta interrupted to say that Minister Goring's office had called. Goring wanted Becker to report to his office at 2 PM that day for a meeting of utmost importance. Needless to say, this caused quite a stir in the office. Becker and Richter speculated about what the meeting would be about.

Becker had Heinz drop him off at Goring's office, and he was immediately ushered into the office. Goring greeted Becker as two gentlemen were leaving.

After Goring and Becker sat down and conversed briefly, Goring said, "Major, do you remember when I told you that you were going to be taken care of when the time came? Well, the time has come. I have a generous offer for you. As you know, we recently announced the establishment of the new secret state police agency. I have a position for you. I think you are the perfect man for the job. I'm sure you are aware that Rudolph Diels has been named director by the fuhrer because of his many years of experience in police work. I would like to have you in the number two position. At least in name, you are number two. Actually you will be working for me and will answer to nobody but me. I have discussed this with Diels, and he fully understands the situation.

"If you agree to take the position," Goring continued, "you will be promoted to the rank of senior colonel. You will have, besides your immediate staff, access to whatever manpower you need to carry out your duties. That includes members of the armed forces. The headquarters of the new secret state police force will be housed in the same building that your office is in now. You can meet with the building superintendent to select new offices for you and your staff. What do you think, major—or should I say colonel?"

"I am overwhelmed at your generous offer, Herr Minister, and of course I accept the offer. You have my deep gratitude. When do I start?" Becker asked.

"You start today. One of my aides will make an appointment with the tailor to get your new uniform. I have also spoken to the fuhrer, and he has made an exception so that you can be an officer of the SS even though you are not a member of the SS. It will add prestige to your rank. That will also allow you a little more selection in choosing your uniform. Himmler, as head of the SS, may be pissed, but that is of no concern. He has been informed of this appointment.

"You may also want to update your automobile. Have your driver report to the transportation department to make that exchange. I assume you will keep those presently on your staff, but that is entirely up to you. You are also authorized to expand your present staff, and you can handle that through personnel. I think that covers everything. Do you have any questions, Colonel Becker?"

"Offhand I can't think of any," replied Becker. "I suppose the first thing I should do is pay a courtesy call to Director Diels."

"That is a good idea," Goring said. He picked up the phone and summoned Diels to the office. Diels appeared shortly thereafter and greeted the new deputy with a hearty handshake. Goring briefed Diels on what had been discussed, and Diels welcomed Becker aboard with a full understanding of his role. Diels was cordial and said he would have one of his aides see that all of Becker's needs were met.

"Colonel Becker, I am sure the minister has told you that our headquarters is going to be in your present building. I have made an appointment for tomorrow with the building superintendent and a state architect to discuss the necessary remodeling. Perhaps you would like to attend the meeting and outline your needs."

"Yes," Becker replied. "I will bring my aide, Captain Schwarz. We look forward to being there. Let me say how pleased I am to be working with you. By all accounts, you have a sterling reputation in the field of police work. That combined with my military experience in the intelligence field should guarantee that we will be quite successful in our new assignment."

"Thank you, colonel," Diels said. "That is very kind of you. And please call me Rudolph, or Diels, if you prefer. I too look forward to our association. The minister and I have discussed the advantages we'll get from having a regular military man of your stature as part of our team. Please have your captain contact our personnel director for any clerical or staffing requirements that you would like taken care of."

"Thank you," Becker said. "Now if you gentlemen have no further instructions for me, I will go get started on my new job. Again, thank you both. Heil Hitler!"

Goring and Diels returned the colonel's salute and bade him a good day.

Becker's first thought after leaving the office was that Goring would have shit if he knew that he had just promoted a Jew to one of the highest positions in the Third Reich. In the outer office, Becker was met by Diels' aide. They discussed the office space meeting and the tailor's appointment. The aide said that he would call Captain Schwarz to discuss additional staff requirements and equipment that would be needed for the new office.

The colonel selected office space on the fifth and top floor, which would house most of the top Gestapo officials, including the director. Becker's next step would be to meet with the tailors for the new uniforms. Becker was brimming with excitement. He couldn't wait to inform his staff of the good news.

When Becker returned to the office, he called a staff meeting to tell everyone about the new assignment. There was, to put it mildly, genuine excitement and happiness. The colonel was inundated with questions, and he answered them all to the satisfaction of the staff. They were mainly concerned with their own fates.

"Major, am I included as a member of the new staff?" asked Berta.

"Yes, Berta, you are. I must correct you on my title. I have been promoted to senior colonel, so from now on you must address me as Colonel Becker." This announcement drew a big round of applause. "There will be additional personnel added to the staff. Captain Schwarz and I will meet with you later to discuss our needs."

This was a big relief for Schwarz, who did not want to go back to active duty in the army. The same was true for Sergeant Heinz. He was overjoyed to learn that the colonel would be getting a new motor car. Over the short time that Becker had known these men, he had developed full trust in them and was sure of their loyalty. As for the civilian personnel, he instructed Schwarz to seek people that would fit into their close-knit operation and that they could have full trust in. Berta was the only female on staff. Schwarz thought Sara Klein would be an excellent addition to the group.

"What do you think, colonel?" he asked.

"Ask her to come over, and we will talk to her," Becker answered. "There is no question as to her qualifications, but I'll have to think about it." Becker had seen Sara frequently over the last few months. Although he had strong feelings for her, he had not acted on them, other than an occasional public embrace and a kiss here and there when the two were alone.

Sara would make a good administrative assistant. She had excellent skills in dealing with the public, especially men. With her good looks and personality, she would be a big plus in dealing with the power structure. Becker knew he could trust her, and that was the overriding question on bringing her on board. He needed people like that.

When Sara arrived for her interview, she did not have a clue why she had been invited. She was breathless and, as always, looked fabulous.

"Sara, do you know why you are here?" Becker asked.

"Hmm, let me see," she said. "Are you going to propose to me, major?"

"Not exactly," he answered, "but the next best thing. How would you like to work for me here at the Gestapo?" he asked.

"Oh, my God," she said. "Are you serious? I would love to work for you. I'll even scrub the floors if that is what you want me to do."

"I don't doubt for a minute that you would make a good scrub woman, but I do have a job for you if you would like to join my staff." Becker then described in more detail what had happened in his meeting with Goring. He told her what her duties would be in the new agency.

Sara could not hide her enthusiasm. "Major, I am so excited. Just tell me when and where to report."

"It's Colonel Becker now, if you please" he informed her.

She was delighted at the prospect of not only working for Becker but being put into such a high-profile position.

"Sara, what will your husband think about you working for Colonel Becker and the Gestapo?" Berta asked.

"He is not going to like it, but this is the best thing that ever happened to me," Sara replied.

Berta announced that a tailor had arrived for a fitting, so the colonel had to drop what he was doing for measurements.

"You have an ideal frame, and your uniform is going to look great on you," the tailor told Becker. "I guarantee it."

"That's fine," replied the colonel, "but when can I expect delivery?"

"I will have your uniforms ready next week, I guarantee it," the tailor said.

True to his word, the new uniforms were delivered the following week. The tailor requested that the colonel try them on to check the fit. Sara and Berta also expressed their desire to see what the new uniforms would look like.

"Sir, I must say that you look fabulous in your uniform," the tailor announced with pride. "May I call in the ladies to get their opinion?"

"Yes, open the door, and move aside lest they crush you coming in here," Becker said.

The tailor opened the door and invited Sara and Berta to come in.

"Colonel, you look absolutely fabulous," Sara said excitedly.

Berta readily agreed. "Sara, we are going to be the envy of the republic, working for the most handsome man in the country."

"Now, ladies, let's don't get carried away." Becker said. He turned to the tailor. "Thank you for doing such a good job. I will spread the word that I have the best tailor in all of Germany."

Becker admitted to himself that the uniform looked good and fit perfectly. After listening to Sara and Berta go on about how great he looked, he finally had to put a halt to it. "You ladies have made your point," he said. "Now I suggest you get on with your work."

As soon as they stopped giggling, they left the office.

Becker decided that maybe this would also be a good time to dress up in his new black uniform and pay a visit to the manager at the *Tiergarten* to discuss new living quarters befitting his new status. He was beginning to feel invincible as he put on the new black dress uniform. Now he would have to put a little more snap in the Nazi salute. Saying "Heil Hitler" was taking some getting used to, but it was a necessary part of the charade. He headed for the hotel.

Chapter Seven

At the hotel, Becker instructed the front desk to summon the manager. Jan Schmidt, the hotel manager, appeared few minutes later. "Good morning, Colonel Becker, how can I help you?" the manager asked, beaming.

"Good morning to you," Becker replied. "Since I have been promoted and have joined the Gestapo, I feel that I must upgrade my living quarters to match my new status. What do you think?"

"Most certainly sir, I am at your service. I think I have just the apartment to fit your new status. If you will follow me, I will show it to you," the manager said.

When they arrived at the apartment, the manager said, "This is our most elegant suite. As you can see, the view is magnificent. It is very spacious, and the furnishings are most expensive but in good taste."

"This place is very nice," Becker said. "It will suit my needs nicely. I'll take it, and, incidentally, I will pay the same rent as I have been paying. You can have your people move me in today. You have been most cooperative. I will vouch for your efficient and courteous service."

"Yes, sir, we will get right on it. If there is anything else you need, please let me know," the manager said.

"Thank you. Have a nice day," Becker said as he left the apartment. *This was an appropriate way to start being a good Nazi and shitting on people*, he thought. The nicer apartment took advantage of his new standing in the social order.

Schwarz and Sara spent the next several days assembling a staff. Meanwhile, work on the remodeling and expansion of the offices was progressing rapidly. The Gestapo was receiving preferential treatment from all quarters. Nothing was too good for the new secret police leaders.

Also at the new colonel's disposal would be whatever manpower he or Captain Schwarz might require, such as armed uniformed and undercover agents. The Nazis also issued a standing order to the army to supply troops and armored vehicles in whatever numbers Colonel Becker requested.

Sergeant Heinz was quite happy trading the old car he had been driving for a bright, shiny, new black Mercedes.

After a couple of weeks, the office construction was completed, and the staff members were told that they could move in when ready. All Gestapo personnel were moving into the building, as well, including the director. The Gestapo was ready for business. No sooner than they had settled in, they started getting reports on various activities that needed addressed. Goring's office was loading them down with requests to investigate a number of individuals, and it seemed like everybody wanted an audience with Becker.

Becker had pretty much perfected his look of contempt toward others without being too unpleasant. He knew that he was living in an atmosphere where a good personality was not necessarily an asset. In some cases, being nice even could cause problems.

The new order had suspended most individual rights. The Gestapo had the power to make arrests on any pretense under the policy of "protective custody." Protective of the new government, that was.

The wholesale arrests and abuse by the Storm Troopers were reaching epidemic proportions. Diels was reluctant to use his authority to curtail such actions. He was afraid to challenge the powerful Ernst Rohm and his Storm Troopers and Himmler and the SS.

Becker felt no restraints. The many arrests and incidents had become one of the foremost problems that Becker's division had to constantly step in and take action on. Without question, the SS and Storm Troopers' main target was the Jewish population. Intervening on behalf of the Jewish people would not be tolerated, so Becker had to proceed with utmost caution. He felt that he could improvise, using tactics that appeared to be pro-government policy but were effectively the opposite. Discretion would dictate his course of action in such cases. Becker had a pretty free hand as long as he didn't get cross ways with Goring. He knew that as long as Goring was in power, others would be reluctant to challenge him, at least openly. That power, however, did not insulate Becker from people like Klein and Nazi officials who were bound to be envious and resentful of his position. They were the ones he would have to be wary of.

Becker noticed that Sara seemed to be troubled about something, so he called her into his office and asked her what was bothering her. "Okay Sara, what is your problem?" he asked.

"Things are not going well with Karl," she said. "He is constantly complaining about everything, but mainly about my job and the fact that I am working for 'that damn Becker.' He has even accused me of being unfaithful. I am just about fed up with him. I have not slept with him in several months, and he has become unbearable. Also, he is hitting the bottle with gusto and becoming more obnoxious."

"Sara, you are not to worry," Becker said. "I will take care of the problem if it should persist or get any worse." He spent an hour with Sara, reassuring her. "I think it's time for you to get back to work," he finally said.

"Yes, sir," she said. She gave him a hug and a kiss and left the office.

Suddenly Berta came into the office crying. "Colonel, I am sorry to interrupt you, but I just received some terrifying news. My teenage nephew has been taken into protective custody by the SA. He has been arrested and is being arraigned before a magistrate at this very moment."

"Berta, pull yourself together and find out where the boy is being held," Becker ordered. "Have Sergeant Heinz bring the car around, and have Captain Schwarz assemble a detail of a half dozen troops to follow us to where the young man is scheduled for a hearing."

About forty minutes later, Becker and his entourage entered the Justice Building. One of the guards on duty directed them to the courtroom of Judge Emil Goetz.

"Are you Judge Goetz?" Becker asked as he entered the courtroom and ordered the magistrate to stop the proceedings.

"Yes, I am Judge Goetz. What is the meaning of interrupting this court proceeding? Who are you, anyway?" the grumpy-looking man behind the bench demanded.

"Colonel Konrad Becker of the Gestapo," Becker shot back. "Never mind what the meaning of this interruption is about. I am taking command of this proceeding. If you fail to cooperate, you will be removed from this courtroom and arrested. Do you understand my order?"

"Yes, sir," the judge answered nervously as he observed the armed troops that accompanied the colonel.

"It has been brought to my attention that a young man by the name of Bernard Stecht is to be arraigned in this court," the colonel said. "I want the prisoner in question to be brought forth at once. I direct the court to tell me what charges are pending against him and what evidence is there to substantiate the charges."

"Will you two Storm Troopers approach the bench?" ordered Judge Goetz.

A couple of storm troopers stood up and approached the bench. They stated that they were the evidence, and that the defendant, while drinking, had made uncomplimentary remarks toward them and then resisted arrest when they tried to subdue him. The judge ordered the defendant, a seventeen-year-old boy, to stand up.

Becker looked at Stecht, a frail lad that weighed 120 pounds. Becker then stared at the two storm troopers, both large goons that would tip the scales at more than 200 pounds. "Are you saying this young boy was foolish enough to attack two big oafs like yourselves?" Becker asked the Storm Troopers.

The judge spoke up, saying that there must be order in his court. He asked that everyone please take a seat so that he could sort things out. The colonel had been told beforehand that the judge was an arrogant, hard-nosed scoundrel when it came to the rights of accused people who were unfortunate enough to appear in his court.

Becker looked at him with a steely stare that would have scared a dead man. "Goetz," he said, "you have been warned. Now hold your tongue, or you will be taken into custody and charged with interfering with the duties of an officer of the Geheime Staatspolizei.

"Are you aware that this young man is the son of a member of my staff?" Becker continued.

The judge turned pale as a ghost. He appeared to be about to fall to the floor, but he managed to grab the bench and steady himself. In a voice trembling with fear he said, "Colonel, I apologize. I assure you, sir, that I meant no disrespect. I will abide by whatever decision the colonel wishes to make in this case."

"Based on the evidence that has been presented, I am ordering that all charges against this young man be dropped and the prisoner released," ordered Becker.

"By orders of this court, the charges against Bernard Stecht shall be dropped, and the prisoner will be released at once. It is so ordered," Judge Goetz pronounced. "As for you two burly storm troopers, you are to clear out of this courtroom and not let me see the likes of you again."

The Storm Troopers complied with the order post haste and headed for the nearest exit.

"Goetz, I will meet briefly with you in your chambers," Becker told the judge. Inside the judge's chambers, Becker made it clear that, if the judge ever saw him again, whether in his court or elsewhere, the judge had better show proper respect for an officer of his standing. "Any deviation from those instructions will ensure your immediate arrest."

"Yes sir. Please accept my apologies. I certainly meant no disrespect, and I beg for your forgiveness," the judge pleaded. All the blood had drained from his face, and it appeared that his apology was sincere.

Becker told the judge that his business had been concluded in the court. "You may now resume the regular proceedings in your court." Then the colonel and his men took their leave.

The courtroom was filled with prisoners, and they were stunned at what they had just witnessed. The judge ordered the courtroom to come to order as Becker left the building. As they were loading up to leave, Captain Schwarz and Sergeant Heinz both saluted the colonel and congratulated him on how he had handled the situation.

When the men returned to the office, Berta was waiting. When she found out what had happened, she was jubilant and appreciative. She went on and on in her gratitude until Becker finally had to tell her to cease and get on with her business.

Sara followed Becker into the office and likewise expressed her thanks and admiration. "Heinz told me about what took place at the hearing and how you practically destroyed the judge and the arresting officers," she gushed.

"Okay, Sara, I think you would admire me if you heard I had gone to the toilet, so how about getting back to work?" Becker replied.

Later, Sara came in again. "Sir, Colonel Richter is here to see you," she announced.

"Show him in," Becker said. He patted her gently on her rear, and she walked out with a giggle. *There is nothing like a happy employee*, Becker thought.

"Hello, colonel," Becker said to Richter. "It's good to see you again. Please have a seat."

"Thank you, Konrad. I just stopped by to tell you how delighted I am with your promotion. It looks like we will still be working together. I have a command in the area, and we will be providing troops as needed for your operations." Richter pointed out that Becker was in the bore sights of certain individuals and that he had better take extra precautions to protect himself.

This was no surprise to Becker, but it was a reminder of something that he knew he must never forget. "Do you have any names in particular?" Becker asked.

"Yes, one of them is a Himmler deputy by the name of Dirk Hartman," Richter replied. "Hartman is a snake if there ever was one. There is another member of Himmler's staff, a Major

Wilhelm Donst, who has been overheard denigrating you and your staff."

Becker filed Hartman's name in his brain to be dealt with when necessary. "Thanks for bringing those men to my attention, and rest assured, I will be wary of them," replied Becker.

"Think nothing of it," Richter said as he got up to leave. "I must be on my way. Let me hear from you if you need anything."

"Thank you," Becker said. "Heil Hitler." They saluted, and Richter departed.

In the short time Becker had been in Germany, he had already developed a dislike for the Nazis because of what he had heard about and seen them do to innocent people. He was also appalled at the hatred directed against the Jews. He called Captain Schwarz into the office.

"Do you know a Colonel Hartman with the SS?" Becker asked.

"I have heard of him, but I do not know much about him," Schwarz answered.

"I want you to do a background check on Hartman and report back to me. I am not going to let any of those bastards get too far ahead of me," Becker said.

He knew he was in a dog-eat-dog situation. He had to stay on top, or he would be history. He had to get in the first bite. Those people played for keeps. Becker was beginning to wonder if he was becoming more like the Nazis. He sensed that he was becoming more aggressive. His justification was that he was dealing with evil people, and the only way to survive was to deal harshly with them. If he was going to make it, he had to be meaner than they were. He had reached the point that inflicting harm and even death on his adversaries no longer presented a problem. The situation he found himself in offered no choice. Weakness would be failure, and strength would be success. There could be no compromise. What was really beginning to bother Becker was that at times he enjoyed the power he had been entrusted with. Those thoughts had to be dismissed. He was doing what had to be done. If the occasion called for force or brutality, then so be it.

As Becker was mulling that over in his head, Sara interrupted him. "Colonel, you just received an invitation from Minister Goring for a reception this Friday evening for the *fuhrer*," she said with excitement.

Becker knew he had no choice but to attend. Absence might be construed as a slight to the fuhrer, which no good Nazi would be guilty of.

"Since you don't have a lady, I would like to volunteer my services," Sara said.

"Okay, but you won't be attending as my lady, but as part of my staff," Becker answered. He certainly did not want to go by himself. "I suppose you will have to ask your husband for his permission."

"To hell with him, I don't need his permission," she replied.

"Well, lady, it's your funeral then. So you are invited to attend as my guest."

"Thank you, sir," she said. "Now I must find something to wear. I know I don't own anything I can wear to such a prestigious event, so I guess I had better go shopping."

"Nonsense, Sara, this is not a fashion show, so don't try to make a fashion statement," he admonished. "As long as you don't show up naked, you will be fine." He knew whatever she wore she would stand out in the crowd.

She laughed and said, "I will find something appropriate, but I will gladly get naked after we leave the party."

Becker smiled and said, "Behave yourself, and send in my next appointment."

The next day, Sara told Becker that Karl was very unhappy when he had heard about the reception. Karl made some veiled threats if Sara carried out her wishes to attend the function. "He has been making unflattering and derogatory remarks about you, sir," Sara said.

"Is that so," Becker said as more of a statement than a question. "Have Sergeant Heinz pick Klein up and bring him into the office."

An hour later, Berta announced that Sergeant Heinz and Klein had arrived.

"Let him cool his heels for a few minutes, and then have Heinz bring him in," Becker instructed Berta.

Once Klein was in his officer, Becker said, "Klein, frankly, I am surprised that you are not honored to have a high-ranking official of the Gestapo escort your wife to an important government function. It has been brought to my attention that you have expressed your opposition to this arrangement, and in the process, you have made some unflattering remarks not only directed toward your wife but to me as well. If I am not mistaken, I told you when I first met you that you should take good care of your wife or somebody else would. From what Sara tells me, you apparently have not followed my advice. Instead you have heaped further verbal abuse on her.

"Sara is a valued employee of the Gestapo," Becker continued. "I must warn you that I will not tolerate any further abuse of her. I don't want to take up too much of your time, as I know you must get back to work, but if you ever threaten Sara again, I will personally see that you pay dearly for it. Without having to draw you a picture, do you understand what I am saying?"

Klein mumbled, "Yes, sir." Becker stood up and walked around from his desk in front of Klein and gave Klein a double slap that knocked the man to the floor. "Now get up you bastard and don't you ever mumble to me again" Becker said. "Yes sir," Klein replied.

"Klein, do you realize that you could be shot for striking or mentally abusing your wife, an employee of the Gestapo?" Becker asked.

By then some of the hostility had subsided, but Klein was still sullen and not a happy warrior. "Sir, I don't appreciate being rousted out of my office like a common criminal and physically abused" he said sarcastically.

"Heinz, get this son of a bitch out of here," the colonel ordered.

"Yes, sir," Heinz said. He grabbed Klein by the arm.

"Heinz, one more thing, let him walk back to his office," Becker added. "The state should not be transporting people on nongovernmental business."

Klein hurriedly left the building without saying goodbye to his lovely wife.

Afterward, Sergeant Heinz informed the colonel that, on the way to Becker's office, Klein had used profanity in describing his wife's neglectful conduct and her infatuation with her boss.

"Heinz, that man was obviously hallucinating. He should be watched," Becker said. "I have the feeling that we will be dealing with this fellow again. Tell Sara to come in here."

"Yes, sir," Heinz replied on his way out.

When Sara came into his office, Becker briefly described to her the meeting that he had with her spouse. "Sara, your husband was complaining to Sergeant Heinz that you have been neglecting him, among other things. Is that correct?" Becker asked.

"I haven't been sleeping with him, if that is what he means," Sara said. "And that's not all. I am not going to sleep with him."

That brought a smile to Becker's face, but he decided not to comment further on the subject, other than to tell her that if Klein ever crossed the line again, he wanted to know about it.

"Sir, he is a very bitter man. You should be careful. He is capable of violence, and you are at the top of his hate list."

"He will just have to get in line, Sara. I have more powerful enemies to deal with than Klein."

Chapter Eight

Becker decided it would be unseemly for an officer of distinction to attend the *fuhrer's* reception without staff. "Schwarz," Becker said, "I would like for you to attend this reception tonight. You can act as a chaperone to keep the lovely Mrs. Klein at bay," he said with a laugh. "You can also introduce me to some of the dignitaries I haven't met."

"Yes, sir, I would be happy to," Schwarz replied.

"A man of my stature should never be without an attendant," Becker added.

Becker's first task at the reception was to seek out Minister Goring, who was holding court with a number of military leaders. Goring greeted them with a genuine show of hospitality.

"Herr Minister, I would like for you to meet my assistant, Sara Klein, and of course you know Captain Schwarz," Becker said.

He could tell by Goring's demeanor that the minister thought Becker's relationship with Sara went beyond that of an assistant.

Goring slyly insinuated as much in their conversation. Goring would not discourage this conduct. It was well known that he respected virile men who had auras of power and machismo. Of course, Sara knew how to play her role. Wearing a pale blue party dress that was not too revealing but accentuated her finer points, she portrayed herself as a femme fatale. With her winning personality, she was quite a hit, not only with the minister but as it later turned out, with every man that she came into contact with during the evening. Fearful that the minister's eyes were going to permanently cross from looking down at Sara's bosom, Becker decided it was time to move on to meet some of the other guests.

"Please excuse us, Herr Minister. We must not take up any more of your time. You have many other guests who are anxious to see you," Becker remarked.

"Thank you for coming, and also for bringing your staff," Goring said.

They left the minister and leisurely strolled on to visit with the other dignitaries. It was obvious that Sara was having the time of her life as Captain Schwarz led them to meet the important officials in attendance. As the evening wore, on Sara seemed to become more and more animated and intoxicated with the ambience of the moment. It reached the point where Becker had to admonish her, in a respectful and affectionate manner, to calm down a little.

"Sara, rather than provide me with all of your attention, you must direct your charm and charisma toward some of those in attendance who might be of some benefit to our office," he said.

She demurely agreed to hide her feelings, or at least to suppress them until the proper time to unleash them on the object of her affection, which she hoped would be later that evening. "Yes, sir, I will carry out your orders as you direct," she said.

It seemed the more Becker tried to discourage her, the more interested she would become. He finally decided he could live with that. After all, he was on a mission, and that mission was not to be sleeping with German women, particularly married ones, although that objection seemed to be losing some of its strength. In his younger years, when he had tried to pursue beautiful young girls, he was rebuffed for being over-eager. How funny it was. Maybe it was true that women wanted what they couldn't have. Becker supposed that he was learning a valuable lesson, but it was a painful lesson, restraining his mind from doing what his body wanted to do.

Becker's thoughts were suddenly interrupted when Captain Schwarz approached him and said that he had some important officials that wanted to meet Becker. Sara excused herself to go to the ladies' room, and Becker accompanied the captain over to a group of uniformed officers.

One of them was Ernst Rohm, the head of the Storm Troopers. After the two were properly introduced, Rohm, a robust and swarthy-looking man, addressed Becker in a condescending tone. "Colonel Becker, I have heard a great deal about you. Nevertheless, I feel that there is a great deal yet to know. My inquiries about you have left me with many unanswered questions and, I must say, a great deal of curiosity. Maybe you can enlighten me," Rohm said with a sneer.

"Maybe you already know more than you need to about me," Becker answered. "However, I will be glad to enlighten you to this extent. I have served as a career officer in the German army and more recently as an SS officer in the Gestapo. I enjoy the confidence of Minister Goring, as well as that of our fuhrer. Beyond that, there is not much you need to know, but your interest has been duly noted. Now, if you will excuse me, I must rejoin my associates. I trust that we will meet again. Heil Hitler."

As Becker and Schwarz walked away, the captain remarked, "Colonel, you never cease to amaze me with your self-confidence. Rohm is a very powerful man, and you just got through cutting his legs out from under him. How do you do it? And aren't you concerned that you may have earned an enemy?"

"No not at all," Becker said. "He is already my enemy. My objective was to let the bastard know that if he fools with me, he will regret it. That is my way of avoiding any misunderstanding as to how far he might go in dealing with me without suffering severe consequences. You might remember that."

Becker smiled. He hoped that Rohm got the message. He certainly didn't need anyone prying into his past. Plus he had another motive that he did not wish to disclose. He knew that Rohm had become an enemy of Goring and Himmler and was becoming less trusted by the *fuhrer*. This would put Becker in good company. Being an enemy of one whose days were numbered could be beneficial. Besides, Rohm was a sordid individual with a less-than-desirable reputation.

"Sara, I trust that you had a pleasant visit to the powder room," Becker said.

"Oh yes, a most pleasant visit" she replied. "I met a number of nice ladies, and after listening to their chatter about you, I have decided that I must take a more active role in protecting my interest. Your presence at this affair has not gone unnoticed by them. Perhaps I shouldn't tell you this, but if you pay attention to any of those witches, I will strangle you," she said with a giggle.

"And just what is your interest to be protected?" he asked.

"Is it not obvious? You have me behaving like a desperate school girl," she replied.

"Sara, you are very amusing. Captain Schwarz, what am I to do with this woman?" Becker asked.

"Sir, you will have to answer that question yourself, but I know what I would do with her if I was fortunate enough to have that decision to make," Schwarz said with a laugh. He knew that Becker had little to worry about in terms of Sara's loyalty and devotion. Sara knew what she wanted, and she was determined somehow to get it.

An announcement was made that the *fuhrer* had entered the building, and the trio got into the greeting line to meet and shake hands with him. After twenty minutes waiting in line, they at last came face to face with the *fuhrer*. Becker gave the heil Hitler salute and shook the *fuhrer*'s hand.

"Colonel Becker, I have heard many good things about you. It is a great pleasure to meet one of Germany's unsung military heroes. We'll continue to expect great things from you."

"Thank you, Mein *Fuhrer*," Becker replied. "I would like to introduce two members of my staff, Sara Klein and Captain Kurt Schwarz."

"Sara is most lovely, and I am tempted to steal her away from you," the *fuhrer* said, ignoring the captain. This brought a burst of laughter from those around them.

Becker thought perhaps it was time to move on. He thanked the *fuhrer* and politely stepped aside. The trio moved around the hall, meeting guests, most of whom were not of any particular importance to them.

That was, until Becker was introduced to a well-groomed officer who stood out among his small group. He had a quintessential Prussian military look. His name was Janz Reinhart. Becker knew he was head of the security service of the SS and was close to Himmler. Meeting Reinhart called for a much different attitude and approach, as Becker certainly did not want to earn the animosity of such a high-ranking officer.

"Heil Hitler," Becker said with a salute. "Colonel Reinhart, it is a pleasure to make your acquaintance. Our busy schedules have unfortunately not allowed us to meet earlier." Becker extended his hand.

"Thank you," Reinhart responded. "I have heard much about you, and I have looked forward to meeting you. May I compliment the lovely lady that you are escorting this evening? She is quite stunning, and it seems we have a shortage of such beauties gracing our halls these days."

"Thank you," Becker replied. "This is Sara Klein and Captain Kurt Schwarz. They are members of my staff."

This disclosure seemed to be music to Reinhart's ears, dispelling the impression that Sara was Becker's date or girl friend. Becker noticed a twinkle in the man's eye as he held Sara's hand for what seemed like an eternity. As usual, she dazzled the gentleman. Becker thought how fortunate he was to have selected her to be part of his group. After a few minutes of conversation, Becker made the customary offer of services to the colonel and, along with his small group, moved on.

Schwarz whispered, "That encounter with Reinhart was quite a contrast to the one with Rohm."

"They have a different status," Becker replied. "Rohm is on his way out, and Reinhart is on the way up. You should learn to recognize the difference." The order of business in the Third Reich, Becker knew, was to never show weakness but to also show respect when the occasion called for it.

The hour was getting late, so Becker had Schwarz order the car, and they left the building. "Heinz, drop me off at my place and then take Sara home" Becker said. She gave Becker a look of disappointment, but being the good trooper she was, she took it in stride. Becker didn't like the idea of sending her home to that scoundrel of a husband, but under the circumstances he thought it best. He found himself in a difficult situation. Becker wanted to be with her, but he knew that this was not the time or place because of the risk involved.

The next morning, Becker told Berta, "I have some business to attend at the bank, so have Heinz bring the car around." As Becker entered the car, he instructed Heinz, "Take me to the Deutsche Bank, sergeant."

"Yes sir," Heinz replied.

Upon entering the bank lobby, Becker was greeted as if he were a celebrity. It seemed that a high-ranking officer with the Gestapo was someone who generated not only fear but great respect. This was not conducive to clandestine operations. The last thing Becker wanted to do was draw attention to his meetings that might create curiosity or suspicion.

A bank employee approached him and asked, "May I be of assistance, sir?"

"I am here to speak to someone about my account," Becker was saying as Fritsch appeared and told the employee that he would assist the customer. They stood in the lobby for a few minutes and talked. This appeared to be a safe place to talk, not subject to prying ears.

"Colonel, I am amazed at your almost instant success in establishing yourself within the highest reaches of the Nazi government," Fritsch said. "The Gestapo's reputation is becoming fearsome in all of Germany."

"Thank you," Becker said. He briefed Fritsch on the progress that he was making and passed on personal information about Goring, Himmler and some of the other players that Becker thought would be of interest to intelligence officials. He knew, of course, that meeting with Fritsch was extremely dangerous and that they must take precautions not to be seen together too much.

"I am delighted at the progress you have made, and I can't wait to file my report to my superiors in England," Fritsch said. "I am equally sure that your superiors in Washington will be most pleased."

Becker wondered about his relationship with this man. Fritsch was the only person in Germany who knew who Becker was and what he was doing there. "It has been a pleasure to meet with you again. I will get back to you when I have something of importance to report back on," Becker said. He bade Fritsch farewell and went to his car, which was waiting on the street. Becker instructed Sergeant Heinz to take him back to headquarters.

The latest big news to hit Berlin was the fire at the Reichstag, the house of parliament. A suspect by the name of Marinus van der Lubbe had been arrested, and there was much speculation about the identities of those involved. The event was publicized by the Nazi's as a serious threat to law and order by communists.

"Colonel Becker, it appears from our investigation into the Reichstag fire that the real perpetrators were Storm Troopers and not that communist van der Lubbe who was arrested," Captain Schwarz said as they started the daily meeting.

"I suspected as much," Becker replied. "I will take it up with Diels and Goring at our next meeting, but I am sure that it will not be a surprise to them. We are sure that this was the work of the Storm Troopers. The incident was just a setup for Hitler to declare an emergency and get the Reichstag to pass the law giving the *fuhrer* dictatorial powers."

Becker wanted Goring and Himmler to know that he was well aware of what really happened. Keeping quiet about the matter to others would, of course, enhance Becker's perceived loyalty to the party.

Schwarz was a smart man and quick to evaluate problems. He also possessed a keen intellect in deciphering the motives of others. Becker was fortunate to have him on his staff. It was too bad that Becker could not divulge his real role, but he could share that with no one. Not even Sara, although Becker felt like she would accept him anyway. *But you never know for sure*, he thought. No, this was something that he had to shoulder by himself. In the short time that Becker had been in Germany, he had built a rapport with all of those under his command. At the same time, there was no doubt that they were deadly fearful of doing anything that would anger Becker. Just the way he wanted it to be.

"Colonel Becker, Sara would like to speak to you as soon as your meeting with Captain Schwarz is over," Berta announced. "Thank you, Berta. Tell her that we are through with our meeting and to come on in. Captain, let me find out what this woman wants," Becker said to Schwarz. "I hope it is nothing involving that *dumbkoph* husband of hers. What a waste of humanity. I think I should go ahead and have him put away."

"Just say the word and his ass is history," Schwarz said as he left.

"Frau Klein, or is it *Fraulein*, what can I do for you today?" Becker asked Sara as she entered the room.

"You can get me out of my horrible marriage and take me away from here," she replied. "Well, my dear Sara, I am afraid I have too much on my agenda to fantasize about such a thing. Have you considered murder or divorce? But in a more serious vein, what do you want today?"

"I am serious, but I guess you are not," Sara said. "I just wanted to let you know that my husband, as you call him— incidentally we no longer share a bed—is up to something, and it involves you."

"How so, *Fraulein*," Becker asked.

"What is this *Fraulein* stuff? The name is Sara. Anyway, I know that Karl has been meeting with a Major Dunst, and he has been trying to hide what they are talking about from me," she said. "I overheard Karl talking on the telephone yesterday, and he mentioned your name. He did not know that I was in the other room and could overhear him. He said he agreed with the caller that Becker 'had to go.' Who is this Dunst anyway?"

"The name is Donst, Wilhelm Donst, and he is one of Himmler's henchmen," Becker replied. "He is a lanky, skinny string bean that I had a few words with in a meeting with Goring and Himmler a while back. I sliced him up pretty good in front of his boss, and I guess he has decided to get revenge. Of course, it could be something deeper because I don't think Himmler is too enthralled with me, either. I am not going into that, but what else can you tell me about what that asshole husband of yours is doing?"

"You may already know this, but Karl has been reassigned in the office of the chancellery," Sara said.

"What the hell does that have to do with me?" asked the colonel.

"I don't know, but getting back to what I overheard, apparently they have done some research on your background. They've come up with nothing so far. It would appear that they have something more sinister in mind from what I could understand. Please, colonel, you must be careful. I don't know what I would do if something happened to you."

"Look Sara, don't you go worrying your pretty head about me. I can take care of myself. What I want you to do, though, is to pretend you know nothing about this and keep your ears open to find out what those bastards are up to. We are dealing with the lowest form of mankind. Donst would not think twice about eliminating you or anybody else that gets in his way. Do you understand me?"

"Yes," she replied, "I do, but I am very afraid, not for myself, but for you."

"I will deal with those snakes in my own way. Instead of divorcing Karl Klein, you may wind up attending his funeral. Now give me a hug and get out of here so that I can get some work done."

"You know that I would like to give you more than a hug, but I guess I'll take what I can get," Sara said as she wrapped her arms around Becker. She gave him a passionate kiss as well.

"Quit forcing yourself on the boss, and tell Berta to have Captain Schwarz come back to the office," Becker said with a smile.

"Colonel you sent for me?" Schwarz asked as he came in a moment later.

"Yes, captain. It looks like my enemies are growing out there. What do you know about Major Wilhelm Donst? Or is it dunce? Ha! Ha!"

"As you know, he is an SS officer and is pretty tight with Heinrich Himmler" Schwarz said.

"Yes, I know he is with the SS. I too have been designated an SS officer by Hitler, but I am not affiliated in any way with Himmler's SS. I have met this fellow Donst before and I found him to be quite lacking in social skills. Obviously I gained his admiration when I cut him down in front of his leader. Based on what Sara overheard, he evidently has decided that one Colonel Becker is too many for him to tolerate. I don't think he would do anything without the approval of Himmler, but nevertheless we have to take this threat seriously. I want you to get me a comprehensive dossier on him."

"Yes sir. I will get on it right away," Schwarz said. "I assume Karl Klein is involved in this matter?"

"Yes, you are absolutely correct," Becker said. "I am not sure how he fits into this puzzle. He has no real standing or power. His involvement must stem from the fact that he is disenchanted with me over Sara. I'm guessing Donst thinks Klein will be a source of information because they think his wife is sleeping with me. Ironically, I have not even bedded her, at least not yet. This looks like a partnership of two malcontents. They have made a fatal mistake in deciding to do me harm. Captain, conduct your investigation discreetly, as I would rather catch those two derelicts by surprise."

"Yes, sir, consider it done," Schwarz said.

"And put both those bastards under surveillance around the clock," ordered Becker.

"Yes, sir," Schwarz said as he left the office.

Chapter Nine

"Colonel, we have received a memorandum from the director that we are to start enforcing the act suspending civil liberties in time of national emergency, whatever that means," Berta told Becker.

"What it means is the Gestapo can do any damn thing it wants to, and it is legal," he said. "So take my advice and behave yourself."

"Yes sir. Did you know that they are also doing a lot of construction work under our building? What is that all about?" she asked.

"That is of no concern to you. Or maybe they are making room for people like you," Becker said. He didn't want to tell her that the construction workers were building facilities for holding prisoners and for interrogation. In other words, it was a torture chamber. The Nazi regime meant business when dealing with dissidents and enemies of the state. The government had already encouraged boycotts of Jewish businesses and institutions.

Goring and others had asked Becker about his feelings toward Jews. Becker told them that he was a soldier and not a social scientist and therefore had no particular interest in the matter. He didn't know how well that went over, but it did not seem to raise any eyebrows. This was an area where he had to maintain caution. He could not afford to be branded a Jewish sympathizer. Being Jewish himself, his natural instinct was to assist that population as much as he could without incurring the wrath of his superiors. This was not an easy task considering the fanatical hatred that the Nazis had for the Jews. The Nazis hated the socialists and the communists, but they hated the Jews more. It was a heavy burden on Becker to restrain his feelings. He knew the time would probably come when he would be compelled to display hostility toward these innocent victims. He dreaded that moment.

Berta told Becker that he had been summoned to a meeting with Goring and Diels at 3 PM that day. *What could that be about?* Becker wondered. He would soon find out.

Becker entered Diels' reception room and was ushered into his office. The minister had not arrived yet. Diels greeted Becker, and they chatted about inconsequential subjects for about thirty minutes until Goring finally showed up with one of his aides.

"Good day, gentlemen," Goring said. "I apologize for my tardiness, but I couldn't get away from the *fuhrer*. I will be brief. Himmler, the *fuhrer* and I are becoming impatient with Rohm. The army is putting more pressure on the *fuhrer* because they fear Rohm's intended takeover of the military. We must double down on our efforts to bring a resolution to this problem. We all know that the pig is not going to go peacefully, so that means we are going to have to kill him. There is no way around it," Goring said, becoming more animated.

"My message is to accelerate your efforts in bringing this

matter to a conclusion. Bear in mind, we are talking about a high-ranking official that controls over one million Storm Troopers. They greatly outnumber the regular army. Rohm has become increasingly defiant and apparently thinks his control over the Storm Troopers shields him from any kind of oversight or authority. His belligerence and arrogance has gained him the enmity of the army and, most importantly, the *fuhrer* himself," Goring ranted. "We expect the Gestapo to gather more evidence and build the case against him. If Rohm becomes aware of our plans, it will jeopardize the whole operation. Are there any questions?"

"Herr Minister, I would remind you of the information and photos that you already have in your possession," Becker said.

"That information has been delivered to the *fuhrer*, but he wants more," Goring replied.

"We can get more, but it is going to be similar," Becker remarked with a look of despair. "Unless we can catch the bastard in bed with a dead man, it is going to be the same old stuff. Maybe with our electronic surveillance we can catch him saying something incriminating."

"Colonel, you are right. It may take something like that for the *fuhrer* to make a decision," Goring replied.

"This is a case against a scoundrel that no one has any use for," Becker said. "His demise will be a blessing, and there will be few tears shed for his departure."

"I suppose you are right, colonel. Get on it, and if we can't come up with something else, then we are just going to have to convince the *fuhrer* that he is in danger and it is imperative that we take action," Goring said.

"In the meantime, we will see what else we can turn up," Becker said. "I will put our people on it today."

"Thank you gentlemen, I must leave now. I have another meeting I am already late for. Let me hear from you," Goring said as he went out the door.

Diels offered Becker assistance with resources and personnel. This was top priority. They called in Captain Schwarz and laid out the program to him. They gave him the responsibility of picking the people that he would need.

"Captain, what is the latest on Rohm?" Becker asked.

"We have nothing new to report, sir," Schwarz replied. "Until we can get a bug on him, we are at a stalemate."

"Captain, our job is to uncover enough illegal misconduct on Rohm's part to warrant his removal, and that is the bottom line," Becker said.

"Sir, I will pull the files on our agents and select those capable and trustworthy enough to accomplish our assignment," replied Schwarz. "I may need to go outside the Gestapo to get the people we want. Is that a problem?"

"No, that will not be a problem," answered Becker. "Just get started on this at once. Unless you have something more to discuss, you are dismissed."

"Thank you, sir. Seig heil." Schwarz saluted on the way out.

Back in his own office, Becker asked Berta to get Colonel Richter on the phone. A few minutes later, Berta announced, "I have the colonel on the phone, sir."

"Leon, this is Becker. I have an idea that maybe you can help me with. You have some knowledge of remote listening devices, so I was wondering if you could stop over and bring me up to date on their feasibility."

"Colonel, I have done some work and experimentation on the subject," Richter replied. "I am not an expert, but I will be happy to reveal what I do know. In fact, I have been wanting to visit with you. If it is convenient, I can drop by your office in about thirty minutes."

"Thanks, Leon, I will see you then," Becker said. He hung up the phone.

It was not long before Richter arrived and was ushered into the office.

"Colonel Becker, I have done quite a bit of research on the subject that we discussed over the phone," Richter said. "There is some technology out there that works to a point. You need to employ an engineer to design an apparatus that will meet your needs. This technology has the potential of being revolutionary. If you can supply me with the engineer, then I will be happy to assist him in perfecting a product. This could be an invaluable tool in intelligence. I am sure it would greatly enhance your investigations."

"Leon, I knew I could count on you," Becker responded. "I will provide an engineer or two. I would like to expedite this project. I will instruct Captain Schwarz to put this in motion. Since this is a clandestine operation, I would appreciate you exercising as much secrecy as possible. If you need approval from your commandant, that can be arranged. My orders in this matter come from the highest authority of the government."

"That is all I need," Richter replied.

"Oh, I see the hour is getting late. I would be most happy if you joined me for a cocktail in the hotel lounge, if your timeframe permits," Becker said.

"I would be honored to have a drink with you, Colonel Becker. May I use your telephone to call my wife and tell her that I will be late?" Richter asked.

After Colonel Richter called his wife, they left the office and went to the Hotel *Tiergarten* lounge to have a drink and relax after a heavy day at the office.

Richter warned Becker of rumors that he had heard regarding Karl Klein. "Konrad, I keep picking up information that this Klein fellow is making waves."

"I am surprised that Klein would exhibit hostile behavior toward me," Becker said with a laugh.

"Colonel, I think you should take Klein's threats seriously since he apparently is now cooperating with the SS," Richter warned. "At least, he has been seen in the company of an SS officer."

"Leon, I do take those threats seriously, and I am aware that Klein is working with the SS," Becker agreed.

They wrapped up the meeting and agreed to keep in touch about surveillance technology. As soon as the piano player finished playing "Ramona," which was one of Becker's favorite songs, they departed with a handshake. Becker went to his apartment and retired for the evening.

Hearing the song "Ramona" had brought back memories of Becker's life back in the good old United States. It also reminded him that his present social life was lacking and in need of a boost. Maybe it was time to change that. He would have to work on it.

On Thursday morning, there was a room full of people in the reception room. "Berta, who are all those people and how did they get past security?" Becker asked.

"All of them have security clearance and are here to discuss various topics, sir," she answered.

"Route them through Captain Schwarz and have him screen them," Becker said. He noticed that one of the people waiting was an elderly, distinguished-looking gentleman. He told Berta to show the old man into the office.

The man introduced himself as Professor Walden. He said he hoped Becker would remember him. He had been one of Becker's teachers back when he was a student at Grand Gymnasium in Munich. Becker pretended to have a vague recollection of the teacher while being careful not to get tripped up by someone who may have been testing him. Becker really needed to get to Munich to check out that old school. He suspected that the subject would come up again in the future, and he didn't want to get caught not having some knowledge of the school.

The purpose of the professor's visit was to talk to Becker about trouble he was having with some storm troopers, supposedly because he had been critical of the hoodlums' antics. Becker listened carefully to the old man's story. While the colonel sympathized with the professor's plight, Becker told him that this was a local police problem.

"Professor, have you reported these acts to the police?" Becker asked.

"Yes, I have, and it has only made matters worse," the old man replied. "The police are afraid of these thugs."

"Let me ask you this, professor," Becker said. "Have you done anything that might give these hoodlums cause for this aggressive behavior?"

"They think I am Jewish, but no, sir. I have done nothing wrong that I am aware of, except I have criticized their behavior. But I am not the only one who is a victim of this lawlessness."

"Are you a member of any group or society that is considered an enemy of or a threat to the fatherland? Are you Jewish?" Becker asked the old man.

"No, I am not, and I have done nothing that could be considered anti-government activity," Walden said. "It appears to me that these are more random acts of violence against law-abiding citizens."

"Professor, can you identify these perpetrators?" Becker asked.

"I don't know their names, but I could possibly indentify some of them if I saw them. They are not always the same people," the professor answered.

"Listen, professor, I will look into this, but here is what I want you to do. The next time you have a problem I want you to call the police and file a complaint. Then you should call my office and notify Berta Stecht, the lady that brought you into my office. She will direct your call to one of our officers. We will take it from there. Understood?"

"Yes, sir," Walden said, "and you have my thanks for taking the time to see me and remembering me from your younger days in my class. Thank you very much, sir."

"Quite all right, professor. Have a nice day, and we will see if we can provide you some relief from the harassment and invasion of your personal life. Good day to you, sir."

Becker called Berta in and instructed her to provide the professor with the phone number and to expect a call from him. Becker told her briefly what the problem was and that she was to inform Captain Schwarz as soon as she received a call from the professor.

Becker also briefed the captain and instructed him to post a couple of agents around the old gentleman's home. The agents were to be instructed to immediately notify the office of any further hostile acts against the professor. They were also to arrest any intruders that inflicted harm on the professor or his property.

"If need be," Becker said, "the agents should hold the perpetrators until our office can send a detachment to bring them in.

Later that day, Captain Schwarz brought in a couple of men who said they were engineers and were there to offer their services. The captain had spent some time with them, and he wanted to bring Becker up to speed on what they had discussed and how the engineers could assist the Gestapo in surveillance activities. Becker was satisfied with their presentation and signed off on the project. The engineers were to begin as soon as they could obtain the necessary equipment and personnel.

After the engineers left, the captain and Becker discussed the day's events further. "Captain, the old gentleman that was in earlier today is a former instructor of mine that I have not seen in years. He has become a target of some of Rohm's hoodlums. This ties into what we are working on with the Rohm project. This is not an isolated event and should help expose the rogue activities of Rohm and his band of outlaws.

"As far as the listening devices are concerned," Becker continued, "I want one put in Sara Klein's residence near the telephone as soon as they are ready for operation. I think listening to Mr. Klein's calls can enlighten us. This has nothing to do with the Rohm case but plenty to do with those who would do harm to the Gestapo. I am referring in particular to that dog Wilhelm Donst."

"I understand, colonel, and I hope we can bring the surveillance program into operation within the next two weeks," responded Schwarz. "As to the old professor, we will have to wait on something over there to happen, but we will be ready to act on a moment's notice.

"Does Sara know about the listening device?" Schwarz asked.

"Not yet, but I will inform her, possibly tonight," Becker replied. "It will make it much easier for our crew to plant the devices with her knowledge and assistance. While I am thinking about it, I will call her and tell her to meet me in the hotel lounge later this evening. You are welcome to be there if you like," Becker said.

"Thank you, sir," Schwarz replied. "I have an engagement with a nice lady later in the evening, but I would like to sit in on your meeting with Sara, and a good stiff drink will certainly be welcome after another tough day here at headquarters. Do you think Sara will mind?"

"She probably will mind if you decide to stay too long, but who cares?" Becker joked. "Actually, I am sure she would be happy to have you join us."

"Colonel you are a fortunate man to have a beautiful woman like Sara who worships the ground that you stand on."

"Captain, you know that Sara is a married woman. I am sure her devotion is more to her job and the fatherland," Becker said.

"Sure," Schwarz said with a big laugh.

"Regarding the listening devices, we need to think about how we can plant a bug in Rohm's office or his residence," Becker said. "We need to get him on record making anti-Hitler statements. See what you can come up with."

After the captain left, Becker called Sara and asked if she would like to meet him at the lounge at seven. She eagerly accepted.

Becker was running a little late that evening. Sara greeted him with a kiss when he arrived, and the captain said hello. "Sorry I'm late, but I had an unexpected call from the minister that I had to take," Becker said. "I see that you two have already ordered."

The waitress appeared, and Becker ordered a beer and took a seat next to Sara. "What the hell is all that noise outside, captain?" Becker asked.

"That is another one of those Storm Trooper parades. They are going to one of their rallies," Schwarz answered.

The sound of the marching band and the goose-stepping marchers almost drowned out the conversation.

"They will pass by in another fifteen minutes," the captain said.

"I wonder who their featured speaker of the evening will be," Becker said.

"Probably that fat pig Rohm," Sara quipped.

"The captain has another engagement this evening, so we can take care of a little business before he has to go," Becker said. "Sara, we are going to place a listening device in your residence. The purpose, of course, is to monitor the conversations of Karl and his co-conspirators, whoever they may be. It is not intended to monitor any intimate conversations or sexual encounters that you and your husband may from time to time engage in," Becker joked.

"Colonel, you need not worry about that," she countered. "Besides, I need to tell you that I plan on moving out as soon as I can find a suitable place. I can hardly stand the sight of that man. The other night he had the gall to ask if he could spend the night with me. Can you believe that?"

"Yes and why not?" Becker replied. "But seriously, I think it might be best if you did find another place. Let's get our listening device planted before that happens. I might even impose on the manager of the hotel to find you a flat here."

"Oh, colonel, would you please?" Sara said. "I would love to live here if I can afford it."

"I think he will cooperate with us on that," Becker said. "He has been most accommodating ever since I became an officer with the Gestapo. I will speak to him about it. In fact, I will tell the waitress to summon him now." Becker motioned to the waitress. "*Fraulein*, will you ask the front desk to have the manager come to our table?"

"Yes, sir," the waitress said before she scurried off to the lobby.

In a few minutes, the hotel manager, a tubby gentleman in his fifties, appeared with a huge grin. "Good evening, Colonel Becker. It is a great pleasure, as always, to offer my services. How sir, may I help you this evening?" Schmidt asked.

"Hello Herr Schmidt, may I introduce two members of my staff? I might add that they are two most important members of my staff, Sara Klein and Captain Kurt Schwarz."

"It is my great pleasure to meet both of you. On behalf of our hotel, we are deeply honored to have such distinguished guests with us tonight," the manager said with a bow.

"Manager Schmidt, I have a great favor to ask of you," Becker said. "This beautiful young lady has decided that she would like to become a permanent guest of this hotel. I wonder if you would be so kind as to find her a suitable apartment here, of course at a reduced rate. After all, you know our public servants must be frugal with their funds because of the inadequate compensation they receive from the government."

"Of course colonel, I will be most happy to accommodate this beautiful lady," the manager answered. "My dear lady, please let me know when it is convenient and I will gladly show you what we have to offer. As a favor to the colonel, you may rest assured that you will be happy with our offering." Schmidt said.

Sara, flashing her beautiful smile, thanked him for his hospitality and told him that she would call the next day to make an appointment to see the apartments.

Becker turned to the manager and said, "Thank you, you have been most gracious. Your generous hospitality and that of this grand hotel will not be forgotten."

"Now that the problem of finding living quarters for Sara has been settled, we can get back to the business at hand," Becker said. "Sara, the captain will set up a time when our crew can meet you and place the device in a location conducive to maximizing the sound. It needs to be close to the telephone so that Karl's conversation can be distinctly overheard from a location nearby. Are we all clear on this?"

Sara and the captain both nodded in agreement. It was time for the captain to leave. He got up and excused himself and said he would see them back at headquarters tomorrow.

After the captain left, Sara turned to Becker and asked, "When can I call you by your first name? It is so unromantic to keep having to say *colonel this* and *colonel that*. I am tired of only getting to say your name while I am bathing, alone thinking about you."

"Okay. Sara, you are now permitted to call me by name when we are alone. Actually, I have never forbidden you to call me by name. At least, I cannot recall such a restriction." "Oh Konrad thank you, I promise you will not be sorry. And getting me that apartment, I just can't believe how lucky I am to have such a wonderful man in my life. I am truly floating in the clouds," Sara said.

"Don't float too high," he admonished. "I admit that you have slipped yourself into my life, but I must warn you that our relationship cannot interfere with my duties."

"I truly understand," she said, "and I promise that I will never do anything that would offend you or cause any problem for you. I would sooner die."

"Let's not take it that far," Becker said. "I think it is time to go as soon as we finish our drinks. It's still early. Would you like to come up to my apartment for a drink?"

Sara accepted, and they went up to the apartment. After mixing a couple of drinks, they sat down on the sofa and relaxed. It really felt good, Becker thought. He was comfortable with her even though he knew he was asking for trouble. Not necessarily from Karl Klein, but from Sara Klein and Konrad Becker.

"Konrad, you are such a handsome man in that black SS uniform. But everyone wonders why you are the only Gestapo officer that ever wears the black uniform. I—and every other woman that sees you—feel faint when we see you."

"The answer is quite simple, Sara. When I was brought into the Gestapo, even though I was not officially assigned to the SS, Hermann Goring thought it would add additional prestige to my position. He prevailed upon the *fuhrer* to make the distinction. I think it probably is the only case, other than the *fuhrer*'s personal guards, in which someone outside the SS is allowed this honor. I did not seek it, but I certainly have no objection to it. I am sure that Himmler is probably not too happy with it, but that's his problem, not mine."

"Whatever the reason," she said, "you are quite an irresistible man, whether in your black uniform or the gray one. You are also mysterious. Nobody knows much about you. Tell me about yourself."

"There is not much to tell," Becker said. "I was born in Munich and went to school there. My father was a general in the army. I come from a long line of military officers. I enlisted in the World War, and after my training I was sent to the front. I was wounded and sent to Berlin to recuperate. From there, I attended the university and studied English. After several years in army intelligence, I was assigned to the German Embassy in America. When I came back, I met you, and now here we are. That is my life, at least up to now. Now you tell me about yourself. I know you married an asshole, but what about your life before that?"

"I was born just outside of Berlin," Sara said. "My father was an employee in a mercantile store, so growing up I lived a frugal life. I practically drove my mother crazy when I was a teenager. She thought I had too many boyfriends, and she worried about me. As soon as I finished my schooling, I left home to get away from my parents' strict discipline. I came to Berlin and got a job as a waitress at a beer hall. That is where I met Karl. He had a good job with the government, and like most young girls, I felt like I needed the security of a man. He promised to get me a job with the government, and so I decided to accept his proposal and, like an idiot, married him. I never really loved him, but I guess I felt like he could support me. My father and mother still live outside Berlin, but sad to say, I don't see them often.

And that pretty much sums up my life, except to say that I didn't know what real happiness was until I met you," Sara said. "I knew the first time I saw you that you were the man of my dreams. I vowed right then that I would never let you get away. I told the girls in the office that I was going to get you. And what Sara wants, Sara gets, my dear Colonel Konrad Becker."

"I have never met a woman like you," Becker said. "Any man

would be lucky to have you. You have a great personality. And you are without a doubt the most beautiful woman that I have ever seen. But as I told you before, I am not in a position to make a commitment."

"But why not?" she asked.

"Right now I can't explain it to you. It is too complicated. You are just going to have to live with that for now. This is a very dangerous time for me, and you are going to have to have patience," he explained.

"Is it because I am still married?" she asked. "As soon as I move out, I am filing for divorce."

"Of course that is part of it," Becker replied. "We can discuss it further after the divorce," Becker said, wanting to buy time. He knew that his mission was the real obstacle to their relationship "Look what time it is. Get up, it's time I sent you home."

Becker could see the look of disappointment on her face when he said that Sergeant Heinz was waiting in the car outside the hotel to take her home.

"I was hoping I could sleep over. Do we have to end the evening so early?" Sara asked.

"I am afraid so, my dear," Becker said. "I am not happy about it, but practicality must prevail. You are going to have to change your marital status before this relationship can get to that point."

It was not the morality question that concerned him. Everyone already assumed they were sleeping together. But that was all it was: an assumption. There was no way of telling how much fallout there would be if the suspicions were true and their relationship became an issue in Sara's divorce case. Involvement of a high-ranking official in the Gestapo in a marital dispute must be avoided.

"I hope you can understand that a marital scandal involving a high ranking Gestapo official is unacceptable," Becker said. "It has nothing to do with the feelings I have for you. Now get that behind of yours off the sofa, and let's head downstairs."

"Okay, you mean man," Sara said with a giggle. She was feeling much better after his explanation. She fully understood, or at least thought she did, what was at stake. Besides, she knew that divorce was not far off. She had waited this long, so a few more weeks wouldn't matter.

When they got downstairs, Heinz was patiently waiting in the car. Becker instructed him to take Sara home. He also told Heinz to wait outside her home for a while to make sure she did not have a problem with Karl Klein. In the event something should happen, Heinz was to intervene immediately.

When the car reached Sara's home, she got out and said, "Thank you, Gerhard, and goodnight."

"You are welcome, Sara. I will wait out here for a while. If you have a problem, just blink the lights for me," Heinz said.

"I am sure everything will be okay, Gerhard, thanks."

When Sara entered the house, Karl was waiting for her and demanded to know where she had been. "I was attending a meeting," Sara said. "You know, I do have a job."

"I guess you were hanging out with that damned Becker, weren't you?" he growled.

"Listen, asshole, I wasn't 'hanging out' with anybody. I was with my boss and Captain Schwarz, if you must know. Now get out of my way. I am tired, and I want to go to bed."

"Go ahead, you bitch," Karl roared. "You will pay for this before it's over, that I can promise you."

"Oh, is that right? Is that a threat? Who is going to make me pay? It is it you and that skinny asshole that you have been sucking up to lately?" she asked.

"I ought to slap the shit out of you right now," he threatened as he advanced toward her.

"Go ahead. Sergeant Heinz is still out there, hoping you will try something like that so that he can blow your stupid head off," Sara countered.

Karl stepped back, startled, and went to look out the front window. He then headed for his bedroom without saying another word. A few minutes after the lights went out, Sergeant Heinz drove off.

Sara Klein knew that it was time to get out, and the sooner the better. Tomorrow should bring an answer as to how soon, that and the placement of whatever the hell they were going to put in the house to listen in on Karl's conversations. The thought of a new life without Karl brought a sudden wave of relief. Sara drifted off to sleep, confident that his fear of the colonel would protect her from him doing her harm.

"Good morning, Colonel Becker," Sara said, beaming, the next morning. "How are you this beautiful day?"

"Hello, Sara. I am doing fine. Evidently your homecoming last night was not too distasteful, judging by your cheery outlook this morning."

"Oh, on the contrary, my homecoming was anything but 'not too distasteful,' as you describe it. My considerate husband was waiting up for me, and his behavior was much more than distasteful. He even threatened to slap the you-know-what out of me," Sara said. "Oh, Konrad, I don't know if I can spend another night under the same roof with that poor excuse for a man. I think he would have struck me if I had not told him that Sergeant Heinz was waiting outside in the car. Konrad, what am I going to do?"

"One thing you can do is to maintain the cheery attitude you came in here with," Becker said. "The other is to get on over to the *Tiergarten* and let Schmidt show you an apartment. I will put a rush on the planting of the device in your home. I don't want you to worry your pretty little head over this. I will make sure that you are taken care of."

"Thank you so much," she answered. "I am so thankful that you have come into my life."

"Never mind that, Sara, you just get back to work and stay strong. You are going to be fine. And tell Berta to set up a meeting with Goring, preferably today."

"Yes, sir, and I will try and get over to the hotel before lunchtime," she promised before she walked out of the office.

"Colonel, you have an appointment with Minister Goring at three o'clock this afternoon. Is there anything I can get for you?" said Berta. "Captain Schwarz would also like to come in when you have time."

"Thanks, Berta, have the captain come on in," Becker said.

A few minutes later, the captain entered the room. "Good morning, colonel. I trust your evening went well after I left last night."

"Yes, quite well, thank you," Becker said. "Sara was not as fortunate when she got home, though. Her husband is not a happy warrior, and he treated her rather shabbily."

"I am sorry to hear that," Schwarz replied. "Sara is such a wonderful person. She deserves better."

"I couldn't agree more," Becker said. "Once she is rid of that bastard, I think things will get much better for her. I want you to expedite our project out at the Klein house. I want her out of there as soon as possible. He is too much of a coward to physically harm her, but there is no doubt that she will feel much better away from him."

"I just spoke to one of the engineers, and he says they should be ready tomorrow to do the job out there," Schwarz said.

"Very good, captain. Coordinate with Sara and get it done."

Chapter Ten

Becker arrived at Goring's office right on time. The receptionist greeted him. "Good afternoon, Colonel Becker. I will tell the minister that you are here. May I get you refreshments or something?"

"No, thank you," he replied. The receptionist beckoned that he should go on into Goring's office.

"Colonel Becker. Please have a seat," Goring said. "It is so good to see you. I am disappointed that you didn't bring that lovely lady on your staff. What's her name?"

"Sara, Sara Klein, Herr Minister. No, she was not able to accompany me this time, although I am sure she would be pleased to be here, but perhaps next time." Becker knew that damn lecher would always like to see a good-looking woman, especially one as pretty as Sara.

"What can I do for you today, colonel?" Goring asked.

"First of all, we are proceeding on the Rohm project," Becker said. "I have encountered another problem that I felt should be called to your attention. It should not cause you concern, but I felt like you should know about it. Sara Klein's husband has apparently decided that I have become dispensable. I am not the least bit concerned that he alone poses a serious threat to me. However, it appears that he has recruited an ally, or more likely, the other way around. The ally may have recruited him."

"You know that rumors travel, and I have heard that you are, shall we say, having your way with the young lady," Goring said. "As far as I am concerned, I just wish it was me instead. That woman is a looker. And I might also add that rank has its privileges. A man of your rank certainly deserves to have some pleasure in life, considering all the sacrifices you have made and will continue to make for the fatherland."

"Thank you, Herr Minister, but truthfully I have not at this time enjoyed the ultimate gift of this fair lady's sexual favors. There are certain impediments that I think should be removed before I embark on that journey," Becker said.

"What a gentleman you are, colonel. I admire your patience in the matter and of course wish you well. What, may I ask, is the problem?" Goring asked.

"There is one caveat to this story that I have not gotten into," Becker replied. "Klein has been approached by Major Wilhelm Donst, an SS officer. A conversation was overheard between the two discussing my demise, a prospect that I find quite unappealing."

"That must be that skinny fellow that has been following Heinrich around lately," answered Goring. "I frankly don't like his looks. You must exercise great care because I suspect that pipsqueak is not acting without some kind of consent from his boss."

"That is exactly what I was thinking, and consequently, I have put into place a plan to counteract their activities," Becker said.

"The Himmler connection is a more serious problem and would indicate that Donst's interest extends higher up."

"I see where you are going with this, Colonel, and I quite agree. That worm Himmler would like nothing better than to undercut my relationship with our *fuhrer*. He has made no effort to conceal his desire to take over the Gestapo. But, colonel, I need someone over there that I can depend on. There are few people that can be trusted these days. I can't even trust my own relatives. So I just want you to be assured that you have my full support.

"We must always keep in mind though that the higher you go, the more interest is out there to bring you down," Goring continued. "At the present time we must take on one adversary at a time, and presently our emphasis is on Rohm. He represents the biggest threat not only to the *fuhrer* but to me as well. But don't let that stop you from protecting yourself from those dogs. That holds true even though they may have the support of people in high positions. That includes Himmler."

"Thank you, Herr Minister," Becker said. "You have reinforced my confidence, and I am prepared to take on whatever they may come at me with. I have an excellent staff, and thanks to you, I have been assured by Colonel Richter that I have a sizable army unit that I can call upon when needed. Now I must return to headquarters unless you have something else that needs attention."

Becker now knew how nauseating playing a role could be. He reminded himself that survival must always be uppermost in his mind. *So Goring is a bloated piece of manure*, Becker thought. *I need his support to succeed. I just have to suck it up and get on with the mission.*

"Thank you for the update," Goring said. "Keep me informed on our main project and any other matters that you think I should be aware of. Heil Hitler."

"Heil Hitler," Becker said, giving the arm salute as he left. As he was going out, the receptionist asked him to say hello to Sara. He thanked her for her hospitality and told her he would relay her message to Sara.

The hour was getting late, so Becker hurried back to headquarters to find out how Sara had fared in looking at lodging at the *Tiergarten*. She popped in to let Becker know how the day went. She was brimming with enthusiasm and couldn't wait to fill him in on the details.

"Oh Konrad," she said. "That Mr. Schmidt is such a gentleman and was so nice I couldn't believe it. I chose a wonderful apartment, although it is not on the same floor as yours, darn it. That is what I wanted, but there was nothing available on your floor. But I know you will just love my new place. And even more delightful is that it's well within my price range. I couldn't believe it when he quoted me the rent. Konrad, pinch me because I can't believe this is all happening to me. I am in love with the most wonderful man in the world, and I am just beside myself. Please forgive me if I am acting like a silly school girl, but I am so happy."

"I'm glad you are happy," Becker replied, "but don't get carried away. You still have some big problems to deal with, so I suggest that you get on with it. By the way, that lady over at Goring's office, Lana or whatever her name is, said to say hello to you. You seem to be moving up in the world."

"Oh she did?" Sara said. "Maybe I am moving up in the world, thanks to you. My mother would definitely approve of you."

"That would be nice," he said. "Now I think the captain is ready to set up a time to plant the listening device, so talk to him and get that done."

After Sara left, Becker summoned his office assistant. "Berta, check with Captain Schwarz and get me an update on the Professor Walden case."

"Yes sir. I do know that our people are out there, so I think we are just waiting for something to happen," she said. Captain

Schwarz will be in shortly, and I will tell him that he needs to give you a report. Is there anything else you need, sir?"

"No, that will be all for now," Becker said.

"Oh, I just remembered, colonel, Director Diels sent word that work in the basement is coming along well and that you should take a look at what they have done so far," Berta said.

"Very well, when Captain Schwarz comes in, we will go down there and check on it."

Later that day Becker and the captain went to the basement to check on the so-called improvements. They were welcomed by the construction supervisor, who started the tour in the area where the "enhanced interrogations" were to take place. What they were seeing sent shivers up Becker's back."Captain, what in the hell is that for?" Becker asked. That is what they call water boarding, an uncivilized practice that creates a sense of drowning and has been outlawed by the Geneva Convention and dates back to the Spanish Inquisition" Schwarz explained. "Then over there is the area for body stretching techniques and electrical shocks, and of course the cell block to house suspects and inmates' he went on.

"Kurt, I think I have seen enough," Becker said "Let's get the hell out of this dungeon. This is not something that I have any interest in. There must be a better way of extracting information from prisoners than this."

The captain agreed, and they returned to the office.

"Can you believe the situation down there, captain?" Becker asked.

"No sir, I cannot. Evidently when it comes to collecting information, somebody means business. It doesn't sound like Diels. This is coming from somewhere else."

They were interrupted by a call for Captain Schwarz, informing him that the crew was ready to do the Klein project. Schwarz and Sara left the office to meet the installation crew at the Klein residence.

En route, Sara thought it would be a good time to engage the captain in conversation about her personal life and feel him out about how the colonel felt about her. She felt insecure and wanted another perspective. "Kurt, you remember the meeting at the hotel the other night when the colonel told me to look for an apartment at the *Tiergarten*? In case you haven't heard, I found the perfect one yesterday. I can't wait to move in. I really am excited about it."

"Sara, you are not very good at hiding your emotions. I think by now everybody in Berlin knows about it. I am very happy for you, and I really hope things work out for you," Schwarz replied.

"Kurt, you must know by now how crazy I am about the colonel," she said. "Sometimes he is so cool and strict that I have a hard time reading him. I think he cares for me, but he doesn't like to show any affection in public, and it keeps me in a state of anxiety. I have butterflies in my stomach just thinking about him. Do you think he cares for me, I mean, really cares for me?"

"You are one of the most beautiful women I have ever seen, and no man could resist your charms," Schwarz said. "As for the colonel, he is hard to read, but I can tell you this: If he didn't care for you, you would be long gone. Seriously, I believe he cares a great deal for you, but you know he is a career soldier, and you are going to have to compete with that. He is a strong man, and I guess he does not like to show affection, at least publicly. Maybe he thinks that showing affection is a sign of weakness. I do know this, if anyone tried to harm you in any way, they would not be of this life for very long. Everybody not only respects the colonel, but they fear him. Nobody wants to get crossways with him except maybe that dumb husband of yours. I even think that Goring and Himmler fear him."

"Kurt, I hope you are right. I don't know what I would do without him in my life. I knew it the first time I laid eyes on him at General Schleicher's office. I only married Karl out of desperation. I was just a young, inexperienced kid that thought I had all the answers. I never loved Karl. I didn't know what love was.

"Please don't mention to the Colonel that we had this conversation. He would kill me on the spot. Oh, stop at the next house on the right," she shouted to the driver.

When the work was completed at the Klein house, the captain and Sara returned to headquarters. They reported immediately to the colonel that the work had been completed. After testing was finished, the system was in operation.

"Sir, all we have to do now is to sit back and wait for the conversations to begin. We don't think anyone paid attention to what we were doing. With Sara present, there was no reason for anyone to suspect anything," Schwarz said.

"Good work, captain. I am sure it won't take long for that fool to start shooting off his big mouth. Too bad we can't hear the other end of the conversations, but hopefully we can obtain enough information coming out of Klein's mouth.

"Sara, I see no reason that you cannot go ahead with your plans to move," Becker continued. "Captain, do you see the need for her to participate anymore?"

"I can't think of anything, sir, unless something goes wrong that would require her to go back inside the house. If some problem does arise, we should be able to re-enter the premises without her participation."

"Good, then let's move on to other business," Becker said. "Sara, you are excused and you are free to proceed with your moving plans. If you need help, Captain Schwarz will see to it that you get it. Okay?"

"Yes sir. Would you like to take a look at my new apartment?" she asked.

"Yes, I would, but I will have to get back to you on that," Becker said. "Call me at home this evening, and we'll see."

The next day, while going through some files on persons of interest, Becker was interrupted by Captain Schwarz. "Colonel, we have just been notified that our agents at Professor Walden's home have apprehended three storm troopers on the professor's property. They reported that there was some resistance, and reinforcements had to be called in, but they are now in custody and on their way to headquarters."

"Good," Becker said. "When they get here, throw their ass in one of those cells in the basement. This will be a good time to break in those facilities."

An hour later, the captain stepped into the office and announced that the special guests had arrived. The colonel accompanied Schwarz to the basement to conduct the interviews. By the time they got down there, the prisoners had been placed in separate cells. Becker and Schwarz went to one of the interrogation rooms, one that regular interrogations could be conducted in, without the equipment for so-called enhanced techniques. The captain instructed an agent to bring in the first prisoner. The agents brought in a big, burly man in his thirties. He had a shaved head and a surly attitude.

"Boy," Becker said to him, "do you know why you are here?"

"Naw, not really, unless it's because we were out at that old Jew professor's house to shape him up and teach him not to disrespect law enforcement," he answered. "And who the hell are you?"

"After I get through knocking the shit out of you, I'll tell you," Becker said as he pulled his Luger out and smashed it into the middle of the man's forehead. "Look, asshole," Becker calmly said, "as soon as you can gather your wits and show the proper respect for an officer of the Gestapo, we will get on with this interview. Do you understand me?"

"Yes sir. I didn't know who you were," the man said as he tried to pull himself up from the floor. He wiped blood off his forehead and stood wobbling for a minute, trying to regain his balance.

"Now that you know," Becker said, "sit down in that chair and behave yourself, or I'll have one of these guards put a bullet in your ass. "Corporal," Becker said to one of the guards, and "hand that bastard a towel to wipe the blood off of his face so he can see me while I ask him some more questions."

After wiping his face, the man sat down, seeming to have a much better understanding of his situation. His hands started to tremble. Becker concluded that the man was finally ready to conduct his interview without any more aggression. Becker had his attention.

"Who is in charge of your little group that we brought in here today?" asked Becker?.

"I guess that would be me," the prisoner said.

"What is your name?" Becker demanded.

"Ludwig Weiner."

"Ludwig Wiener what?" Becker shot back.

"Ludwig Wiener, sir."

"Wiener, who told you that Professor Walden was a Jew?" Becker asked.

"I don't remember exactly, but everybody knows he's a Jew, sir. We have orders to put them kind in their place."

"Whose orders?" asked Becker.

"My superior officers, and we just follow orders," answered Wiener.

"Well, you ignorant son of a bitch, it just so happens that the professor is not a Jew. Do your orders specify that you take it for granted that a person is Jewish? Do you think you can use your own judgment in making decisions like that?" Becker asked in rapid fire.

"That's pretty much the way I understand it," Weiner whined. "You can tell by looking at 'em."

"I can look at you and tell that you are an asshole, but I can't tell if you are Jewish or not," Becker countered. "Just because you are wearing that uniform does not give you the authority to abuse respectable citizens who have not broken any laws. You are going to stay locked up until you wise up.

"Take him to the medics and let them sew him up, and then put him into a holding cell," Becker ordered. "On second thought, put him into the cell that is occupied by those two rowdies that are being held for killing a policeman."

"Yes, sir," one of the guards said as they whisked Weiner out of the interrogation room.

"Does the SA have any minimal qualifications for their personnel, captain?" Becker asked.

"Colonel, based on what I have seen, the answer is clearly no. Shall I bring another suspect in?"

"Yes, let's see if we can find anyone in this bunch that has a brain," Becker said.

The second man was escorted into the room and seated in the witness chair. Apparently he had overheard part of what went on in the earlier interview, because he was quite subdued. He was a large man that could easily bully others.

"What is your name?" Becker asked.

"Otto Brimer, sir" the bully answered.

"Who was in charge of the group that was harassing Professor Walden?" Becker asked.

"That would be Ludwig Weiner, sir."

"Who is his superior officer?"

"Sergeant Erich Hauser, sir," Brimer answered.

"Whose orders were you following when you went on the professor's property?" Becker asked.

"I don't know for sure. I guess it was Hauser," Brimer answered. "We had been out there before, and the old man was sassing us, so Ludwig said it was time to pay another visit. Besides, ain't that old man a Jew?"

"He is a German citizen and comes from a long line of upper-class Germans," Becker replied. "Do you have standard guidelines from your superiors to determine whether or not a person is a Jew? What criteria do you use in making that determination?"

"Cri-what? What is that, sir?" the detainee asked.

"Never mind, listen to me," Becker ordered. "Do you have a family? If you do, and you do not answer my questions truthfully, your family will never see you again. Do you understand what I am saying?" Becker asked.

"Yes, sir, I do have a family. I understand what you just said, and I swear to tell you the truth."

"Do you know the name of Hauser's superior officer?" Becker asked.

"I guess that would be Captain Bruno Stern."

"Captain Schwarz, have Hauser and Stern picked up and brought in for questioning," Becker ordered. "These louts know nothing. That is all the questions I have for this man. Have him returned to his cell.

"Captain, can you believe these imbeciles have been out on the streets playing soldier?" Becker asked. "If these people are representative of the SA, there may be over a million more just like them. No wonder Goring and Himmler want Rohm's head. It seemed like such a waste of time dealing with these lowly swine, but it may be the only way that we can establish a link of misconduct and abuse carried out by the SA that extends all the way to the top."

"I agree with you, sir," Schwarz answered.

The following day, Becker was advised that Hauser and Stern had been picked up and were waiting in the basement to be interrogated. Becker and Captain Schwarz went down to the interview room.

The captain told one of the guards to bring in Hauser first, so he could work up from there with his interrogation. The prisoner was led into the room. He appeared nervous and avoided eye contact with his interrogators. He was disheveled in his brown uniform and did not exhibit the qualities and appearance that one would expect from a soldier. He was physically out of shape, which led Becker to believe that they could expect little in the way of intellect. Becker's initial impression would quickly prove to be on the money. Becker let Captain Schwarz begin the questioning.

"What is your name, rank and your area of responsibility at the SA?" asked the captain. "Erich Hauser. I am a sergeant, and I am responsible for supervising my detail," he answered.

"You will at all times address me as sir. Do you understand that?" Schwarz demanded.

"Yes, sir," Hauser answered.

"How many men do you have in your detail?" Schwarz asked.

"Forty, sir," Hauser answered.

"What are the functions performed by your detail?" asked Captain Schwarz.

"What do you mean, sir?"

"Hauser, don't you understand plain German? What do you and your detail do for the fatherland besides inflicting harm on innocent citizens?"

"We don't do that, sir," Hauser said.

"All right, I am asking you again, what the hell do you do? And don't waste anymore of my time," Schwarz said.

"Yes sir. We enforce the law and arrest criminals and enemies of the state."

"What do you mean when you say enemies of the state?"

"Sir, we are supposed to find people who are not loyal to the Nazi party and our *fuhrer* and see that they are punished for it," Hauser said.

"Do you have any law enforcement training? And what is your occupation?" Schwarz asked.

"No, sir, I have not had formal training, but we do have a manual that we follow. I am a butcher, but I only work part time. I spend more time doing my job with the SA."

"Who is your immediate supervisor?" Schwarz asked.

"Captain Bruno Stern, sir. He is our gruppen(group) leader."

"Is that the other man that was brought in with you?"

"Yes, sir," Hauser said.

"This manual, does it say that you have the authority to detain citizens or interfere with their activities?"

"Yes sir."

"What is the authoritative source of that manual? By that I mean, what law is it based on, and who is the person responsible for issuing the manual?" Schwarz asked.

"Sir, I guess that comes from the chief of staff, Ernst Rohm. I don't know nothing about the law."

"Hauser, are you aware that you can be prosecuted for interfering with the lives of innocent German citizens?"

"Sir, we don't do that. We just go after Jews and communists."

"Are you familiar with the Professor Walden case?"

"Yes, sir, I am. He is on our list."

"On our list," Schwarz repeated. "And what list is that? He is not a Jew or a communist, so what the hell is he doing on your list?"

"Sir, I don't know the answer to that. I just carry out my orders," Hauser answered.

"And your orders were to go after all of the names on your list, is that what you are saying? Where did you get the list? Who gave you the order to pursue names on that list?"

"The list is from SA headquarters, and the orders come from Captain Stern," Hauser answered meekly.

"Hauser, you are going to be held in custody and your case will be turned over to justice officials for prosecution. Guards, take this man back to his holding cell and bring in Stern."

A guard said, "Colonel Becker, some of the prisoners have complained about the noise coming from the cell with the two police killers and that storm trooper detainee. They are saying they can't sleep because of the hollering coming from that storm trooper fellow."

"Then you may move him to another cell if you think he is ready to change the way he acts," Becker replied. "If not, maybe he should spend another day in there with those two psychos."

"Thank you, sir, I don't think he will cause us any more trouble," the guard said.

Becker was becoming restless, spending what he considered his valuable time listening to the interrogations of all of these simpletons. It was obvious that the prisoners were not going to provide the Gestapo with a smoking gun that would lead directly to Rohm. Captain Schwarz suggested that he continue the process even though the results so far were disappointing. Becker instructed Schwarz to go ahead with the interrogations, and Becker would return to the office.

The captain later reported to Becker that Stern provided basically the same information as Hauser. That did, however, move the chain up a little higher. There was no doubt that Rohm was aware of what was happening generally with his agency, even though he was probably unaware of the Walden incident itself.

Becker was officially restrained from going after these people for their attacks on Jews, but there was nothing to stop him from making life on earth miserable for the sorry bastards for doing so. Becker and his staff continued to build the case against Rohm piece by piece. It was just be a matter of time before they would be able to present more to Goring.

Chapter Eleven

The next morning, Becker called Sara into his office. "Sara, I am going to Munich. I want to visit my old school and refresh my memories. The old professor has already brought back such fond memories," he lied.

"Oh, yes, that would be terrific, colonel. I would love to go."

"My dear, I would love to take you, but I do not plan to go by motor car. It is just too far to drive. Will you please arrange an airplane flight for me tomorrow?"

"Yes sir. When do you plan to return?" she asked.

"Schedule me to return the day after tomorrow. That should give me plenty of time to complete my business. Notify the Munich headquarters of my arrival time so that they will have a car there to meet me. Also, arrange for lodging for the night."

This wasn't a good time for Becker to leave, but he thought he should get the trip out of the way. The real reason he wanted to go to Munich was to cover his tracks because somewhere, sometime, somebody was going to hit him with that part of his early life that he was not ready to confront.

Sara reported that the travel plans to Munich were complete. "Colonel, you are scheduled to leave at 10:30 AM tomorrow and should arrive in Munich in the afternoon. I also have made a reservation at Eden Hotel Wolff. Gestapo headquarters has been notified, and a car and two officers will be there to meet you at the airport. Are you sure you can't take me with you?" she pleaded "I promise to be on my best behavior."

"I am sure you would be a good girl, but this trip is about business, Sara. I am sure you must have packing and other things to do in preparation for your move to your new apartment. Incidentally, what can you tell me about that Eden Hotel Wolff?"

"Sir, I am told that the hotel is right across from the railroad station and has a sterling reputation."

"Hmm. That's interesting," Becker said. "It gives me an idea. Cancel the flight plan and book me on the train. Make if for the day after tomorrow. I know the trip by rail will take more time, but I would like to see the countryside and maybe relax along the way. I will need a private compartment and seats for my escort detail."

"Does that mean that I can go with you?" she asked. "Please?"

"Oh, all right. But listen, this is a business trip and I expect you to keep your distance and act accordingly, at least in public or in the presence of others. Is that clear?"

"Yes, yes, I will make the arrangements right away. Thank you. And how big a detail shall I tell the captain to provide for you?" Sara asked.

"Four should be adequate," he answered. "By the way, have you heard anything from Klein?"

"I have heard nothing, and I hope I never hear from him again."

"On your way out, Sara, tell the captain that I need to see him."

After a few minutes Captain Schwarz appeared and asked. "Did you have something for me colonel?" "Captain, I have decided to make a short trip down to Munich. I am going to visit the Grand Gymnasium where I attended the school in my earlier days and thought this would be a good time to revisit." Becker said. "Get in touch with that old professor, Walden, and see if he would like to make the trip with me. I am sure it would bring back some fond memories for the old fellow, and he can show me around. I changed my mind about flying down there and decided to take the train so we will have plenty of room for him"

"Yes, sir, I think the train will be more enjoyable, and it will give you a little more time to relax," Schwarz said.

"I know it will take longer to get there and back by rail, but what the hell. You can look after things here while we are gone, captain. By the way, I'm taking Sara and a four-man escort detail," Becker said. "Follow up on that, captain, and see that everything is taken care of, and have Sara come in" Becker ordered.

"Yes sir, colonel. Have a nice trip, and we will take care of things here in Berlin."

"Colonel, the railway arrangements have been made, and we leave the day after tomorrow at 8:45 AM," Sara announced as she entered the room. "I have been assured that you will have one of the finest compartments reserved for important officials. It accommodates six for seating and has two sleeping berths."

"Sara, that is fine, but there is not likely to be much sleeping on this trip. I don't know whether the captain told you, but I have invited that old professor that was in here recently to go with us. I hope that doesn't interfere with your plans. He most likely will spend a great deal of time in the compartment with us, and our escort detail will occupy space outside to ensure our privacy and security."

"Yes, sir, it does interfere with my plans," she joked. "But I'll have to live with that since I have vowed to act like a lady and keep my distance."

"Okay, you may go home now and finish packing for your move. By the way, how is that coming?" Becker asked.

"I hope to finish tonight," she replied. "All I am taking are my clothing and personal effects. Lucky for me, the new apartment is fully furnished. Are you going to be a gentleman and help me with my moving?"

"Actually, the answer to that is no," he answered. "But I will do this for you. I will have Berta and Heinz help you. How would that suit you?"

"That suits me just fine, thank you, and I will try and do it tomorrow if that is okay," Sara said.

"Done, now go see if we have heard back from the professor. I am looking forward more and more to this trip. It should be educational and therapeutic, at least for me. And you?"

"I am excited and can't wait to get on that train," she said.

"Colonel," Captain Schwarz interrupted as Sara was leaving the room. "I have been in contact with Walden, and he is grateful for the invitation to go to Munich. He has asked me to convey his thanks and says he will be at the train station at seven in the morning. Also, your escort detail has been selected and will be well-armed for the trip. They will report to the station at eight. We have also notified our Munich headquarters, and they have adjusted their plans accordingly. They will meet you at the train station in Munich and make arrangements for visiting the school. They have also alerted the school officials to expect you, and they are making the necessary preparations for the visit. Your trip should be enjoyable, as everyone there is excited.

"I am also pleased that you are taking Sara with you," Schwarz continued. "She is definitely flying high these days. I have advised her to tone it down a little because I am sure those people in Munich have rarely seen the likes of a woman as glamorous as she is. They might get the wrong impression. I am also told that the mayor of Munich would like to meet with you, as well as some party officials at the Brown House, the Munich headquarters of the Nazi party. Of course I told them that all of this is subject to your approval and at your convenience."

"Captain, you have done a fine job on this," Becker said. "If need be, you can get in touch with me through the Munich office. As for tomorrow, you may see that Berta and Sergeant Heinz are available to assist Sara in her move. I think she would like to do this before our trip. You can give them whatever time they need during the day to make the move."

"Yes, sir," Schwarz replied.

"As for that mayor and party officials, I'm not going down there to spend time with a bunch of politicians, so make up some excuse for me," Becker ordered.

"Yes sir." Schwarz replied.

The next day was fairly routine, even quiet, with most of the office staff out helping Sara move. Becker felt this would be a good time to touch base with Goring to inform him of his plans to go to Munich. Becker decided to drop in on the minister at his office. Becker informed the temporary office assistant that he was off to the Reichskanzlei Building and would be in the Minister's office.

Goring had an affable personality and got along fairly well with the military. Becker knew, of course, that Goring was a dangerous man and adhered to the evil practices of Hitler and the Nazi Party. Being in the presence of people Becker didn't like and being friendly toward them was extremely difficult, but as time went on, Becker became more adjusted to it. *Like broccoli, you just cut it up into small pieces and mix it with your potatoes to hide the taste,* Becker thought.

When Becker arrived at the minister's office, he was told that Goring had a visitor and would be with him shortly. Just as Becker sat down, the door to Goring's office burst open, and the minister asked Becker to come on in. Goring had someone he would like to introduce Becker to.

"Colonel, I would like for you to meet my dear, dear friend, Anna Gelding." Anna Gelding, a well known actress with the National Theater, is Goring's long time companion. A very attractive woman, she appeared to be about ten years older that Becker, although he later found out she was only five years his senior.

"This is indeed a great pleasure, Ms. Gelding," Becker said. "I have heard so much about you. Of course your fame precedes you. I must say, however, that your photographs do not capture your true beauty," he fibbed. Anna was a well-endowed woman above the waist but fairly petite below. Certainly she was easy on the eyes.

"Oh, thank you, colonel," she said with a smile. "I am flattered. I, too, have heard a great deal about you, sir. It seems that you are the most eligible bachelor in all of Germany and a topic of admiring conversations among the ladies, both single and married. I can certainly see why they are interested."

Becker had never met Karin, the former Mrs. Goring, as she had passed away some time ago, but the minister seemed to have good taste in his ladies, at least from Becker's point of view. On second thought, Becker thought, maybe he should limit that opinion to the ladies that Goring associated with in public. From all accounts, Goring was less discriminating in his secret liaisons.

"And please call me Anna, colonel."

"Forgive me, Anna, for intruding on your meeting with the

minister," Becker said. "I came over unannounced, taking the chance that the minister would be in the office. What a delightful surprise it is to meet one of our most famous actresses."

"Thank you again, colonel, for those very kind remarks. If you gentlemen will excuse me, I must go. Hermann, I will see you later this evening, and Colonel Becker, I do hope to see you again. Hermann and I would like to have you as our guest in a social setting."

"Thank you again, Anna," Becker answered, "and I would love to spend time with you and the minister on a social occasion. I look forward to it."

Goring walked Anna to the door and gave her a kiss on the cheek. She left the office.

"Colonel, what brings you out this fine morning?" Goring asked.

"I wanted to let you know that I plan to be out of the city for a few days, Herr Minister. I am taking the train to Munich tomorrow morning and was wondering if I might be of some service to you while I am down there."

"Offhand, I can't think of anything, colonel. Are you taking that delicate flower with you? What's her name, Sara?"

"Yes, Herr Minister," Becker said. "I am sure you know how difficult it is to perform your duties without the assistance of a trusted and competent aide. I am also taking an old professor of mine. He was one of my teachers in my early school days in Munich."

"What school did you attend down there, colonel?" Goring asked.

"Grand Gymnasium," Becker replied.

"Oh, yes, I have heard of that school. In Schwabing, I believe. Where did you receive your military training?"

"I attended the military academy in Berlin," answered Becker. After the war, I was given a leave of absence from my military duties to attend Ludwig Maximilian University in Munich, where I studied the English language. I became quite proficient in English, and that was a great influence on my being assigned to our embassy in the United States.

"Oh, yes, and your father, General Becker would be very proud of you," Goring said. "And a great soldier he was. Colonel, you have an outstanding background, and your English speaking ability certainly enhances that. The *fuhrer* will be pleased to know that you speak English so well. There may be a possibility that you may be of use to the fatherland in future diplomatic assignments. There are so few of our army officers that the *fuhrer* trusts—in fact, zero."

"One more thing before I leave, Herr Minister" Becker said. We arrested a few of Rohm's clowns the other day. They had been out stirring up trouble, specifically, abusing an elderly gentleman who happens to be the old school teacher who I mentioned earlier. They had on other occasions beat the old man, and I had a stakeout put in place that apprehended them when they returned. During their interrogation, it was revealed that their motive in attacking this old man was that he was a Jew and that he was showing a lack of respect. It turns out that the professor is not a Jew and comes from an old-line, respectable German family.

"There is no doubt but this type of activity is being encouraged and sanctioned from the top of the SA without the proper safeguards to protect our true German citizenry," Becker continued. "We have included this case in our ongoing investigation of Rohm, and I'll check in with you after we return from Munich to update you on that project. That is all I have, so I will let myself out. Heil Hitler." Becker saluted.

"Heil Hitler. Have a good trip, colonel, and say hello to your assistant for me."

When Becker returned to the office, it was in a flurry of activity.

"Colonel, all hell has broken loose," Schwarz announced. "Some of the top SA people are in a snit over the arrest and retention of their troopers."

"Thanks, captain. That's good. Let 'em get their asses up in the air. Have you done anything to settle them down?" Becker asked.

"No sir, I just talked to a caller who identified himself as SA *Gruppenfuhrer* Karl Fleischer. I made it clear to him that unwarranted attacks on German citizens will not be tolerated and offenders are going to be arrested and prosecuted. He didn't take that well and said he would take the matter up with SA Deputy Papen."

"Good work, captain. Have you heard anything from the movers?"

"No sir, I have not," Schwarz answered.

"I think I am going home, myself," Becker said. "I need to get some things ready for my trip tomorrow. I'll check in on Sara when I get to the hotel. I'll see you when we get back from Munich."

"Yes sir. Have a good trip."

When Becker got to the hotel, he went up to Sara's apartment to see how she was doing. Her door was open, so he walked in. The place was a mess.

"Hi, colonel," Sara said. "Welcome to my new home. We have moved everything over here, but now the fun begins putting everything in the right place. I didn't realize that I had so much junk. I am pooped out already, and I have a long way to go."

"It looks like it to me. Do you have to do it all today?" Becker asked.

"I guess not," she replied. "but I want to do it as soon as I can.

I know Berta is about to flop. I don't know what I would have done without her and Heinz. Can I get you a drink, colonel?"

"No, thanks, I think I will go on to my apartment. I still have some things to do tonight. I will see you in the morning. Sergeant Heinz is to pick us up at eight, so be ready," he reminded her.

"Yes, sir, I'll be ready. I will see you in the morning unless you would like to come back later for a drink," she said as he walked out the door.

Sergeant Heinz picked them up the next morning at eight, and Sara was right on time. Becker didn't know how much sleep she had gotten, but she was bright and sassy, as usual. At the station, the escort and the professor were waiting. Walden said he had been there for over an hour and was ready to go. They all boarded the train and pulled out of the station about fifteen minutes later.

"Professor, if you don't mind," Becker said, "please be seated next to the young lady who is one of my trusted aides. Sara Klein, this is Professor Walden."

"I met the professor when he came to headquarters to report those attacks. It is so nice to see you again, professor," Sara said. "If I can get anything for you on our trip, please let me know."

"Hello again, Fraulein Klein, or is it Frau Klein? Oh, yes, colonel, I remember her. How could I forget such a beautiful young lady?"

"Sir, at present I am married, but I expect my status in that regard will change very soon," Sara said, glancing at Becker for a sign of approval or joy. "But you can just call me Sara. Thank you so much for the compliments."

"Sara, it is my great pleasure to be seated beside such a vivacious young woman," the old man said with obvious pleasure.

"Professor, Sara is married to a wonderful chap who I think works at the Chancellery," Becker said.

"Professor, you must not pay attention to the colonel. He takes great delight in teasing me about my miserable marriage," Sara said as she pointed a finger at Becker.

This trip was turning out to be a fun and interesting time for Becker, with these two sitting across from him. After the train pulled out of the station, it wasn't long before Becker started to see the countryside and a peaceful feeling fell over him. He watched the beautiful scenery flash by and listened to the clacking on the rails as the train picked up speed.

"Professor, when did you leave the old school, and how did you wind up in Berlin?" Becker asked.

"Sir, I was born in Berlin. When I retired in 1921, I returned with my wife to live in the old house that my parents had owned and in which I spent my early childhood. My wife Anna, bless her soul, passed away three years ago. Since that time, I have lived alone. I miss her terribly. With all the turmoil and problems I have encountered recently, I feel sometimes that maybe it is time for me to join her. Being invited on this trip has greatly boosted my spirits. Colonel, you have my gratitude for that. It is so kind of you to extend such a courtesy to me. Thank you again, sir, from the bottom of my heart."

"Think nothing of it, professor. Why, this trip would be quite boring without you. Isn't that true, Sara?"

"Why, yes, of course," she lied. "And I am so sorry to hear about the loss of your beloved wife. But let's not look back and dwell on the past. Rather, let's look ahead and enjoy our trip to Munich, where I am sure the both of you can rekindle some of the fond memories of the life you enjoyed in those years gone by."

The professor smiled and leaned back in his seat, and Becker could tell the old man was already thinking about the good times when he was a young man trying to corral young rascals like Becker. The happiness was written all over his face, and Becker felt much better about bringing Sara on this trip. She had a way of making people feel good. *It is generally assumed that women of great beauty are more interested in themselves than others,* Becker thought. *Not so with this one. She really cares about others.* Becker was thankful that he had found her. He wondered what she would think if she knew his whole story. He knew he might never find out.

"Professor, when did you start teaching at Grand?" Becker asked.

"I started when the school opened in 1901. I was one of eleven teachers when the school started."

"I enrolled at the school in 1908, when I was ten years old," Becker said. "I graduated in 1916, when I enlisted in the army. Sad to say, but my memories of my days at the school are somewhat fuzzy. Forgive me if I sometimes appear to be detached from those early years. So much has happened to me since then, I guess I have blocked out the early days."

"Colonel I understand. All of the pressure and the responsibility that you have taken on must have taken its toll. I too have memory lapses, but mine are due to my advanced years. I will soon be seventy nine years old," the professor admitted.

"Does anybody know how long it will take for us to get to Munich?" Sara asked.

"We should get there sometime before dark," Becker answered. "Sara, if you like, you are free to check out the other passenger cars or go to the dining car. Or maybe you just want to stretch your legs."

"Thank you sir, I think I will do that. Will the guards permit me to leave our car?" she asked.

"Of course, but you must exercise caution," Becker replied. "In fact, I suggest you have one of the guards go with you, just to be on the safe side."

As Sara left the compartment, Becker turned to the professor and said, "Tell me more about the Grand school. I would like to hear about it from a teacher's point of view."

"We started out with about 300 students, as I recall. We had twenty classrooms and a sports hall. Our headmaster was a gentleman by the name of Arnold Gustafson. Mr. Gustafson was strict but fair if you performed your duties to suit him. I am sure you remember Mr. Gustafson. He must have been headmaster through your entire stay at the school. I believe he left in 1916 or '17. I think his health was failing him. He died a couple of years after he retired.

"He didn't hesitate to use corporal punishment on you boys," Walden continued. "No doubt you were among those on the receiving end of some of those whacks. Oh, boy, those were the days. They didn't have any women teachers in those days, and they probably still don't. If you studied English, you probably had Mr. Smythe. I think his first name was Gordon. A rather stuffy sort, but I am sure you probably remember him. He was tall, thin, with spectacles and a mustache. He came to the school after me, but he was there for a long time. After the war started, Smythe caught a lot of flack because everybody thought he was an Englishman, but he was born in Germany and was a German citizen. His parents were English, though."

"Yes, I remember the old gentleman," Becker lied. "I got along with him quite well, as I recall. Now professor, refresh my memory about Mr. Gustafson, the headmaster."

"He was probably in his sixties when you were there, colonel. He was a heavy set man and losing his hair. Students referred to him as Old Baldy—behind his back, of course. I am sure you students had a name for me, too."

"No, professor, I don't recall any names for you," Becker said, "but as I said, my memories have really faded. I suppose that comes with age."

That brought a laugh from the old man.

"By the way, professor, what is the name of that street the school is on?"

"*Leopoldstrasse*," Walden answered. "Colonel, I have noticed that you do have a sense of humor after all. You must be in your early thirties," he guessed.

"Thirty-five, but feeling like fifty sometimes, professor."

While they chatted, Sara returned to the compartment and took her seat. She listened to the conversation intently.

"I see that the noon hour is fast approaching," Becker said. "Perhaps we should move to the dining car. Sara, since you have toured the train, you may head us in that direction."

After lunch, they returned to their car and took their seats. Becker was trying to soak up as much of the scenery as he could so that he would at least have passing knowledge of what this country looked like. He finally dozed off for a bit while Sara and the professor carried on conversations about subjects ranging from *A* to *Z*. Sara was a good listener, but she was able to hold her own when it came to talking. Becker awoke when the conductor announced that they would be in Nuremberg in an hour, and there would be a short stop to pick up and let off passengers.

After Nuremberg, they continued the journey to Munich, arriving at seven that evening. They were greeted by the local Gestapo commander and some of his soldiers. Sara and the professor were impressed with the grand reception.

Sara remarked, "Colonel, your reputation is growing by leaps and bounds. These people treat you almost like the *fuhrer*. I guess I am not the only poor soul that is in awe of you."

"Cool down, Sara," Becker said. "You can save the behind-kissing for when we get back to headquarters."

"Is that a promise?" she said as she laughed. It seemed that he just could not get under her skin. Fortunately, no one else heard the conversation.

"Your luggage is being delivered to the hotel, Colonel Becker," said an agent. "Welcome to Munich. We are at your service. Will you need transportation for this evening, sir?"

"No, inspector," Becker replied. "We will remain at the hotel this evening. I trust that the hotel has a quality restaurant?"

"Oh, yes, colonel, they do. The food is excellent. What time should we be at the hotel in the morning for a tour of the school facilities?" the agent asked.

"I would like to get an early start, eight in the morning," Becker said. "You will provide us with a motor car for me, the professor and my aide. You should also have a truck to accommodate my security detail and transportation for yourself and whatever additional personnel that you intend to provide."

"Yes sir. We will be here at eight in the morning. Please enjoy your stay in Munich. Good night, sir."

With that, they entered the hotel and were escorted to their rooms by the bell captain and his bell boys. The hotel was nice, and the décor was early Bavarian. *Splendid taste*, Becker thought. He was glad to be in the rooms and freshen up for dinner. The professor was in the room to the left of Becker, and Sara was in the room to the right.

He told both of them that they would meet in the dining room at eight, even though he was sure Sara would have liked more time to make sure that she was at her best. He didn't need to worry, though. She couldn't help looking less than fabulous. But being the woman she was, nothing short of perfection would be acceptable to her.

Sara and the professor were waiting when Becker entered the dining room, and they were promptly seated. As expected, Sara was ravishing. For a fleeting moment, Becker wondered if it had been a good idea to bring her on this trip. Maybe he was taking unnecessary chances. Those thoughts quickly faded as he glanced over at her while she was ordering a glass of wine. They enjoyed a fine dinner, and after consuming an after-dinner drink, they all retired to their rooms for a good night's sleep.

Sara conducted herself quite appropriately, and Becker was sure the professor was unaware of any intimacy between the two of them. At least he did not indicate any such suspicion but you never know about educators, especially wise old professors like Walden. It is instinctive for intelligence people to be suspicious and curious, but wise old educators also have an instinct for recognizing magnetism that exists between and man and a woman. Here in Munich, it really did not matter. Goring suspected that Becker was having sex with Sara despite Becker's denials and had no objections. No objections, that is, as long as they were discreet. Ironically, Goring had given Becker the impression that he hoped that Becker was sleeping with her. After all, in Goring's way of thinking, it was an injustice for a woman like Sara to go unattended. Goring even said on occasion that it would be a waste to allow someone as beautiful as Sara to go without "proper servicing," as he put it.

The next morning, they met the inspector and set out for the school. After a thirty-minute ride, they arrived at Grand Gymnasium on Leopoldstrasse. The buildings were what one might have expected of an older facility. The grounds were well-manicured and, considering how long the school had been in existence, Becker thought it was quite attractive. They entered the main building and were ushered into the headmaster's office. The headmaster was named Rudolph Doch, and Becker guessed he was in his late forties.

"Welcome to Grand Gymnasium, Colonel Becker," Doch said. "It is such an honor to have you as a guest, sir. The students were quite excited when we told them that we would be honored with the visit of such a distinguished officer of the Gestapo."

"Thank you, Herr Headmaster," Becker said, "The pleasure and honor to be here is mine. Allow me to introduce my companions. First we have Professor Walden. The professor taught here when the school opened and spent a number of years here. The young lady is my administrative assistant, Sara Klein. Herr Doch, this brings back old memories for me. It has been seventeen years since I left this school. There appear to be some changes, but basically everything looks the same," Becker said with a straight face.

"Shall we begin our tour, colonel?" Doch asked. "The students are anxious to see you."

Becker said yes, and they began the tour. The students were friendly. They could barely contain their enthusiasm at the sight of the soldiers in their uniforms. Becker could tell the old professor was really enjoying himself by the expression on his face. He seemed to be rejuvenated by the experience, and that made Becker feel better about having invited him. They spent an hour making the rounds of the complex and then returned to the headmaster's office.

The headmaster asked if he could have a word with the colonel in private. Becker instructed the staff and his escorts to remain outside while he and the headmaster were seated in the school office.

"Colonel Becker, I do not wish to be indiscreet, but I feel that I must inform you that I have had some recent inquiries about you and your attendance at Grand. I was told that I was not to disclose the inquiries, but I feel as if I can confide in you without any repercussions."

"Of course headmaster, I assure you that what you say here will be kept in the strictest confidence," Becker assured him. "Tell me the circumstances of the inquiries and who made them."

"Sir, the first was made by a gentleman named Klein, a civilian who claimed to be working for the SS. Later a Major Donst of the SS was here. They both asked questions regarding your tenure here at Grand and if I was aware of anything negative about your character.

"Naturally I was not here when you were a student," the headmaster continued. "I know nothing about you or how you may have behaved here at Grand other than what our school records show. Those records contain no negative information about you, other than a few minor scholastic infractions here and there. I gave them my opinion, based on the records, that you were an exemplary student. They both seemed disappointed in my response. I bring this to your attention because I thought it strange that they would be looking into the background of a person of such a high rank and distinguished military record."

"Thank you, headmaster, for bringing this matter to my attention," Becker said. "I will take care of it. If you hear from these men again, or from others making such inquiries, I expect you to advise me promptly. I will leave the number of my senior aide in Berlin for you to call. His name is Captain Kurt Schwarz. If he is not available, then ask for Sara Klein. Thank you for the tour of your fine school, and thank you for the information that you have given me. You have been most gracious. You are a true servant of the fatherland and the Third Reich."

Becker gave the heil Hitler salute, and he and his entourage departed the school and headed back to the hotel. What the headmaster had told Becker about Klein and Donst was no surprise. He knew they were nosing around, but he hadn't known to what extent. Now he knew. He was amused that Klein was passing himself off as an SS operative.

"Sara, book us on the next train to Berlin," Becker said. "Our business here is finished." "Oh, darn, I was hoping we could stay another night and do some sightseeing," she said. "We never seem to have enough time to spend together."

"You call this 'together' with all of these people around?" Becker laughed. "Now get us on that train."

"Yes, sir, the next one leaves at three this afternoon. It will arrive in Berlin at midnight. Is that okay?" she asked.

"Fine, do it. Tell the professor and the sergeant that we will leave on the three o'clock."

Becker couldn't afford to spend any more time in Munich. He had learned a great deal about his old school and was now ready to field questions about his tenure there. In the process, he had picked up the additional information that those two twits were looking into his background. He couldn't have asked for more— other than spending a little quality time alone with Sara.

They left Munich on schedule. Sara made the arrangements for Heinz to pick them up when they arrived in Berlin. On the way back, the professor and Sara did most of the talking. Becker spent the time thinking about what his next move was going to be when he got back. They arrived just after midnight, and dependable Sergeant Heinz was there to pick them up. He dropped Sara and the colonel off at the hotel and then took the professor home. It had been a long day, and Becker couldn't wait to get to bed and get a good night's sleep. As for Sara, Becker figured she felt the same way. He saw her to her door and gave her a goodnight kiss.

Chapter Twelve

When Becker got to the office the next morning, Berta was there to greet him with a handful of messages. She said the captain was waiting to see him. Becker told her to send the captain in, and he sat down and briefly went over the messages.

"Colonel, good morning, how was the trip?" asked the captain as he came in.

"Just fine," Becker said. "In fact, better than I thought it would be. It was good to see the old school again, but I also found out that Klein and Donst had already been there. They made separate trips there and talked to the headmaster. Just as we thought, they were trolling for information. The headmaster was eager to fill me in on their fact-finding mission. He did so even though he was warned not to reveal the nature of their visit."

"That is interesting, colonel. I also have a report on our eavesdropping operation at the Klein house. It seems that Klein is not spending a lot of time at home these days, but we did pick up on one conversation he had. Although we could not identify who he was talking to, the conversation was definitely involving you, and there was some mention of Sara. Klein is furious at the latest turn of events. He made several derogatory remarks about 'the bitch' moving out on him and how it was going to limit him in getting information on your activities. He said that it would not adversely affect his standing with the SS. We don't know what was said on the other end, but when Klein hung up, he made obscene remarks about the situation. There is a strong possibility that he may have outlived his usefulness to the SS," Schwarz said.

"Captain, does Klein have an office? And if so, where is it located?"

"I am sure that he is over at the *Lichterfelde Kaserne(Headquarters of the SS)*, where that nest of SS pigs is headquartered. I know that is where Donst's office is located, but I am not sure about Klein," Schwarz said.

"I think he is working at the chancellery," Becker replied. "That's the last I heard about him. We will have to check with Sara."

"Colonel, do we have anybody at SS headquarters that we can trust? Is there a possibility that we can plant a bug?"

"Good question, captain," Becker answered. "That is something I can take up with Goring. Maybe he can plant someone in there. It's worth a try. We need to stay on top of this situation, because those bastards are playing for keeps. Goring needs to understand how important this is. In the long run, Himmler is more of an obstacle to Goring than I am to Donst or Himmler. It is no secret that all of those bastards are in a constant battle to gain an advantage over the others."

"I totally agree with you, sir. What about Sara?" Schwarz asked. "Do you think that nutty Klein might try to do her harm? He has all the earmarks of mental instability, particularly where she is concerned."

"Can you blame him?" Becker asked. "But you bring up a good point, captain. I think he may eventually try to hurt her. He has developed a mentality of 'If I can't have her, no one can.' I guess we are going to have to take him out. I don't want to take a chance on him doing something stupid. I'll let you know when the time comes. As for the Klein house, give it another week. If nothing develops, pull the plug on the operation and reassign the agents."

"Yes, sir, and to be on the safe side, I think I will assign one of my men to keep an eye on Sara. No need to take chances. I'll tell her so that she doesn't get spooked if she sees someone shadowing her."

"Good idea, captain. By the way, does Sara own a firearm?" Becker asked. "Find out, and if she doesn't have one, issue her a Luger and get somebody to show her how to use it."

"Yes, sir," Schwarz replied.

"What is happening on our Storm Trooper case, captain?" Becker asked.

"All of the prisoners have been turned over to the state justice office for prosecution, sir," Schwarz answered. "That one guy that you put in the cell with the cop killers was very subdued when he left here. He also seemed to be having trouble walking. I'm not sure he will be fit to return to duty anytime soon. His attitude did seem to be improved. As for the SA higher-ups, we have not directly heard from them, though I understand that they are still fuming. The police are being deluged with complaints against the Storm Troopers and their brutality."

"We must continue to monitor that situation. Their outrageous activities may be the key to finding the justification to bring Rohm down," Becker said. "And I will take up the matter of finding a plant for the SS with Minister Goring this evening."

Later Becker stopped by the minister's office on his way home to discuss this issue.

"Herr Minister, I just returned from my trip to Munich, and the trip was successful. I learned while there that Major Donst with the SS and one of his flunkies had preceded my visit. They questioned the headmaster about my record at the school and solicited negative information regarding my past. I would like to suggest that we place a confidant in the SS to keep us informed as to their operations. That way we can see if they have an interest either in the Gestapo or the minister's office," Becker said. "It would be most helpful if you could find a loyal individual who can keep tabs on Donst and others that could be working against us."

"Colonel, that sounds like a good idea. Let me see if I can come up with a person that would fit that profile. It should not be a problem, but as you know, this sort of thing is sensitive. We must be careful not to do something that might come back and bite us in the ass."

"Absolutely, Herr Minister," Becker said. "I agree, and that is why the person chosen should be someone who is willing to work with us in all respects."

"Give me a couple of days, and I'll get back to you on that," Goring said. "By the way, Anna was quite impressed with you. She suggested that we invite you to my place the next time we have an event. She and I would like to have you as our guest one evening at Karinhall. In case you are not familiar with Karinhall, it is one of my homes and is about forty-five miles from Berlin. And of course we insist that you bring that assistant of yours, that lovely young lady, I am sorry but her name escapes me at the moment."

"That would be Sara, and we of course would be delighted to accept your invitation. Just let us know the date, and we will be there."

"Good, then it is settled. We will have some other guests out for the evening, maybe even the *fuhrer*, so I will have my secretary get the invite to you. Is there anything else I can do for you this evening?" Goring asked. "If not, then I must rush out of here. I have a meeting with the *fuhrer*, and he is not very patient with lateness."

"No, Herr Minister, I have covered everything I wanted to talk about today. Have a good day, and please give my regards to Anna."

Becker looked at his watch. It was past six. so he decided to pack it in for the evening and headed out for the hotel.

A week later, Becker got a call from Goring. He had someone that he wanted Becker to meet and asked if he could get over to his office right away. Becker hurried over, and the receptionist told him to go right in. Becker took note of an SS officer standing with the minister. The man was well-dressed in his gray uniform and black boots.

"Good morning, Colonel Becker," Goring said. "I would like for you to meet one of my old acquaintances, Major Albert Koenig. Major, this is Colonel Konrad Becker with the Gestapo."

"Major Koenig, I am pleased to meet you," Becker said as he extended his hand.

"The pleasure is mine, Colonel Becker. I have heard a great deal about you, not only from Minister Goring but from others as well. From all accounts, you are held in very high esteem."

"Thank you, you are very kind."

"Colonel," Goring interrupted, "as you can see, Albert is an SS officer and someone who I feel can help us with the subject that you and I discussed last week. I have complete confidence in him. I have known him for many years. I went over the plan with him extensively yesterday and briefly while we awaited your arrival this morning. While this fits the description of a covert operation, we must be clear that Major Koenig will be serving in this capacity as an emissary of the *fuhrer*. Of course he will act through this office. His duties, as always, are for the purpose of advancing the interests of the Third Reich."

"I understand, Herr Minister," Koenig said.

Becker spoke up. "In other words, he is not a spy or double agent."

"Exactly," Goring replied. "He will be reporting to you regarding any activities, either directly or indirectly, that might involve you or the Gestapo. Are we all clear on that?"

Both the major and Becker nodded their heads in the affirmative.

"At this time, we should have an open discussion of the matter," Goring stated. "Colonel, you go first."

"Thank you, Herr Minister. Major, are you acquainted with or do you have any knowledge of a Major Wilhelm Donst?"

"Yes, I know him," Koenig replied. "I am not closely associated with him, but I have attended some meetings at which he was present. I have heard some opinions of others who know him."

"And from your own observations and the opinions of others, what can you tell me about him?" asked Becker.

"Sir, as you know, he is on Herr Himmler's staff. In my personal observation, I have found him sometimes rude and always self-centered and arrogant, except when in the presence of Herr Himmler. He has a reputation for being what some have termed a 'suck up' and others a 'suck-ass' with his superiors. He is not well-liked and has few friends in the SS. He appears to be quite intelligent, however, and must not be sold short. Outside the SS, I know nothing about him."

"Major, I concur," Becker said. "I too have formed a very unfavorable opinion of the man and consequently consider him a threat to our service to the Third Reich and the *fuhrer*. We must be extremely careful in how we deal with this termite. For the time being, we must monitor his activities. I know that he has undertaken an investigation of me. To what extent, and for what purpose, I don't entirely know yet. This is where you come in, major. I want to know what he is doing with his investigation. I want to know what his motive is. It surely must be more than a personal pique over my putting him down at a meeting. Is he acting on his own, or is he acting on behalf of others? I want to know if anybody is involved with him.

"I do know that he has been assisted by a Karl Klein, a malcontent and former high-level employee in the chancellery during the Hindenberg years," Becker went on. "Klein's estranged wife is on my staff. Some of the information on Klein's role in this matter has come from her, so we know it to be reliable. What do you think, major? Are we on the same page?"

"Yes sir, I fully understand what is expected of me. All I need is for Minister Goring to sign off on the program, and I am ready to begin."

Goring said, "The reason I brought you into this is because I would like to get to the bottom of it. Colonel Becker has been placed in the position he is in because I have full confidence in him. I expect him to protect my interest and that of the fatherland. Any attack on Colonel Becker is an attack on me. I have tried to make that abundantly clear to all concerned, including Himmler. I fully approve the plan, and it should be put into action at once. Understood?"

The major and Becker agreed and both gave the heil Hitler salute as they prepared to leave. The major and Becker exchanged private phone lines to reach each other. After a few more minutes of conversation, they left the minister's office and returned to their respective headquarters.

Upon returning to headquarters, Becker called Captain Schwarz in and briefed him on the meeting. "Kurt, my meeting with Goring went well. I met a Major Albert Koenig, and he is going to be working with us at SS headquarters. I gave him your name and number in the event he needs to get in touch with me and I am not available. He shares our views on Donst. As a matter of fact, it seems Donst is generally held in low esteem by those who work with him. Koenig will keep us posted on what he finds out.

"Now here is what I want you to do," Becker continued. "Get those engineers that worked on the Klein house project and have them design us some equipment that an agent can carry on his person. We want to be able to listen in on conversations within normal hearing range without being detected. There should be some way that these devices can be amplified to pick up sound outside of normal hearing without wires. I also want you to assign agents to monitor the comings and goings of Klein and Donst. I want to know who they are seeing and where they hang out. At present, this need not be done on a twenty-four hour basis, but it should cover most of their work-day activities."

"Yes sir. I'll get right on that. I also talked to Sara," Schwarz said. "I told her that for the time being we had assigned undercover agents to see if anyone was following or stalking her. She is a little skittish about giving up her privacy, but she understands that it is for her protection. Hopefully we can pull them off shortly, depending on how things play out. Colonel, I think it would ease her mind if you touched base with her. She seems to be really happy in her new apartment."

"Yeah, I'll do that," Becker said. "If I don't have time to see her before we go home, I'll catch her this evening."

One thing that kept bothering Becker was not being able to be straight with Sara. She really was a nice person. The lies and the false representations he made to the Nazis meant nothing because it was part of the job. It was different with her. She was innocent. He had no way of knowing how she would react if she knew the truth about Colonel Konrad Becker. She was a German, but she didn't seem to be enamored of the Nazis. She had pretty much admitted that she was committed to him and wanted a permanent relationship.

He was sure, that someday, if he was lucky, he would leave here and go back home. While he was living a glamorous life, Becker knew that it could change abruptly. But for the time being, he had everything he wanted, including admiration. It just happened to be in the wrong country and on the wrong side. He still worried that he was beginning to enjoy what he was doing. He would just have to make the best of it. In the process, he could find no reason that he shouldn't take advantage of the situation and enjoy himself. As for Sara, he would just have to wait and see. Since he couldn't stop thinking about her, he called her in.

"Sara, if you like, I will pick you up at seven and take you to dinner," Becker told her.

"It's a little late to be asked out, but let me check my schedule and see if I can make it." She laughed. "You are in luck, sir. I see that I am free this evening, so I will expect you at seven."

Becker picked her up at seven. She insisted that he see her apartment now that she had settled in and had everything in place. He looked the place over. Sure enough, she had everything spic and span, and it really looked nice. The place was all Sara.

"Sara, you have done a great job on this place. It certainly has the woman's touch. And you look great as well," he added.

"Thank you, sir. I did it all for you," she said as they left the apartment to go to the restaurant.

She obviously was a happy young woman. Looking down at her, Becker felt at that moment that she was not the only one who was happy. He too felt good having her with him.

The next day in a meeting, Captain Schwarz briefed Becker on the surveillance program. "Colonel, you told me a couple of days ago to ask our engineers about electronic eavesdropping technology. I did so, and they have been working on it. At this moment they are out actually doing some test runs. They promised to have us something that might do the job in a day or two.

"I also assigned agents to track Donst and Klein, and I have something on that, too," Schwarz continued. "Donst and Klein have been sighted in the club at the Adlon Hotel. Further surveillance will determine whether or not this is a regular meeting place. They were seen sitting in a booth in the bar, and adjoining booths may afford us the opportunity to pick up on their conversations. They do have entertainment in that bar at certain times, and the noise may interfere with our ability to hear what they are saying. It does look promising, however, and we will stay on top of it. The Klein house operation has not panned out as we had hoped. But it did provide us with some valuable experience in fine-tuning our eavesdropping capability."

"Good report, captain" Becker commented.

A week later, an invitation arrived requesting the presence of Colonel Konrad Becker and his lady at a cocktail reception at Karinhall, hosted by Interior Minister Hermann Goring and Anna Gelding. Becker called Sara into the office and showed her the invitation.

"Sara, are you free that evening to accompany me to the party?" Becker asked.

"Oh my God, colonel, you bet your last *Reich mark* I will," she answered. "How exciting, but it is only two weeks away, and I have nothing to wear."

"I have heard that before," Becker said. "No doubt this will be a formal gathering, and you should be appropriately dressed. I suggest you go to Marlene's or some other upscale boutique and pick up something and put it on my account."

"Oh, my dear colonel, I can't do that."

"You can, and you will," Becker said. "Now move along unless you have something else to discuss. The reception, as you can see, is being held at Goring's Karinhall estate, which is forty miles from Berlin. Tell Berta to schedule Heinz for that evening."

"Colonel," the Captain interrupted. "I just received a call from a Bruno Wetzel, one of Rohm's deputies, and he has requested a meeting with us as soon as possible to discuss the recent arrest of those Storm Troopers."

"Oh, shit, captain, I don't have time to mess with those bastards right now. You can take care of it," Becker replied.

"Sir, he indicated that it was extremely important and did not want to meet with any subordinates," Schwarz said.

"Okay, captain, set up a meeting in the conference room tomorrow. I want you there because I am sure he will bring some of his associates to the meeting. They don't seem to have a manpower shortage over there."

The captain later informed Becker that Wetzel and his entourage would be there at ten the next morning.

The next morning when Captain Schwarz and Colonel Becker arrived at the meeting about twenty minutes late, they found five Storm Troopers sitting at the table. They gave the heil Hitler salute, and the Storm Troopers all sprang to their feet and returned the salute. After the captain introduced Becker, he asked who was in charge of the delegation. A beady-eyed, overweight man stood up again and introduced himself.

"Sir, I am Bruno Wetzel of the SA," he said. My position is deputy to Chief of Staff Ernst Rohm. The other men here with me are members of my staff. Would the colonel like for me to introduce each of them?"

"No, sit down, Wetzel, and state your business with the Gestapo," Becker curtly replied.

"Well, err, uh, we are here to protest the unlawful arrest of several of our troopers recently," the red-faced Wetzel replied.

"Just what do you mean by 'unlawful,' Wetzel?" Becker

demanded. "Do you not know that the Gestapo has the authority to arrest anyone that, in our opinion, has violated the laws of the Third Reich? That would include you, as well. Our people were acting on my orders when those hoodlums wearing SA uniforms were arrested. Need I remind you that under the enabling act I have the authority to order the arrest of anyone suspected of misconduct of any nature, subject only to override by the *fuhrer* himself?"

"Sir, that authority to arrest anyone does not apply to SA officers doing their duty. The authority also would be subject to court interpretation," Wetzel shot back.

"Wetzel are you a lawyer?" asked Becker.

"No, sir, but—"

"But nothing," Becker cut him off. "You have heard my position on the matter. If the SA feels they have a different interpretation of the law, then take it to the courts. Meanwhile, as far as I am concerned, your stated position is irrelevant."

"Sir, what did our men do that was illegal?" Wetzel asked. "Our position is that they were doing their duty by identifying and rounding up undesirable elements who pose a threat to our country and the *fuhrer*."

"Wetzel, what is your definition of undesirable elements?" Becker asked.

"Jews, socialists, communists and people like that," Wetzel answered.

The colonel knew he had to choose his words carefully here. He could not be seen as protecting any members of those groups. "We here at the Gestapo understand the need for ridding our country of undesirables, but my question to you is, what criteria do you use in determining whether or not a person fits into any of those groups?" Becker asked.

"We instruct our people to use their own judgment in making those decisions," Wetzel said.

"Judgment based on what?"

"Sir, usually we can look at these people and tell. In some cases we act on reports or complaints," Wetzel said.

"Wetzel, are you aware that the victim who was the target of those men that we arrested is not Jewish, nor a member of any of the groups that you named. In fact, he is an innocent citizen whose German ancestry is unquestioned. He is a retired professor and a law-abiding citizen. There is no legal authority for you to arrest and cause injury to innocent citizens of our country. Are the procedures you followed approved by Chief of Staff Rohm?"

"Yes, sir," Wetzel replied. "Our procedures are approved by our chief of staff, and it is our duty to enforce those procedures."

"Wetzel, now hear me on this. Under the enabling act, only the Gestapo has the power to detain individuals on suspicion of illegal or threatening activities. It makes no difference whether or not our suspicions are well-founded. The SA does not have that authority, and if you or your men continue to engage in activities such as the one involving the professor, then you will be arrested and prosecuted. Do you understand that?"

"Okay, colonel, I hear you, but we will just have to see about that. I don't think that Chief of Staff Rohm is going to like what has happened here today."

"That's just too damn bad," Becker replied. "Captain Schwarz, this meeting is over. Have someone escort these people out of the building. We have more urgent business to attend to. If this bastard gives you anymore trouble then throw his ass in one of those holding cells in the basement and let him challenge the enabling act from down there."

Wetzel was fuming, but the man knew better than to push it any further. Becker suspected that he had not heard the last of this, but with the anti-Rohm sentiment among the Nazis, Becker doubted Rohm would find much support to do anything about it.

After Wetzel and his men had left the building, Captain Schwarz commented, "Rohm is probably going to retaliate against us."

"Let Rohm him bring it on," Becker said. "We will be ready. I don't like the dirty son of a bitch anyway."

"Colonel, one thing can be said of you, and that is, you have got balls," Schwarz said. "That bunch left here with their tails tucked between their legs. I would sure love to be a fly on the wall to hear the reaction when they get back and report to their chief."

"Captain, you can't let people think you are weak. They will invariably take advantage of you. After this meeting, that fat bastard Wetzel will not like me, but he sure as hell will think twice before he takes me on. It's the only way to deal with thugs like that. They have no respect for men of good will. Remember that. It's the law of the jungle. Only the strong survive."

Chapter Thirteen

Though Becker's plate was getting full with his various investigations, he still had to get information on what the new German government was doing that might lead to threats against the United States. He had information that the army was increasing its manpower by hiding additional personnel with the police and other agencies. He had previously relayed information on the subject through Fritsch, but what he had now was much more detailed information. Becker had learned that the re-arming of the military was much more extensive than what he had previously reported. It violated the Versailles treaty entered into between the allies in the World War and Germany. In order to avoid detection, the Nazis were manufacturing military arms and hardware in other countries, particularly in Russia.

It was incumbent upon Becker to get this information to the U.S. war department through his contact at the bank. That was something else he had to worry about. What happened if Fritsch and his activities were exposed? Becker knew nothing about the man. Would he talk? Becker knew that the Nazis had means to make people talk. Becker had doubts as to the value of using torture to gain information, but as far as Becker was concerned, it was a moot question. He was a sitting duck if Fritsch was caught and tortured and started to talk and name names. It did not slip Becker's mind that he might have to deal with that problem in the future. As part of Becker's training, he had been supplied with shortwave radio instructions. But without access to radio equipment, that training would be useless. He needed to work on getting access to the equipment. There was no British or American spy network in Germany other than Fritsch and Becker. For now, he must depend solely on Fritsch. Meeting at the bank was rife with danger. A senior-ranking Gestapo officer in uniform was too conspicuous. He remembered the last meeting they had, with all of the heads turning and looking. Becker had already decided to use another officer at the bank to conduct his banking business. He would have to devise another way of making contact and exchanging information. He would have to carefully think it through.

Becker was getting more reports on the surveillance activities, and it appeared to be paying off. For one thing, Klein and Donst had more meetings at the Adlon Hotel. This was a pattern, and it led Becker to conclude that this was their regular meeting place. The bartender confided in the Gestapo agents that the two usually sat in a booth in a back corner, where there was less noise and more privacy. Becker's people were able to place a microphone, or bug, under the table and run the wire to another table close by. The two operatives, one male and a female, were then positioned to intercept the conversations. The female agent listened on the ear phone and took down the conversation in shorthand. In spite of the usual bar noise, the audio was good enough to gather information and make a transcript for the investigation. Everything was now in place to find out what the two conspirators were up to. The engineers would keep working to develop more sophisticated equipment, but for now the wire would serve its purpose.

At the first meeting, it all began to bear fruit. A transcript of the conversation was as follows:

Klein: That bitch of a wife of mine went off somewhere with Becker last week. I don't know where they were going, but there was a detail of soldiers with them. They were probably going somewhere to carry on their affair, and the soldiers were there to protect that damn Becker. I would give anything if I could get that son of a bitch off by himself. Donst: Don't be stupid. He would probably beat your ass to a pulp. He has a reputation for not only being tough but mean as hell. If you hadn't let that damned wife of yours get out of the house, we might have been able to uncover some useful information on Becker. As it is, I have been questioned about the usefulness of having you around.

Klein: But, major, I'll do whatever you want me to. I can still help bring this guy down. As for her, I treated her like a goddamn queen, and look where it got me. She is going to pay for the way she has treated me. I can promise you that."

Donst: You don't have to promise me a damn thing. As for treating her like a queen, that's bullshit, and you know it. We all know about your whore-hopping and amateurish Casanova activities. So let's cut the bullshit and get down to business. You are going to have to produce, or your ass is out the door. Got it?

Klein: Yes, sir. What do you want me to do?

Donst: We will mull that over. You may have to eliminate Becker yourself. And you can throw that damn slut of a wife in, too. We are getting impatient with you on this project. When you came to us, you said you had a plan and had it all worked out to get Becker. So far all we have seen is your marriage flop. You have produced no credible or worthwhile dirt on Becker.

Klein: I have already thought about ways to deal with him,

but you know he always has a detail guarding him. If I tried to kill him, they would blow me into a million pieces. Hell, getting to him right now would be almost as hard as getting to the *fuhrer*.

Donst: Well, Klein that is your problem. I'll just leave you with this thought: Get it done, or else. It's time for me to get home, or my woman may do me the same way yours did you and leave my ass. But at least she won't be leaving me because she found a better lover.

Klein: Major, you don't have to put it like that. You don't know how much it hurt me to lose that woman. I think she mainly left me because she saw a chance to move herself up in the world.

Donst: Yeah. Well, you can still dream about that one, but the man just outgunned you, and you are too dumb to admit it. By the way, did you get anything when you went to that school in Munich?

Klein: Nothing negative, but I did manage to get names of students that attended when Becker did.

Donst: Yeah, we got those names, too. We are sifting through them trying to come up with someone that may know something and will cooperate with us. Meanwhile, I'm going to have to reassess our business with you unless you can come up with something better. We will be in touch. I am running late. Heil Hitler. *End of transcript.*

"Colonel, that pretty much summed up the first meeting that we were able to monitor on Klein and Donst," Captain Schwarz said.

"Captain, it looks to me like Klein may become a non-factor in this conspiracy," Becker said with a slight laugh. "His days seemed to be numbered over there based on what we have heard today."

"You are right about his problems with Donst and the SS, but

I think it would be a mistake to ignore the little bastard," Schwarz said. "Colonel, he is going to somehow work up enough nerve to harm both you and Sara. Mark my words on that."

"Maybe you are right, captain. I was mainly referring to what may be his brief and short tenure with Donst and the SS. But captain, our main concern here is Donst and whoever it is that's backing him. There is more to this than his pique at being insulted or belittled at a meeting. Maybe if his old lady is not too ugly, you can take a shot at her and show him that he's not any more of a man than that fool he was just making light of."

"No thank you, colonel, I can't imagine any woman hooked up with him being the least bit appealing to me. I guess I am a little like you when it comes to women. I am used to nothing but the best."

"Captain, that reminds me, we need to get our ladies together soon, or we might wind up like those two losers we were just listening to," Becker said. "By the way, I'm taking Sara to a reception at Goring's place next week. Sorry that it is not for the common folk, but I am sure you understand that rank has its privileges."

"I understand very well, sir, but I have an idea of a better way of spending some time with my woman. And if you want my advice, you need to find a little more quality time to spend with yours."

"Captain, I don't have a woman. And you are not telling me anything I don't already know, but I have to put business of the state ahead of personal pleasure." *At least for the time being,* he thought. It would be nice if he could spend leisure time with friends for a change.

The next few days were routine. The office received a directive that the SS had opened a labor camp at Dachau. The purpose of the camp was to house political prisoners and enemies of the state.

That described just about anybody. It seemed that local jails and other detention facilities were overcrowded with inmates, and there was a need for relief from the influx of new prisoners. The SA, in particular, was hauling people in by the thousands.

At the time, the Gestapo only had a few hundred men, but Becker and Diels had access to unlimited army personnel. If they needed manpower, all they had to do was to issue an order for an unlimited number of troops. The manpower would be available immediately. The regular army troops were much better-trained and -disciplined than the SS or SA forces. The SA was being used primarily as an auxiliary police force, and it was spiraling out of control. This was causing major problems for the *fuhrer*, not only with German citizens, but with the generals and other armed forces leaders who felt their power was threatened by the ragtag, undisciplined force with overwhelming numbers. In fact, the SA greatly outnumbered the regular army. This was a time when the *fuhrer* had indicated to his staff that he needed to shore up his power with the army, as the SA Storm Troopers had outlived their usefulness. The defense minister had warned Hindenberg in 1931 that it was dangerous to allow non-state organizations to conduct military operations. The warning was later heeded, and paramilitary groups like the SA were banned. However, after the new defense minister, General von Schleicher, was appointed the next year, the recommendation was reversed. That allowed the Nazis to utilize the Storm Troopers, who would eventually cause the downfall of the Weimar government.

Pleased with the success of the eavesdropping operation, Becker instructed the engineers to start research on more sophisticated equipment, such as wireless technology. Becker did not want this technology revealed to any other sources. In the hands of the wrong people, it could prove dangerous to privacy and civil rights. The category of "the wrong people" pretty much fit anybody but those who had the technology.

As Becker and Captain Schwarz talked after analyzing the Klein/Donst transcript, the subject of what should they do about Klein came up again.

"Captain," Becker said, "after thinking about Klein I have decided, at least for the time being, that maybe we should shore up his status over at the SS and with Donst. From what we see on these transcripts, it appears that he is in jeopardy of being cut loose. It may be in our best interest that this doesn't happen, at least for awhile. What do you think?"

"I agree, colonel. I see an opportunity for us to make some use of him by providing him with false information that he can pass on to Donst."

"Exactly," Becker said. "We will need to use Sara to accomplish that. Let's get her in here and discuss it with her."

After a minute, Sara came into the office.

"Hello, Sara. The captain and I have been going over the transcripts of Klein and Donst. I know you have not had a chance to read them. I think you should do so after this meeting. There are several complimentary references to you. That is, if you don't mind being called a bitch. I am sure you will find them interesting.

"After talking it over, we think, at least for the time being, that it may be in our best interests that the relationship between Klein and Donst be maintained," Becker continued. "As you will see, Donst has become somewhat disenchanted with Klein and his, shall I say, lack of production. By the way, Sara, is Karl still working in the chancellor's office?"

"After the *fuhrer* took office, he was reassigned to another department," she said. "I am not sure what he does, but he has not been happy with his new position. He always liked to play the big shot, but he no longer is playing that role."

"No wonder Donst is ready to dump his ass," Becker said. "If he cannot supply the SS the information they need, then he becomes dispensable. So Sara, you can assist us by contacting Karl for whatever reason, maybe about your impending divorce action or something, whatever you think appropriate, and feed him some information that he can take back to Donst to shore up his fragile relationship over there. Do you follow me?" "Yes sir, I am not anxious to have anything to do with Karl, but what do you want me to do?" she asked.

"When you call him, you can drop some reference to being invited to a reception at the Goring lodge," Becker suggested. "I know that is not earth-shattering news, but it is a start. And while that information appears harmless, it does give him something to take back to Donst that implies that he still has access."

"Colonel, as I said, I am not thrilled about calling him, but I will do it," she said. "I don't think he is going to be thrilled at the prospect of me going to some reception with you."

"Well, that's pretty selfish on his part," Becker joked, "but I understand. Without coming right out and saying it, you might give him the impression that he may still have a source of information from you. This may be his only ticket to continue his working relationship with Donst. I just don't want you to give him the slightest idea that reconciliation is possible."

"Colonel, you need not worry about that," she said. "I can't stand the sight of that man. Like I said before, I want nothing to do with him. I would prefer that I never saw or talked to him again, but I know that is not possible for the time being."

"All right, Sara, but be careful how you do this. I am not really comfortable putting you in this position. If you have any reservations, then I don't want you to do it. Does he know where you are living now?" Becker asked.

"Yes. He has called several times and asked if he could come over and talk to me. I have told him no, but he doesn't want to take no for an answer," she answered.

"Okay. Let's give him a couple more weeks with this plan, and then we will pull the plug on him as a source of information. After that, captain, I want you to make it crystal clear to Mr. Klein that he is not to contact, interfere with or go anywhere near Sara. If he fails to comply with that message, then we will see if we can't have him sent to the new labor camp at Dachau. I am sure they won't miss him over wherever it is that he works; at least he won't be missed by the *fuhrer*."

"Yes, sir," Schwarz replied.

"That will be all, captain," Becker said. He turned to Sara. "Sara, you stay for a few minutes." After Schwarz had left, Becker asked, "Have you completed your shopping for the reception?"

"Yes, I have, and you are going to love my new outfit. It is very sexy."

"Let's not get carried away," he said. "I don't want you to show too much skin to that crowd."

"It is not objectionable," she countered. "I just think I look good in it, and I think you will be proud to show me off. Besides, I am dressing for you."

"I'm sure you will be a knockout, Sara, so get going. I have some work to do before the day is over."

With that, she said goodbye and left the office. As she walked out, Becker thought to himself, *that woman gets better-looking every day, if that is possible.* He had no doubt she would knock them out at the party.

On the night of the reception at Goring's, Sergeant Heinz picked Becker and Sara up at 6:30 so that they could make the drive and arrive around eight.

"Sara, you were not exaggerating about your dress," Becker said. It was pale green and highlighted her modest bosom while hugging her body like a glove. "You are absolutely gorgeous, and the dress is in perfectly good taste."

"Thank you, I knew you would like it," she said.

They arrived at the lodge at eight, and uniformed troopers met them at the entrance gate and escorted them to the main building. Upon entering the lodge, they were greeted by none other than the host and hostess, Hermann Goring and Anna Gelding.

"Good evening to you, Colonel Becker, and your lovely young lady, and welcome to our home. Anna, you have met the colonel, but I would like to introduce Colonel Becker's beautiful young lady, Sara Klein, who also is an important member of the Gestapo."

"Hello, and welcome Sara," Anna said, embracing the younger woman. "It is such a pleasure to finally meet you. And you are even more beautiful than I had been told. I am not surprised, however, considering you are being escorted by Germany's most eligible and handsome bachelor."

"Oh, thank you so much," Sara said flashing that great big grin of hers and her beautiful white teeth. "I am flattered beyond belief to receive such a compliment from Germany's first lady of the theater."

"If I may get a word in," interrupted Becker, "it is a great pleasure to see you again, Anna, and it is always a pleasure to see the minister. Thank you both for having us as your guests tonight. We are truly honored," Becker lied.

"You ladies get acquainted while I show the colonel around Karinhall," Goring suggested.

"Becker," Goring said as they headed into the main reception area, "I have some important people here that I would like for you to meet. The *fuhrer* is not here tonight, but most of the guests are captains of industry and big business."

They made the rounds, meeting mostly people that Becker had never heard of. They were all very friendly, to put it mildly, no doubt due to Becker's rank and position with the feared Gestapo.

Meanwhile, his young assistant was monopolizing the

attention of the male guests to the extent that the other ladies in attendance were beginning to chafe a bit. Becker felt it was time for him to intervene, so he went over to a small group of men surrounding Sara and apologized for the interruption.

"Excuse me, but I feel compelled to rescue my lady before she succumbs to the charms of you gallant and charming gentlemen," Becker said.

One of the men responded, "Colonel, we are not to blame. We have been captivated by this charming and beautiful young woman. Where in the world did you find such a treasure?"

"That, sir, I cannot tell. You know that the Gestapo is a secret police force. I cannot reveal our innermost secrets." They all laughed.

As Becker and Sara moved away from the men, he asked if she was having a good time, already knowing the answer. "I am having the time of my life," Sara said. "All of these men are so nice and attentive. Some have even offered to steal me away from you and shower me with wealth beyond my wildest dreams. They were, of course, not totally serious, but it has been flattering since I never hear anything like that from you."

"I'm glad you are having a good time, but don't overdo it," Becker said. "Some of the wives are getting jealous. You need to spend a little more time fraternizing with them."

"How about you, Konrad?" she shot back. "Don't think I haven't noticed that you have been doing some of your own fraternizing with these women. Particularly that pretty little wench in the red dress. She looked like she was going to jump you any minute."

"Now, Sara, don't let your imagination get the best of you. I was just carrying on conversations with the ladies, which are just a part of my duties as a high-ranking official of the Gestapo."

"Bullshit, Konrad. I saw the way you were looking at that hussy," she fumed.

"Okay, Sara, maybe you better go easy on that wine. I don't want to have to carry you out of here. Now get your sweet little ass in there and mingle with those old ladies, and for God's sake, stay away from that woman in the red dress," he ordered.

"All right, but I want to be with you," she said. "Why can't we get out of here and go somewhere where we can be alone?"

"No, now that is enough," Becker said, his voice rising slightly. "That is just wine talking. We can spend some time alone in the car on the way back home."

"Yeah, with Heinz in the car, hoopty doo," she shot back.

With that brief exchange, they went their separate ways to interact with the other guests. Becker was still thinking about her defiance. She had spunk, he would have to give her that, and strangely he felt good about it. Maybe it was the wine. Whatever it was, it was pretty obvious that she was getting to him, and he thought she was well aware of it.

Becker joined some male guests and entered into conversations, while Sara did the same with some of the ladies. Goring was definitely hanging with the big money boys. Financially, Goring seemed to be doing quite well himself. This place had to set him back a few *Reich marks*, Becker thought. This was just one of several homes Goring owned. Becker asked Goring how he knew all these wealthy people.

"Colonel, I have known most of these people for years. I am not one of those typical party members from the streets, like Rohm and some of the others. They wouldn't know how to act around the elite. How about you? Are the dogs still barking?" Goring asked.

"Yeah," Becker admitted. "We picked up some more conversations between Klein and Donst. They appear to be on the verge of parting company. Evidently the split between Sara and Klein has shaken the confidence of Donst and whoever his backers are about getting any more useful information from Klein."

"That has to be Himmler, colonel," Goring said. "He has his eyes set on taking over the Gestapo. I know he will dump Diels and put Reinhard Heydrich or some other stooge in charge if he takes over."

"What would that mean for me?" Becker asked.

"Don't worry, Colonel Becker," Goring said. "You will be taken care of, and that is a promise. I am still number two, and my say will prevail over Himmler. Besides, that has not happened yet, and they will have to accommodate me before it does. Meantime, you can do as you please in dealing with the scum who are tracking you. They are acting at their own peril. If they are dealt with, there is nothing Himmler or the others can do about it. Just handle it discreetly.

"I have pretty much convinced the *fuhrer* of your importance to the Third Reich," Goring continued. "You are insulated from any harm from your adversaries, whoever they might be, except for your personal safety. None of us are afforded that luxury. Right now our main emphasis is to remove Rohm. Himmler is still on board with his removal, even though he and Rohm once were big comrades."

"Will he stay on board?" asked Becker.

"Sure," Goring answered. "Quite frankly, Himmler is deathly afraid of Rohm now. He knows that Rohm is drunk with power with those hordes of thugs he has assembled at the SA."

With that, Goring suggested that they should get back to the other guests. After spending another hour chatting with other guests, Becker could tell that Sara was getting restless. She kept giving him that let's-get-out-of-here look. He motioned to her to join him, and they bade farewell to the host and hostess, complimenting them on their hospitality and thanking them.

The ride back to Berlin was relaxing after all the back-slapping and boring conversations. Becker asked Sara if she had a good time.

"I had a great time until you forced me to spend more time with that bunch of snooty old dames. But the men were so nice. They liked me, even if you don't," she pouted.

"I like you sometimes, at least when you are behaving yourself," he said.

"I would behave myself a lot more if you would pay more attention to me," Sara said. "You are too stingy with your affection." She snuggled next to him."

"Maybe I will be more affectionate when I get to know you better," Becker said with a laugh. She seemed content with that and gave him a hug. "Heinz, do you think we should drop this woman off and let her walk home?"

Before Heinz could answer, Sara chimed in. "Oh, I just remembered something, colonel. I forgot to tell you, but I did as you asked and called Karl a couple of days ago. I told him about the reception tonight."

"And what did he say?" Becker asked.

"As I thought he would, he cursed you out and then told me how sorry he was and that if I would just give him one more chance, he would make me happy," she said. "I told him that he could never make me happy, and after I told him that, his mood changed quickly. He became quite agitated and accused me of being unfaithful and an opportunist."

"An opportunist, what did he mean by that?" Becker asked.

"I don't know," she said, "but I finally just hung up the phone on him. Why didn't you ask me what he meant by unfaithful?"

"Look, Sara, everybody knows you have been unfaithful," Becker joked.

"I have not," she hotly denied. "I confess that I would have been if not for you."

"Not so loud. Do you want Heinz to hear you?" Becker whispered.

"I don't care," she replied. "It's the truth, and you know it."

141

"Okay, but what did Klein say about the reception?"

"That really got him going. He said, 'I guess you think you are somebody, and you have a lot of nerve going to such a high-level outing with another man.' He also said, 'You know that they all think that Becker is screwing you.' I told him that they would be wrong, but that I wish to hell that it was true. When I said that, he became verbally abusive, and that's when I hung up on him," Sara said. "Please don't make me talk to that man again, Konrad."

"Okay, you did well, Sara, and we are through with him. We will see if he does anything with it, but otherwise that's it."

They arrived back at the hotel and got out of the car. Becker walked Sara to her apartment and gave her a goodnight kiss. She was still a little tipsy from the wine.

"Is that all I'm getting?" she asked.

"Yes, you know I don't sleep with married women, even though I may take them to fancy receptions and parties," he said with a smile.

"But I am getting a divorce, remember?" she said.

"Goodnight, Sara."

Chapter Fourteen

The next morning at the office, Captain Schwarz came in and greeted Becker. "Colonel, we have just received a transcript of a later meeting between Klein and Donst. This took place on the seventh. That's a couple of days before you attended that reception at Goring's. Do you have time to discuss it now?"

"Yes, let's take a look at it," Becker replied.

Klein: Heil Hitler. Good evening, major. How are you today?

Donst: Heil Hitler. I'm fine. What have you got for me that was so urgent?

Klein: I spoke with my wife, and during the conversation, I found out that she and Becker are going to a reception at Goring's place, the lodge.

Donst: Your wife? Is that what you still call her? Don't you mean Becker's woman? And so what if he took her to a reception?

Is that all you have to report? We know that Becker is Goring's fair-haired boy, so what's the big deal about him and your wife or ex-wife going to a reception?

Klein: Sir, that may not be important, but what it does show is that I still have an ear as to what they are doing.

Donst: Bullshit. Listen, how dare you waste my time with trivial shit like this? We are looking for viable information that is helpful in our investigation of Becker. The next thing you know, you will be coming in here telling us that the man went to the toilet. Do you think I am going to run to my superiors with something like that? Klein, I have just about had it with you. You fool. That woman probably planted that little tip on you hoping that you would run with it. I canceled a card game this evening to meet you, and this is what I get.

Klein: I am sorry, sir. I thought that you would be glad that I was on speaking terms with my wife. And yes, she is still my wife. If she doesn't stay away from that son of a bitch Becker, then I will do the job on him myself.

Donst: If you want to take him down, then that is fine, but you had better not leave any tracks back to me. Do you realize how risky that will be? You are talking about taking out a top Gestapo official. The only way I see you accomplishing that is for you to sacrifice your own life, because you can rest assured, you will not leave the scene. Do you know that, and are you prepared to sacrifice your life to get him?

Klein: I hadn't thought about it that way. Of course I would have to have a well-thought-out plan, one that would not put my own life in peril.

Donst: Klein, I'm afraid that we are going to have to cut you loose. All I hear from you is that constant whining about somebody humping your old lady. We already know that. You are turning out to be more of a liability for us than an asset.

I am responsible for bringing you in on this operation, and if something goes wrong, then my ass is in the fire.

Klein: But, sir, I can deliver. Just give me a chance.

Donst: You have had your chance. You forget you ever saw me. If you breathe one word about any of this, it will be the last breath that you take. You got that? Don't say another word.

"What do you think colonel?" asked Schwarz.

"I would say that Klein is history. In fact, he may have saved us the trouble of dealing with him. If the mere hint of that conversation was revealed, Klein would have been lucky to have had us enroll him as a new resident of Dachau. He would be fast-tracked to the nearest graveyard. Captain, go ahead and pull the plug on Klein, but have our crew continue listening to Donst. We are not through with that asshole. He is going to lead us to whoever is in on this thing with him."

"Yes, sir," Schwarz said.

Meanwhile, another meeting was taking place at SS headquarters between Colonel Dirk Hartmann and Wilhelm Donst and monitored by Becker's agents.

The transcript of that conversation follows:

Hartman: "Wilhelm, how is the Becker inquiry coming along?"

Donst: "Sir, we have had a few snags here and there, but we are working on it. I had to dump one of our informants, the Klein fellow. He is the one that is married to one of Becker's aides. The damn woman ought to be in movies instead of working for the government. Anyway, there is talk going around that the colonel is smoking her. To top it off, that fool Klein wants her back. What a *dumbkoph*."

Hartman: "What happened to Klein that warranted his 'dumping,' as you call it?"

Donst: "Sir, he proved to be unreliable, and his effectiveness was compromised when the wife kicked his ass out and filed for a divorce. We were not getting anything out of him but trivia. The latest bit of information that he provided was that his wife was attending a reception at Goring's with Becker. The man turned out to be a total disappointment. We already know that Becker is Goring's stooge. Being invited to a reception by the fat man is nothing unusual or newsworthy. Klein was not coming up with anything of any consequence. As for what bits and pieces of information he was feeding us, we could have gone directly to Becker and asked him for it, and he probably would have been happy to give it to us."

Hartman: "So where do we go from here? There has to be something out there on Becker. What about his ancestry?"

Donst: "We researched that, and it is beyond reproach. As you know, his father was a respected general and war hero. His grandfather was an army officer."

Hartman: "What about his associates or acquaintances? There must be someone out there that can shed some light on this fellow."

Donst: "Sir, we are working on that, and we have identified several individuals that may be able to help us. We expect to conduct interviews soon. We are also mindful that we have to be cautious in dealing with this man. The reports indicate that he is cunning and has no qualms about using force and violence. To make matters worse, he doesn't seem to care who he uses it on. This is something that he picked up in America, because from what we have learned from some of those who knew him before he went over there, he previously showed no tendency toward violence. He has become a person who seems to relish using force against anyone who gets in his way."

Hartman: "That is interesting, major. We know that the Yanks are violent, and that is why they must ultimately be destroyed.

I have heard about that Capone thug and those wops from Italy who have no compunction about gunning each other down on the streets. But getting back to Becker, we need to come up with more than just his illicit relationship with that other man's wife. From what I hear, every man in Berlin would like to engage in calisthenics with her. Ha!"

Donst: "If you have seen her, sir, then you can certainly understand why. Using their relationship as an attempt to bring him down would be laughable since Goring and everybody else is aware of it. The fact that he would invite the woman to a reception attended by leading business leaders indicates that he couldn't care less. My guess is the fat man (Goring) himself would like to bag her."

Hartman: "You have made your point, Major Donst. Let us concentrate on the former acquaintances. There must be somebody out there that Becker has crossed or that dislikes him or knows something about him that would be useful to us. We have to come up with something to help Himmler convince the *fuhrer* that the Gestapo would be in better hands under the leadership of Himmler and the SS. Diels is not a problem. Becker has too much power, and therefore we have to remove him one way or the other."

Donst: "Colonel I couldn't agree more. The man is not only a threat, but he is unbearable. In line with what you just suggested, we do have Klein, who would like very much to kill Becker. Klein expressed his desire to me and left little doubt in my mind that he would do it if he thought he could pull it off. I scoffed at his rant because of the difficulty in accomplishing the act without considerable resources. There is little chance of one man getting close enough to Becker to bring it about. Klein just may fill the bill for a dupe. He has the perfect motive, and therefore there would be little speculation about the involvement of others, particularly the SS. I think maybe we should give the idea consideration.

There would have to be careful planning, and Klein lacks the brainpower to carry out such a mission. He could, however, be the tool for such an incident. Like they used that idiot van der Lubbe in the Reichstag fire, Klein may well be our van der Lubbe in this case."

Hartman: "Very good idea, major. I like it. You have my permission to proceed with this plan. I must warn you, however, that this is a dangerous plot and must not be traced back to you or me. The penalty for killing a high-ranking Gestapo official is execution. You have been dealing with Klein, and he can implicate you if the plot fails. He does not know, nor must he ever know, of my participation in the plan. Do you understand?"

Donst: "Yes, colonel, I understand. I intend to see that preparation and planning for this will be foolproof, or I will not want to proceed with it. I am well aware of Becker's disposition and skill. If he gets wind of this, I am a goner. Also, I must think Klein's involvement through. I do not trust him that much. I may have to have a third-party deal with him."

Hartman: "Do as you like, major, but remember, once this plan is put into action, you are on your own. If there is a failure and the trail leads back to you, it stops there. Is that clear?"

Donst: "It is crystal clear, sir, and rest assured that you will be protected."

End of transcript.

Discussion of transcript follows:

"Colonel, what do you think about that?" Schwarz said.

"That cocky little bastard Donst was lying," Becker said. "He would do whatever he could to save his own ass. He would not give a second thought about throwing Hartman to the wolves. Let's call it a day, captain. I'm tired and Colonel Richter is waiting to see me. Would you ask him to come in?" Becker asked. "Yes sir" the captain replied as he went out of the office to get Richter.

Colonel Richter enters and salutes. Colonel Becker, I will only be a minute. I just want to let you know how pleased I am with the electronic state of the art spying apparatus that you have assembled. Putting Captain Schwarz in charge of that covert operation was a very smart move. Richter said. "Thank you" Becker replied. We have added a dozen agents to that detail and they are thoroughly trained in all phases of electronic eavesdropping." "Good, then your next step will be to plant the bugs in areas where your intended targets congregate" Richter said. "Just thought I drop by and compliment you on the covert operation and now if you will excuse me I must run" Richter said as he headed for the door. "Thank you again colonel and I will get with you later in the week if time permits" Becker said.

For weeks now, Becker had been contemplating checking out the entertainment facilities at the Adlon Hotel. Since it was a place that Donst frequented, Becker thought it was a good time to mix a little business with pleasure. He was curious who else might be hanging out there. Becker invited Sara and Captain Schwarz to join him for dinner to find out.

"Captain, you and I and Sara are going out for dinner this evening at the Adlon," Becker said. "We are going to do a little socializing, so I'll pick up Sara, and we will meet you there at, say, eight?"

"Yes, sir, that sounds good to me. I'll be there," Schwarz said.

That evening, Sergeant Heinz picked the colonel and Sara up at 7:30 at their hotel and drove them to the Adlon. Captain Schwarz was waiting in the lobby when they arrived. The bell captain ushered the guests into the club lounge, where the head waiter seated them at one of the best tables, usually reserved for prominent government officials. Sergeant Heinz stood nearby with his Schmeisser MP28 submachine gun at the ready.

After the three had ordered a round of cocktails, Sara said, "Colonel that is a lovely song the orchestra is playing. Do you know the name of it?"

"Sara, that's an American song that I heard quite often when I was stationed overseas, but I can't think of the name of it."

"I love it," Sara said. "They write such beautiful music in America. Someday I would love to visit there. Maybe you can take me there on our honeymoon."

Becker looked at her and smiled. "What a vivid imagination you have," he said. Captain, have you ever met anyone quite like this one?"

"No, sir, I have not, but I haven't given up hope," Schwarz said. They all laughed.

"Captain, obviously our surveillance of Klein and Donst took place elsewhere in the hotel," Becker said.

"Yes, sir, that is correct. That was done in the cocktail lounge. If you like, we can take a look in there while we are here."

"Yes, let's do that. Sara," Becker said, "will you excuse us while we go to the lounge?"

The captain and Becker, followed by the trusty bodyguard, went into the lounge and spent a few minutes observing the location where the bug had been placed. Then they returned to their table.

"Sara has anything happened while we were away?" Becker asked.

"The orchestra went on intermission, and I have been ogled quite a bit," she said. "I am happy you are back. I feel much more comfortable with you two beside me. Some of these people give me the creeps."

"Colonel, don't look now, but one of your admirer's is heading this way," Schwarz pointed out.

An SS officer appeared at the table and gave the heil Hitler salute. Becker and Schwarz returned the salute.

"Good evening, Colonel Becker," the SS officer said. "What a great pleasure to see you here this evening."

"I'm sorry, but do I know you?" Becker said with a straight face. He knew his failure to recognize the man would insult and embarrassing the man.

"I am Major Donst of the SS, at your service, sir. We previously met at a conference we attended with Minister Goring and Heinrich Himmler."

"Oh, yes, major, how forgetful of me," Becker said. "Major, I would like for you to meet two of my most trusted aides, Captain Kurt Schwarz and Sara Klein. I believe you may know Sara's husband, or shall I say, about to be ex-husband, Karl."

"No, I am sorry, but that name does not ring a bell," Donst lied. "But I am delighted to meet such a beautiful young lady and see you again, captain. Colonel, you have excellent taste in your staff."

"Well, major, you take what they give you, but you are correct, I am very fortunate to have these two," Becker answered.

"I also see, colonel, that you have brought your protection with you," Donst said, looking over at a menacing Sergeant Heinz.

"You are quite correct, major. You never know what to expect these days with all of the enemies of the state lurking about, as well as Rohm's roving hoodlums. Are you with someone this evening, major?"

"Yes, sir, I am," Donst replied. "I am with that lovely lady in the blue dress sitting at that table." He pointed at an attractive young woman.

Obviously, she was too good-looking to be married to this buffoon, Becker thought. "Major, she is quite attractive. Give her my compliments. And give my regards to Herr Himmler," Becker said dismissively.

"Heil Hitler," Donst said.

"Heil Hitler."

"So that's the vermin you told us about, colonel," Sara remarked after Donst was out of earshot.

"Yes, that's him, a friend of your husband," Becker said.

"I wonder who the woman is that's with him," Schwarz said. "I am sure she is not his wife."

"Yeah, probably one of his aides," Becker said with some sarcasm. "It fits the profile. It typifies some of these high-ranking German officers, appealing to young, star-struck women who are subject to their whims and command."

"Now you just wait a minute, colonel," interjected Sara. "Some of us star-struck young women have a good reason for our admiration, and it has nothing to do with rank. So there."

"Sara, you do have a sense of humor, and I compliment you for it, but surely you didn't think I was referring to you," Becker said. "What do you think captain?"

The captain, who had consumed a couple of drinks laughed heartily. "Sara is above all of that, of course. Maybe she should apologize for making such an inference," said the captain.

"Shut up, Kurt. You both are just making fun of me. Please excuse me," she said, "I have to go powder my nose." With that putdown, she headed for the ladies room.

"Colonel, what are you going to do with her? You know she is crazy about you," Schwarz said.

"Yeah, I know, captain, but under the circumstances, I am unable to do anything about it. She is still a married woman, you know. She does grow on you, that I will admit. Let's put it this way. I wouldn't want to be here without her. And, by the way, what did you think about Donst lying about knowing Karl Klein?" Becker asked.

"Just what you would expect from scum like him," replied the captain. "It makes you wonder how someone like that can rise to the rank of major."

"Remember, captain, he didn't come up through the ranks

in the army. He is just a part of the trash that we have seen come out of paramilitary groups like the SA and SS. Look at that pig Rohm, for instance.

"Here is our fair lady coming back from the ladies room," Becker said.

"Did you miss me?" she asked. "Never mind, don't answer that," she quickly added. "Guess what? That woman with the major came in while I was there and commented on how lucky I was to be in the company of such unusually handsome men. She said her name was Lenore, but I don't remember her last name. Anyway, she had the nerve to ask me which one of you was I with. I told her both. She said that was obvious, but she guessed that I was with the colonel because it was so plain to see. Am I really that transparent? Besides, she said that her escort had already told her that I was the colonel's. Can you believe the nerve of that woman?"

"Yes, Sara you are that transparent," the captain chimed in.

"Well, Kurt, guess what else she said?"

"What?" he asked.

"As she was leaving, she said with a big smile that she wished that she was with that captain."

"You are lying," he replied.

"No, seriously, she did say that. I guess she is not particular about who she goes out with." Sara laughed.

"Captain, there's your chance to strike back at the enemy," Becker said. "She looks pretty good to me."

"Colonel, maybe you are right," the captain replied. "I just might have to make a run on her. It would serve that little bastard right."

"I'm sure we can find out who she is," Becker said.

"And just what did you mean when you said she looked pretty good to you?" Sara asked as she gave the colonel a look of disapproval.

"I meant she looked pretty good for the captain," Becker said."

"All right, that sounds better," she said.

They had dinner and ordered one more drink for the road.

"Captain, I think that woman really meant what she said in the ladies room. Every time I look over at their table, she is looking at you," Sara commented.

"Yeah, Sara, I caught that. I gave her a smile, and she winked at me, so I guess I have no choice but to follow up. Maybe the colonel is right about her looking good. I guess there is only one way to find out, and that is to check it out for myself," Schwarz said.

"Good idea, captain, but we better get out of here before that half pint comes over here and mops up the floor with you over flirting with his woman," Becker said. "It's also getting a little late. Are you ready to call it a night, Sara?"

"No sir, do we have to? I am having a marvelous time, and it's only eleven o'clock." "It's bedtime for little girls like you, so we must leave," Becker said. With that, the colonel and his party departed with a half-tipsy Sara wishing the night would never end.

The next morning, the colonel called the captain and Sara into his office for a meeting. "Captain, I want a bug planted somewhere so that we can keep closer tabs on Donst," Becker said. "Preferably in his office, if we can get in there. I want to know what the little bastard is up to. Last night his friendly greeting was nothing more than a farce. I'm sure he thought he was pulling a fast one with all of that phony conversation. We probably need to find a spot that will yield the most and best results. His office, of course, would be the best, but that is probably going to be the hardest place to access."

"Probably, colonel, but let us check it out," replied the captain. "There may be a way. I will try to get an agent in there. What about that major that you met at the minister's office? What was his name?"

"Albert Koenig, that's him. I have his number here somewhere. Yeah, here it is," said Becker.

"Thanks, colonel. I'll talk to him," Schwarz said. "He has access to Donst's office. All we have to do is find out when Donst is going to be out of the office and then plant our bug. It will work better if we have a permanent location so that we can set up a listening station nearby and not have to worry about moving around. I'll put our crew on it today."

"Right, captain, that's a good idea," Becker said. "Maybe you can pick up something on that floozy girlfriend of his."

"Oh, colonel, I have something on that," piped in Sara. "I did a little checking this morning and found out that she is a secretary and works in one of the government buildings on *Wilhelmplatz*. No doubt she owes her job to Major Donst. I also have a phone number for her."

"Good work, Sara. Give it to the captain. Incidentally, I had a good time last night, and I think maybe we should do that sort of thing more often," Becker offered.

Sara and the captain echoed their agreement almost simultaneously. "Colonel, you certainly are innovative. You keep coming up with such good ideas lately," Sara said.

"Sara, this is business," Becker reminded her.

"Yes sir, by all means. I would never suggest otherwise," she said, tempted to stick her tongue out at him. At one time he might have had her discharged for such a thing, but maybe she was beginning to get to him now, she thought.

Her thoughts were interrupted when Becker said, "Yeah, I'll bet. Sara, do you ever see your parents? I never hear you talk about them. Are they still living?"

"Yes, sir, they are, but they live three hours away, so I don't see them as often as I would like. As I may have told you, my relationship with them was strained when I left home. I was a silly, naïve young girl that wound up marrying the wrong man."

"If you don't hurry up and get that divorce, you might wind up being a silly, naïve widow," warned Becker. "From the looks of things, if Karl's newfound friends don't get rid of him, somebody else will. He might be just dumb enough to do something foolish, so captain, it may be a good idea if you had someone keep an eye on him. After getting his walking papers from Donst, he may be desperate enough to do something reckless."

"Yes sir, colonel. Sara, do you know whether or not he is still staying at home?" the captain asked.

"No, I don't, captain," she replied. "We were renting that place, and I would not be surprised if he moved somewhere else. I wish it was China."

"I take it, then, that it is over between you two," the captain teased her.

"Okay, let's get back to work," said Becker. "I have to work up a report for the minister. Has anybody seen Diels lately? I need to touch base with him. Sara, tell Berta to set me up a meeting with him one day this week."

"Yes sir," she replied.

"Colonel, Berta handed me a note that we just received a call that there is a situation at the Weimar Center. There has been a clash between the SA and members of the Communist Political Party. It doesn't look good" Schwarz said.

"Okay, captain, tell Sergeant Heinz to have the car ready. And call Colonel Richter and have him dispatch an initial complement of fifty troops down there and issue an order for an unlimited number on standby upon further request," Becker ordered. "As soon as you get through with that, meet us at the car. You can fill me in on the details of the disturbance on the way to Weimar."

"Yes, sir," replied the captain. Becker and his aides quickly left the office and when they got to the street, Heinz was waiting with the car.

"Where to, sir?" asked Heinz.

"Sergeant Heinz, take us to the Weimar Center and have your weapon ready. There is some kind of disturbance going on there," Becker said. As their car sped off in the direction of the Weimar Center, Becker addressed Schwarz. "Captain, fill me in on the details."

"Yes sir. It seems that a large group of KPD (Communist Party of Germany)members was staging some kind of rally, and a number of Storm Troopers moved in on them. It escalated from there. Colonel Richter will have the detachment of troops that you requested on the way. The soldiers will be armed with submachine guns."

"How far away are we away, sergeant?" asked the colonel.

"About five minutes, sir," Heinz replied.

"I guess I had better check my Luger," Becker said. "I haven't fired this thing in a couple of months. Hopefully we will have enough manpower to quell any further deterioration of the melee. We may have more trouble with those goons from SA than from the commies."

Upon arriving at the center, the trio bolted from the Mercedes. The fifty-man contingent sent by Colonel Richter was waiting out front.

"Who is the officer in charge?" asked Becker.

"I am sir, Lieutenant Mench reporting for duty sir."

"Okay, lieutenant, I am Colonel Becker, and this is Captain Schwarz with the Gestapo. Follow us, and have your men prepared to use their weapons on command."

"Yes, sir, colonel," Mench said.

They entered the lobby to find a number of Storm Troopers milling around. Many were armed with night sticks and a few with handguns. Colonel Becker demanded to know who was in charge. A rather large brown-shirt trooper emerged and stated that Captain Schneider was.

"Get his ass out here, and let's find out what this shit is all about," demanded Colonel Becker.

"Yes, sir, I'll get him for you," the portly trooper replied. A few minutes later the officer appeared and introduced himself as Captain Schneider.

"All right, captain, tell me what this is all about," Becker said.

"We have things under control, colonel."

"Did I ask if you had things under control?" asked Becker. "I don't have time to stand here and listen to your bullshit. Are you ready to tell me what is going on here, or am I going to have to order one of these soldiers to put a bullet in your ass?"

"Yes, sir," the now-trembling captain replied. "We were called down here because these communists were staging a protest of some kind, and we were in the process of restoring order. We have three females in custody, and there are about a hundred demonstrators behind the stage in the auditorium. Five of the communists are wounded. Four of our men are dead, and ten suffered injuries, mostly non-life threatening. We think they may have a few dead, but we are not sure because we can't get back there. The ones behind the stage are armed. They are holding hostages, but we don't know how many."

"Do you know who the ringleaders are?" asked the colonel.

"The main one is a man named Shamkov."

"Have you had any contact with him?" asked the colonel.

"Only from a distance, sir," Schneider replied. "He has a bullhorn, and we can see on the stage."

"Captain, I am issuing you an order to withdraw your men and return to your headquarters," Becker announced. "The Gestapo will now take command of this insurrection."

"But, sir, I have my orders to—"

"Hold it right there, captain. I don't have time to listen to your excuses or explanations of why you are here. I have issued an order, and unless you obey that order, you will be taken into custody."

"But—"

Before Schneider could finish his appeal, the colonel spoke to one of the soldiers. "Soldier, seize that man and place him under arrest. If he resists, shoot him. Now who is next in command of these Storm Troopers?"

"I am, sir, Sergeant Fulcher."

"Fulcher, you heard my order to your captain," Becker shouted. "Now execute it, or you will suffer the same fate as your commander."

"Yes sir, colonel. Attention Storm Troopers. Evacuate the premises and reassemble outside," Fulcher shouted into a bullhorn.

Once the Storm Troopers had vacated the building, Colonel Becker turned his attention to Captain Schwarz. "Captain, hand me one of those bullhorns and have all of the wounded removed and taken to the nearest medical facility. Lieutenant Mench, you and your men follow me into the auditorium with your weapons on ready. Hold your fire until I give the order," Becker instructed.

"Yes, sir," Mench replied. "Detail, attention" Mench shouted. "I want twenty men on the right side of the auditorium and twenty on the left. Sergeant Dietz, you and the remaining contingent will remain in the lobby. Let's move in" Mench ordered.

The colonel entered the auditorium with the bullhorn. "Will the leader of the demonstrators step forward?" Becker commanded. "Do not fear being harmed. Our purpose is to begin negotiations for the release of hostages."

A man in his forties stepped forward and introduced himself. "I am Ivan Shamkov," he announced.

"Shamkov, I am Colonel Becker with the Gestapo. I understand that you are holding some hostages, is that correct?"

"Yes, sir, we do have five Storm Troopers backstage," Shamkov answered.

"All right, first of all, I want you to release those hostages. Failure to comply with my order will result in unnecessary bloodshed. Believe me. I have no qualms about shooting all of you, including your hostages. Have them walk out in single file. If you comply with my order, you will be treated fairly and given a chance to present your grievances. Do you understand my order, Shamkov?" Becker asked.

"Yes, sir," Shamkov said. He addressed one of his associates. "Dimitri, release the hostages."

Once the hostages came out, they were escorted outside to reunite with their unit.

"Now, Shamkov, how many demonstrators are with you?" demanded Becker.

"Sir, there are about thirty-five of us," Shamkov replied.

"I want you and your fellow demonstrators to form a single file and walk toward the lobby. If you have any firearms or other weapons, you are to lay them down now. Understood?" Becker said.

"Yes sir. I will lead the way," Shamkov said.

After all of the demonstrators had filed into the lobby, they were taken into custody.

"Mench," ordered Becker, "take these prisoners to Gestapo headquarters for incarceration and questioning."

"Yes sir, colonel. Attention, prisoners. Fall in line and move out front to the street, where you will be loaded on trucks," Mench ordered.

"Thank you, Lieutenant Mench," Becker said. "After the prisoners are secured, you and your detail will return to your regular duty. Heil Hitler." Becker turned to Captain Schwarz.

"Turn this facility back over to the custodian so he can clean up this mess, and we will head back to headquarters. And have the medics remove the bodies."

"Yes sir, colonel. I'll be right with you" Schwarz replied.

At headquarters, Becker told Captain Schwarz to interview Shamkov and some of the other detainees and report back to him.

"Shamkov, I am Captain Schwarz, and I will be conducting the interviews with you and some of the other members of your group. First of all, do you have a statement that you would like to make before we begin the interview?"

"Yes, captain. We were exercising our rights to peaceful assembly when those Storm Troopers showed up. I was making a speech on the street outside the center when all of a sudden the troopers started cursing and beating our people with clubs. That's when we grabbed some of the troopers and went inside the center to protect ourselves from being injured by them. They also shot and killed ten of our people, and a number were wounded by the SA beatings with clubs."

"Were any members of your group in possession of weapons? Were there any firearms, knives or clubs?" Schwarz asked.

"No sir. All of our people were unarmed. We took a couple of handguns and billy clubs from the Storm Troopers. We didn't want to give the police or the Storm Troopers any reason to attack us."

"Are you aware, Shamkov, that these types of demonstrations are illegal under the laws of the Third Reich?" Schwarz asked.

"We do not recognize those laws as being valid," Shamkov answered. "They violate our rights of free assembly."

"You are going to be turned over to the police, and it will be up to the courts to determine your rights under the law. Are there any other leaders among your group that we should talk?"

"No, I am the leader of the group," Shamkov said.

"You were wise to surrender to Colonel Becker. He would not have hesitated to use the force that he had at his command," Schwarz said. "If you hadn't surrendered, you and I would not be having this conversation. Unless you have something else you would like to say, this interview is over. You will be turned over to the police shortly for further questioning."

"Colonel, it is all over the news that you quelled the riot at the Weimar Center. The headline of the special bulletin reads, 'At Least Fifteen Killed In Riot; Gestapo leader diffuses dangerous confrontation between Storm Troopers and KPD Demonstrators.' In the article, it further reads: 'Under the leadership of Gestapo Colonel Konrad Becker, a cadre of army troops quickly squashed a potentially explosive situation at the Weimar Center today. The quick and decisive action by Colonel Becker has been credited with saving hundreds of lives. Chancellor Hitler and Minister Hermann Goring both commended the colonel, an-oft decorated army veteran of World War I. At the time of this news bulletin, Colonel Becker had not been contacted for comment. SA Chief of Staff Rohm refused to comment on the incident. Some observers said the initial response and overreaction by the SA contributed to the confrontation with an initially peaceful assembly of KPD party members. The initial crowd was estimated at more than 1,000.' Colonel, that story has been running on all of the radio stations, too," Sara said.

"All right, Sara, just calm down and let me see a copy of the newspaper," Becker said. "Here it is. Colonel, we are so proud of you. You are truly a national hero. Director Diels and Minister Goring would each like to see you as soon as it is convenient," she said.

"Thank you, my dear Sara. You are very thoughtful. But with all of these people around, I suggest that you curb your enthusiasm and save it for a more convenient time and place. Now call the director's office and tell them I am on my way to see him," Becker ordered.

"Yes, sir," Sara said and went to the telephone.

The director was waiting for Becker when he arrived at Diels' office. "Colonel, congratulations on the way you handled the situation at the Weimar Center."

"Thank you, Herr Director," Becker replied. "That brings up a subject that I have been meaning to discuss with you for some time "I am sure you already know that Minister Goring and *Reichsfuhrer* Himmler have already informed me of the need for change over at the SA. We are, of course, working on that and have made a great deal of progress. This recent incident at the center only adds to the mounting evidence in making the case for the removal of the SA leader," Becker explained.

"Yes, colonel, I am aware of the situation, and I understand the important role you are playing in the elimination of that scoundrel Rohm."

"Herr Director, we have also been monitoring certain individuals who are also plotting to take over the Gestapo," Becker informed the director. "We have placed wiretaps, or bugs, as they are sometimes referred to, in certain places and have been monitoring and making transcripts of their conversations. They are recent activities, and we feel like it is time share this information with you. Some of the conversations that we have monitored include officials at the SS. One of the SS Deputies, Colonel Hartman and a Major Wilhelm Donst, an aide to Himmler, have been the subject of some of these eavesdropping activities. There is no question but that there is a move to bring the Gestapo into the SS, under the direction of Himmler," Becker explained. "Minister Goring will do everything he can to oppose that, but there it is in a nutshell."

"Thank you very much, colonel, for informing me about this

matter. I am not surprised, by any means, but it certainly is something that we must be concerned about. There are a number of devious people in the SS, and I dread the thought of them seizing control of this agency. I'm sure you know who I am talking about. We are fortunate to have men of your caliber. Again, I want to commend you on the good work you are doing for this agency and for Germany."

"Thank you, Herr Director," Becker said as he stood up. He bade Diels good day and wished him well, then returned to his office.

When Becker returned to the office, Berta took her turn giving her congratulations and compliments. She also passed on the many calls that had come in praising the colonel. While it had been a very good day for Becker and the Gestapo, the opposite was true for Rohm and the SA. The riot was humiliating for the SA, in spite of the fact that the confrontation was with the despised communist workers party. Rohm had to be seething, and Colonel Becker knew Rohm's frustration and anger would be directed toward him. Becker could care less what Rohm would do. By all accounts, the original mission that he had embarked upon was proving to be a spectacular success. He had reached the highest level of power in a government that he was dedicated to bringing down. He had managed, through his British contact, to dispatch a great deal of information to England and, ultimately, to his superiors in the United States. He was also disappointed in some of the information that he had relayed back to his country. It was almost common knowledge that the Germans were rearming, and the United States and England did not need spies to tell them that. Hopefully time and patience would bring about an even more important role for him in the hierarchy of the Nazi power structure, and therefore give him access to more important information. The temptation was strong for Becker to become a celebrity and attend an unlimited number of social functions. This clearly did not fit into his plans. He had to continue his work in the power structure but a high profile did not fit into the plan. In fact, it most likely would be counterproductive. He was in an atmosphere where, the higher his profile became, the larger the target he would become. That meant he had to tap down the celebrity angle. His mantra would be, he was a soldier, not a politician or a celebrity. It would suit him well. Those who were in power were wary of newcomers and potential rivals.

The next day the colonel was summoned to meet with Minister Goring. Arriving at the minister's office, Becker was greeted as a conquering hero by the staff and immediately ushered into the minister's office.

"Good morning, colonel. You are no doubt receiving the accolades of the populace, judging by the reception you just received from my staff. How does it feel?" Goring asked.

"Herr Minister, I am, quite frankly, overwhelmed and would be happy to move on and leave it all behind," Becker said.

"You are too modest, colonel. I would like to add my congratulations for your outstanding achievement in reigning in that bunch of rowdies at the center. Your quick action and leadership has reflected very well on me and my office. Even the *fuhrer* took the time to call and offer praise. Please sit down. Would you care for a drink?" Goring asked.

"Why, yes, thank you, Herr Minister. I will have a glass of that favorite wine that you keep on hand."

"Certainly, I'll have one myself," Goring said as he retrieved a bottle from his wine cabinet. "Colonel, you realize that your action at the center has managed to turn the chief of the SA into an uncontrollable rage. He has even paid a visit to the *fuhrer* to express his outrage and indignation over the matter. The *fuhrer* listened to him and sympathized with him, but privately the *fuhrer* was quite pleased with what happened, even though he thinks the communists should be hanged for their treachery. The bottom line is that your action saved the government from what could have been an embarrassment of monumental proportions.

"There were several innocent bystanders that were killed by the SA," Goring continued. "It is a tragic reminder that we must remove that bonehead before he does something that could bring us all down. The generals are becoming increasingly impatient with an out-of-control paramilitary group that outnumbers their own forces by several million men. The *fuhrer* is in fear of a possible coup from a despot who doesn't know what the word loyalty means. With this latest episode, we think the *fuhrer* is nearer a decision to eliminate the problem. What is your assessment, colonel?"

"We have accumulated additional evidence of the man's erratic behavior, as well as his well-known participation in illicit sexual activities," Becker answered. "We are prepared to take whatever steps that are needed to rid society of this swine. Just give the order, and it will be done."

"Colonel, I am reluctant to involve you in this thing personally," Goring said. "I do want you to act in an advisory capacity on how the plot is carried out. It must be professional and in a manner that leaves no room for error. The *fuhrer* is leaning in the direction of openly leading the effort in the final act. We just need to work out the details. One thing that is definite, though, is that it must come as a complete surprise.

"Now colonel, what about your SS detractors?" Goring asked.

"Herr Minister, they are alive and well. We are in the process of planting a bug in Donst's office. I have some competent engineers that have been working on our electronic eavesdropping technology, and I am happy to report that a great deal of progress has been made in that field. Our people are revolutionizing the art of listening devices. It is allowing us more leeway in placement, as well as enhanced listening capability. They have done an outstanding job. Koenig is coordinating with them on when they can access and place a device in Donst's office without rousing any suspicion."

"Say, colonel, I am very interested in that technology," Goring said. "I just might have some use for it. In fact, I will come up with some names that I need to keep tabs on."

"No problem, Herr Minister. Just let us know who they are, and we will get it done."

Chapter Fifteen

B ack at headquarters, the colonel was confronted with a number of important developments, among them, the eavesdropping matter.

"Colonel, the captain would like to see you regarding the latest developments on the eavesdropping case," Berta said.

"Thank you, Berta, ask him to come to the office," Becker said.

"Yes, sir," she said as she swished her ample rear end out of the office. No doubt the woman was still growing.

A few minutes later, the captain strolled into the office and took a seat. "Sir, our bugs have been put in place and are working perfectly. We have rented a room at the Hotel *Kaiserhoff* that is close enough to pick up a very good signal. The transmission is good, and we are manning the station from eight in the morning until seven in the evening. This should give us the best possible coverage, as there is little activity over there after six o'clock.

The first day of operation yielded little in the way of useful information. Mostly routine stuff, and there was no mention of you or the Gestapo,"

"That is interesting, captain," Becker said. "As soon as you pick up something useful, I want to know about it. It is imperative that we stay ahead of those bastards. I just returned from the minister's office, and Goring is quite happy with the way things went at the Weimar Center. Even the *fuhrer* was pleased with our intervention. Goring also expressed an interest in our wiretap technology. Seems he's anxious to put it to good use on some of his own crowd. Boy, these people don't trust anybody, and my guess is that they are more than justified when you take a look at some of the people that they are associated with. They are strictly the bottom of the barrel. Anyway, we need to expect a call soon requesting our surveillance crew for the minister. It looks like we may have to expand our personnel in that department. You should start looking for some good men." "Yes, sir, I still have a list of names that Colonel Richter had recommended," Schwarz said. "I'll start looking at that list as soon as I leave here. Our stock has taken quite a rise since the Weimar Center episode. I have applicants for positions with us coming out of the woodwork. We have a few applicants from the SS and others from army intel."

"Just make sure that we don't bring in any trash, or worse, ringers," warned Becker. "I much prefer a lean machine to a big operation with too many misfits."

"I am on the same page, colonel," Schwarz replied. "I'll get Sara to help me look over the applications."

"Speaking of Sara, how is she holding up, captain?" Becker asked. "I haven't seen her since the mini-riot at the center."

"She is fine, sir," Schwarz replied, "but she says she is lonesome. Maybe you should take her out to dinner this evening. I think that would boost her spirits."

"I don't know about that, captain," Becker replied. "There is a lot on my plate right now, and I can't afford any serious diversions, even with her. Not that I wouldn't like to, mind you. How about that Lenore woman? Anything doing on that?" Becker asked.

"Not yet. Been busy, but I'll get to her a in a day or two," Schwarz replied.

A few days later, Captain Schwarz brought in new transcripts for Colonel Becker to review. "Colonel, we have several days of conversations coming out of Donst's office," Schwarz said. "Most of them are routine. We did pick up two that are very interesting. I am sure you will agree. The first is a conversation between Donst and Hartman. Here is your copy. Let's look it over."

Donst: Colonel Hartman, I'm sure you remember that I told you we were looking at former acquaintances and others who had some type of relationship with Konrad Becker. We have talked to several, and two of them have real potential. One of them attended Grand Gymnasium with Becker. The other served with Becker at the military academy and also had some contact with him after the war. He claims to know Becker well and should be a good possibility for us. The first one is Jared Hersch, and he is presently employed by I. G. Farben in Frankfurt. The other fellow is Dieter Hawes, a captain in the army, stationed at Hammelburg. I have made arrangements to have both of them come in for interviews.

Hartman: Excellent, major. I trust these interviews will be conducted without delay?

Donst: Yes, sir. We should finish both of them next week. I will report back to you then.

Hartman: Very good. Have you had any further contact with that fellow Klein?

Donst: "No, sir. He has attempted to contact me by telephone on several occasions, but I have not spoken to him. I am still trying to decide what I should do with him.

Hartman: I see our friend Colonel Becker made some news and catapulted himself into the spotlight with that circus at the Weimar Center. Do you have any details about what really took place?

Donst: We have the news accounts and also the official report. We have pretty much verified what was in the official report. We have concluded that Becker acted appropriately and have not found anything negative. The man appears to be quite lucky. It was almost like a setup to have those buffoons at the SA incite the entire mess and then let the Gestapo and Becker ride in on a white horse and salvage the operation. But don't worry, sir, we will catch him doing something, and when he does, we will make him pay.

Hartman: I wish I shared your optimism. Thus far, he has performed quite brilliantly. He is riding high at the moment, so I would suggest that you redouble your efforts and come up with something that we can use to bring him down.

Donst: Yes, sir. I am breaking my ass and riding our people hard to do just that. But rest assured, we will get him one way or the other.

Hartman: Thank you, major. I have to go. Heil Hitler.

Donst: Heil Hitler.

"This next one is a conversation between Donst and an unidentified female," Schwarz said.

Female: "Hello, major. Are you busy?"

Donst: "Come in, and close the door and lock it. [Sound of door shutting.] Come over here and sit in my lap.

Female: I have missed you, Willy, and the other willy, too.

[Sound of movement.] Why haven't you called me? It's been more than a week.

Donst: For one thing, I have been busy, and for another, that wife of mine has been all over my ass about being gone too much and neglecting her. It's the same old shit all the time. Give me another kiss, baby.

Female: Why don't you leave her ass? If my husband did that to me, I would run his ass off.

[Knock on door.]

Donst: Oh, shit. Get up and pull up your underwear, quick. [Louder] Hold on. I'll be with you in a minute.

[After a brief interval, sound of the door opening.]

Male voice: Excuse me, major. I did not know you were in conference.

Donst: Sorry, captain, I was just giving some dictation. That will be all for now, Gertrude.

"Colonel, that is pretty much what we have for now," Schwarz said. "The rest of the conversations were of no concern. Thought you might get a kick out of the last conversation. Our Major Donst appears to be somewhat of a philanderer, if not worse. Evidently he fancies himself a ladies' man. No wonder Frau Donst is on his sorry ass."

"Yeah, that was very interesting, captain, as well as amusing," Becker said. "Let's talk about the conversation between Donst and Hartman. It looks like they have managed to locate a couple of people from way back when. I don't remember either one of those names mentioned, although the name Dieter Hawes sounds familiar."

"Colonel, he is the one that is in the army. He must be infantry if he is stationed at Hammelburg. I'll put a tracer on him. In fact, I'll send one of my men over now to look at his army records."

Schwarz stepped out for a few minutes and returned. "I have

a man on his way over to the records department. I'll also put out some feelers on the other fellow, Hersch. IG Farben is a chemical company, so he must be a chemist or somehow connected to the chemical industry. Donst didn't mention where his interviews would take place, but most likely they will be in his office," Schwarz said.

"Right, captain, if that's where they are, our people will be able to monitor them. I noticed that they mentioned our friend Klein. So evidently Donst is still pondering what to do with him," Becker added. "Hopefully they will continue to ride that dead horse. All right, I guess that pretty much wraps it up for me, unless you have something else. I need to make some phone calls."

Two hours later, the captain returned to the office. "Colonel, I have the lowdown on Hawes."

"Good, let's have it," Becker said.

"He's thirty-five years old. Weighs 190 and is six feet tall. He's been in the army for almost seventeen years, and I was right, he is infantry. No meritorious stuff in his jacket. That's probably why he has not advanced higher in rank. He's married with three children. He was born in Stuttgart, and his father was an army officer. He did attend the military academy in Berlin about the same time you did. He has been stationed in a few other locations. That's about it, sir. Does any of that ring a bell?" Schwarz asked.

"Only the academy," Becker answered. "I may have run into him somewhere else, but I have no recollection of it. Maybe we can get more insight into him after his interview, providing that we can listen in on it. We will just have to wait and see. Thanks, captain, and let me know when you have something on Hersch."

"Yes, sir," Schwarz said as he left the office.

The next two days were uneventful, and the colonel devoted most of his time to routine matters. Sara was in and out on several occasions. She was getting used to living at the hotel and was happier than at any time of her life, according to Berta and others around the office.

"Colonel, I am counting the days until my divorce is final, so where are you going to take me to celebrate?" Sara asked.

"I haven't given it much thought," Becker answered. "Maybe we could go to the opera or the theater."

"Konrad, you must be joking," she replied. "I'm talking about a real celebration. Where is your sense of romance? Wouldn't you like to spend the night with a woman who wants to celebrate her freedom?"

"Sara, you just may be too wild for me. Or if you get right down to it, you just may be too wild for any man. Now come down from your high horse and get back to work."

"I'll make you pay for ignoring me all this time," she threatened.

"How?" he asked.

"Just you wait and see," Sara said.

At that time, the captain came into the office. "Colonel, are you busy?"

"No, not at all," Becker said. "I'm just trying to get Sara out of here, but she doesn't seem to be able to take a hint."

"Okay," she said, "I'm going, and I may never come back." She walked out the door.

"What do you have, captain?" Becker asked.

"I have a report back on Jared Hersch. He is listed as a salesman with that company and has been with them for eleven years. He has a wife and two kids and lives in a middle-class neighborhood. Has a drinking problem. All in all, he looks like a good candidate for bribing. He doesn't appear to be a womanizer, which is somewhat of a surprise for a salesman. The bottom line is that nothing stands out about him. His physical description is not flattering, either. He is five-foot-ten and weighs 250. Maybe that explains why he is not a womanizer. That sums up our Mr. Hersch. From all appearances, colonel, it looks like Donst is wasting his time on this character," Schwarz concluded.

"From what you have just told me, captain, I would have to agree with you. Their best bet with that poor fellow is to try to refurbish him, hoping that he can make up some tall tale. What a waste of time. I guess they have plenty of time to waste over there. Nothing in your report gives me the slightest recollection of the man. No, the one to bear watching in this thing is going to be Hawes," Becker said. "Maybe the thinking with Donst is that somehow these people are going to say I'm not Becker. This is probably based on the fact that I either failed to recognize or just plain ignored some people. I guess we are forced to play their stupid game.

"I think we should now devote our time to something more important, like did you ever call that woman that was with Donst that night at the Adlon?" Becker asked.

"Colonel, guess what?" Schwarz said. "I finally got around to calling and made a date with her. I took her to a bistro on the north side of town. She didn't want to go to the Adlon or any other place where she might be recognized. She tells me that old Donst is into her pretty good and is very jealous. She said that she is obligated to him because he got her a job and is helping her with her expenses. She said if it were not for that, she would have nothing to do with him."

"That is interesting," Becker commented. "What else?"

"She is only twenty-two years old and a little naïve, but I like her," Schwarz replied. "We hit it off pretty good. I'll probably take her out again, if for no other reason than to keep tabs on Donst. She has no qualms about talking about him. According to her, he has knocked her around a couple of times, but she is afraid to leave him."

"That sorry bastard," Becker commented.

"I really feel sorry for her," Schwarz said. "Among the other things I found out from her is that she comes from a good family, but dire financial problems forced her into the relationship with Donst. Also, and this may come as a surprise, he despises you and has vowed to get you one way or the other."

"Captain," Becker said, "you are to be commended for making such a sacrifice for your country."

"Actually, colonel, I didn't get that far. She is a nice girl. I didn't want to take advantage of her, so I didn't push it too hard."

"Good for you, captain. She may well be a good source of information for us, so don't discourage her association with Donst."

"Right, sir, I think I am going to enjoy this assignment," Schwarz said. "During the course of the evening, Lenore reminded me more than once about Donst's obsession with you and the Gestapo. I had to convince her that you were not the monster that he portrayed you to be. She was also very complimentary of Sara. Thought she was not only beautiful but very sweet and said she would like to get to know her better."

"Captain, I'm not sure that is a good idea. I don't think we will travel down that road. Speaking of Sara, did you ever find out if she had a weapon?" Becker asked.

"No, sir, she did not, but she has one now and has been taking lessons on how to use it," Schwarz answered. "She carries it with her everywhere now. I think she likes the idea of packing a weapon."

"Call her in here, and let's find out whether she knows what to do with it," Becker ordered.

A few minutes later, Sara came in. "Yes, colonel, did you want to see me?" she asked.

"Yeah, what about that weapon you were issued? Are you

making good use of it, and more importantly, do you know how to use it?"

"Yes, sir, I certainly do know how to use it. I have taken some lessons and have been down to the firing range."

"Just make damn sure you don't shoot the wrong person with it," he teased. "Don't go anywhere without it either."

"Yes, sir, I even sleep with it. Thanks for thinking about me. I guess I am becoming indispensable around here."

The captain laughed and the colonel cracked a slight smile. No doubt, she knew how to push the right buttons.

A couple of days later, the captain popped in with new transcripts to review.

"Who are these conversations with?" Becker asked.

"One of them is with that Hersch fellow, and the conversation didn't last very long. Here they are," Schwarz replied.

[An unidentified voice introduced Jared Hersch to Donst.]

Donst: Pleasure to meet you, Herr Hersch. I'll get right to it. You are here because you attended Grand Gymnasium in Munich with a Konrad Becker some fifteen years ago. Did you know Becker?

Hersch: Yes, sir. I sure do remember him. He was a bully and picked on me and some of the other kids. I attempted to fight him when I was about sixteen, and he beat me to a pulp. After that I tried to stay as far away from him as I could get.

Donst: Do you remember whether or not he had any identifying marks on him? By that, I mean a scar or something like that.

Hersch: No. I just remember him being bigger than me.

"Colonel, the interview went downhill from there," Schwarz said. "As you said before, they were probably wasting their time with that fellow. At the end, you can tell that Donst realized he was wasting time and hustled the poor bastard out of the office like he was three-day-old fish. Here is the other one with Hawes."

Donst: Welcome to Berlin, Captain Hawes. It is my pleasure to meet you. We are pleased that you were able to come down here and perhaps shed some light on an individual by the name of Konrad Becker. Rest assured that anything that you say here will be kept in the strictest confidence. The SS operates under a serious code of secrecy.

Hawes: I am honored to meet you, Major Donst. I am well aware of the SS and its reputation for security.

Donst: Thank you, captain. I don't want to take up too much of your time, so tell me what you can about Becker, how you met him and so forth.

Hawes: I first met him at the military academy here in Berlin in about 1917. We were roommates for a while, so I got to know him quite well, or I guess I thought I did.

Donst: What do you mean by that?

Hawes: Well, I thought we were friends. I had a steady girlfriend at the time, and I cared a great deal for her. Later on, I found out that Becker was taking her out on the sly, and much to my dismay, he knocked her up. Of course he tried to tell me that she had seduced him when I was on a weekend pass visiting my parents.

Donst: I'll be damned. You don't mean that. That sorry son of a bitch.

Hawes: That's not all. I confronted him with it and threatened to give him a good thrashing.

Donst: Then what happened?

Hawes: He beat the living shit out of me, that's what happened, and believe me I haven't forgotten it.

Donst: How do you know the baby was not yours?

Hawes: I thought she was a virgin. She and I never had sex.

Donst: That makes sense. What happened to the girl and her baby?

Hawes: She went off somewhere and, I guess, had her baby. I was later sent to the front, and when the war was over, I never saw her again.

Donst: What was her name?

Hawes: Pauletta. Pauletta Bauer. Everybody called her Paula.

Donst: That is interesting. Becker has a child roaming around somewhere. The child would be about sixteen by now. Any idea where Pauletta may have gone?

Hawes: No. Like I said, I lost track of her.

Donst: I see. Do you remember the name of her father? We may want to look into it. Do you think Becker would remember you?

Hawes: Of course he would. After the war, I heard he had gone back to school in Munich for a while. I heard that he was wounded in the war. Should have some scars on him, I suppose. Paula's dad's name was Joff or something like that. That was a long time ago, you know.

Donst: Can you think of anything else that you might know about him or that he might know about you? Nicknames for example?

Hawes: Now that you mention it, he always called me "Pootie." I don't know where the hell he got that, but that's what he called me. We all called him Becker.

Donst: Pootie. That is interesting. We have talked to several people that knew him before he went to America. They said that they ran into him after he got back and he acted like he didn't even know them.

Hawes: He always thought he was better than anybody else.

It is probably because his father was a general. I could see him snubbing people.

Donst: Maybe, but it looks funny to me. Some of the one's he snubbed weren't just peasants. Captain, we have a proposition for you. We would like to set up a meeting between you and Becker, or maybe arrange for you to "accidentally" run into each other. To see what happens. Would you be amenable to assisting us in this matter?

Hawes: I would be happy to help you and the SS any way that I can. Just tell me what you want me to do.

Donst: We will work up something. Do you know what Becker does now?

Hawes: No, I haven't heard anything about him in probably ten years.

Donst: He is a colonel now and is the number two man at the Gestapo. He acts like he's number one, and for all we know, he may be number one.

Hawes: Holy shit, major. What are you getting me into? The Gestapo? That may be a little more than I bargained for. I don't know about this whole deal.

Donst: Don't go getting cold feet on us, Hawes. I can guarantee that you will be protected. As far as you are concerned, this will just be a casual meeting, and all we want is a report back from you as to what was said and what happened. No one will ever know about your association with the SS. You have my word on that.

Hawes: The Gestapo? That's bad enough, but you don't know this man. Major, I could wind up getting killed or worse. I have a family to think about, and from what I remember about this fellow, he takes no prisoners.

Donst: It's not going to hurt anything if you just accidentally run into one another.

Hawes: Let me think about it. I am not going to call him, that's for sure. He would see through that in a minute.

Donst: While you are thinking about it, we will try to find an event or something of that nature where you could just happen to run into each other. We will find out when and where Becker may be present. You can return to your home, and we will contact you when we find out something. Or if you like, we can make arrangements with your commandant to allow you to spend some time in Berlin.

Hawes: I don't want to stay here. I have to get back home, but right now it looks like the only thing I can get out of this situation is something very bad. I'll have to think long and hard before I walk this gangplank.

Donst: Hawes, you do that, but I think you had better think twice before you turn down an offer from the SS.

Hawes: If I decide to go through with this, just what do you want me to do if I do run into Becker?

Donst: All you have to do is see if he remembers you. Just engage him in conversation. Like, do you remember this or that? What happened to the girl that got pregnant? Let him see if he remembers her name. Also, see if he remembers your nickname, just something like that to test his memory. That is all we are asking you to do. There may be a little bonus in it for you. I'll check on that. How about it?

Hawes: All right, but I expect you to keep your word about protecting me, and I want to hear more about that bonus. My decision is going to ride on the bonus.

Donst: Hawes, you are doing the right thing. As soon as I get something on the bonus, I will get in touch with you, and we will get this thing going. It was a pleasure meeting you. Have a good trip home. Heil Hitler.

Hawes: Thank you. Heil Hitler.

"There you have it, colonel. Looks like you may be a papa. Is all that shit true?"

"Maybe," Becker answered. "I am not admitting anything until I see my lawyer. It looks like they are going to talk that poor fellow into their little scheme, so we are just going to have to be prepared for it when it comes down. I do feel a little guilt about Paula, though. I wonder what happened to her. Maybe you can do a tracer on her. Her father's name was Joff. They lived in Berlin, so there may be something on the family. I'm just curious about Paula and the kid," Becker said.

Becker was a little surprised that Paula's name had never come up when he was being prepped for his present role. The real Becker had a child out there somewhere. It was likely that he overlooked a few things that happened fifteen or so years ago. Anyway, the original Becker was a very young man at the time, and he would want that child to be cared for, the new Becker thought. Maybe the colonel owed him that much, to find out about the offspring. It should not be a problem. He could play along with them and not really admit to anything. He could always take the approach of letting bygones be bygones. He could be as dismissive of Hawes as he had been of others. There was nothing unusual about not wanting to talk about one's past. There was also no harm in being accused of being high-handed and rising to the top without acknowledging old friends and acquaintances. It happened all the time. So they labeled him an asshole. So what? There was plenty of company out there in that category.

"Colonel, you were a very naughty young man," Sara said, interrupting his thoughts. "I don't know whether to be angry or relieved."

"What do you mean by that, Sara?" asked Becker. "I mean, I don't know whether to be angry that you had sex with another woman, or whether I am relieved that you are capable of having sex."

"Boys will be boys," Becker said dismissively, then turned to Schwarz. "Captain, it looks like we have pretty well covered their conversations. We will wait and see what their next move will be. At least I will not be surprised if I happen to run into an old buddy in the near future. My guess is they probably will end their search for old acquaintances, except for Pauletta Bauer," he surmised. "They may think there is some fruit to pick there."

"I agree with your assessment, colonel," Schwarz replied. "Is there anything else I need to do before I go back to the office?"

"I can't think of anything offhand," Becker replied. "Maybe we should start doing more socializing in high-profile places. We seem to pick up on quite a bit when doing so, but that might eliminate your newfound friend Lenore, since she is allergic to such places."

"Right, colonel, I'm ready when you are," Schwarz replied. "I am always ready to socialize. As for Lenore, I think she would go if I asked her, but for the time being, we need to keep her underground. If Donst knew that she was fraternizing with the enemy, she would be toast. He would see to it that she lost her job."

"Captain, tell her for the time being to just lie low. If it ever comes down to it and she works out to our satisfaction, I'll give her a job with the Gestapo," Becker allowed. "Maybe if she knows that, she will feel more secure and work harder to get us what we want."

Schwarz agreed.

After some more thinking on the idea of high-profile socializing, the colonel decided to start at the *Kaiserhoff* Club. The *Kaiserhoff* Hotel was the headquarters for Hitler and the Nazi party and would offer fertile ground for nightlife. Becker called Sara in.

"Sara, what do you know about the *Kaiserhoff*?"

"Colonel, I have never slept there."

"I'm not talking about the hotel," he said. "Don't they have a club or lounge?"

"Yes, they do have a nice club," she said. "My soon-to-be ex used to go there once in a while, and I have had some friends tell me that there is good entertainment there. The problem is that too many Nazi big shots hang out there, and the young crowds are going elsewhere."

"I told Kurt to scare up a date, and we would meet them somewhere and do some high-level socializing. Are you interested?" Becker asked.

"Do you have to ask?" she replied. "All I need to know is when so I can hop in the tub and get dressed up, and I'm ready to go."

"I kind of thought you might accept an invitation," he said. "Go home and get ready, and I'll pick you up around eight."

That was all it took. Sara ran out of the office like the building was on fire.

Chapter Sixteen

As Becker leaned back in his chair, he wondered, what the hell was he doing? He wasn't sent to Germany to socialize and party. While he had attained spectacular success in establishing himself in the highest ranks of the Third Reich under Adolph Hitler he began to go over his actual accomplishments other than his personal achievements. Sure, he had dispatched messages revealing the rearming and manufacture of military products, but so what? They were not earth-shattering revelations. And the duties Becker had performed with the Gestapo were minimal at best, he thought, at least in so far as they carried out his spy obligations. In fact, he had more or less engaged in routine police activity. In spite of the high rank he had attained, he had become no more than a glorified policeman. Oh, he had knocked a few heads and put a few hoodlums in their place, but it bothered him that he had not done more. This must change, or he might as well abort the mission and turn tail to return to the United

States. No, that was not an option. There was too much at stake. The position he was in was almost unbelievable. What he had accomplished in embedding himself into such a powerful position was phenomenal. It was beyond anything that he or the American officials had ever envisioned. The problem now was that he had not taken full advantage of the power and rank that had been bestowed upon him, mostly by luck. Now the question was how he could turn it around and do what he was sent to Germany to do. It was true that there never was a master plan on how the mission would be carried out. It was more improvised, and that is where Becker felt like he had failed to perform up to his capabilities. It was time to get down to business.

That meant that he had to get that woman out of his head, for one thing. No question but that Sara had become a distraction. He blamed himself to a certain degree for allowing her to think that there was a future for the two of them, although he had repeatedly told her otherwise. What should he do with Sara Klein? She was everything a man could ask for in a woman. She was also a loyal and devoted confidant. Her performance as an employee had been exemplary. Here was a woman that clearly would give her life for him. She deserved better. Whatever he did, he would have to do it with compassion. Whatever changes he made in the relationship would be have to be subtle. That was the least he could do. It certainly was no time to act precipitously. He still needed her. There was time. Hopefully it would work out somehow, but in the meantime, he had to come up with a new plan that would be more beneficial.

One thing that popped into Becker's head was the idea of attending high-level Nazi staff meetings, where plans were being made for the future of the Third Reich. Why not? He certainly had the credentials that would permit him and his staff to attend those meetings. With his military background, he would easily fit in at those staff meetings involving generals and other high-level military officers. Civilian officials were not as high of a priority since he already had access to Goring. Still, it would probably be of some benefit to attend those briefings, particularly where military matters were under consideration. That was the new plan. The next question was when to implement it. He decided that now would be as good a time as any, so first on the list would be to call Sara and cancel plans for the evening.

"Sara, sorry but I have to cancel our plans for tonight. Something has come up that has to be taken care of. Call Captain Schwarz and let him know," he said.

"Konrad, I am so disappointed, but I understand," she replied.

Knowing she had gone to the trouble of getting herself ready, Becker told her, "Okay, Sara, if time permits and it is not too late, I will stop by your apartment on the way home," he said.

This brought her spirits back up, and she told him that would be even better than going out. After making some phone calls and wrapping up paperwork, Becker headed home, arriving at the hotel a little after nine o'clock. He knocked on Sara's door, and she opened it, welcoming him with a passionate kiss.

"Can I get you anything?" she asked.

"Yeah, a beer would be fine if you have some," Becker replied as he watched her head for the refrigerator. Watching that woman's fantastic body walking away was almost too much to endure. This was not exactly the way he had planned to start the evening. *But, hey, that's life*, he thought.

"Here you are, your highness," she said. "You look tired."

"Yeah, I guess I'm a little tired," Becker replied. "This has been a rough week."

As Sara sat down beside him, she rubbed his shoulder "I know it's that damn Donst. I could kill him with my bare hands," she said.

"It's not just Donst, Sara. It's the SS and the SA. They have this country turned upside down. It is getting more dangerous every day out there."

"Well, I have my little gun, so just say the word, and I'll go get them myself," she offered.

"Sara, these people are extremely dangerous. They not only kill women, but children, as well. But thanks anyway. If it gets too bad, then maybe I'll turn you loose. I don't doubt for a minute that you couldn't hold your own, but right now you are too valuable a member of my staff to be put into danger," Becker said as he took a drink of beer. "If the 110 pounds of dynamite underneath that dress was unleashed, they would surely come to their knees."

"You betcha," she replied.

"I guess I am going to have to become a little more aggressive in dealing with the sons of bitches," he said. "When you get into the office in the morning, call Colonel Richter and see if he can come by the office sometime tomorrow."

"Okay, but meanwhile make yourself comfortable, relax and quit thinking about those terrible people," she advised. "I worry about you all the time. If something were to happen to you, I don't know what I would do."

"Fine, Sara, you tell me to quit thinking about those people and relax, and then you start talking about them yourself."

"I'm sorry," she said. "Let's change the subject and talk about you. What were you like when you were a little boy? I'll bet you were so cute. Did you get into a lot of trouble? I'll bet you were a handful for your mother. And what was she like?"

"Hey, slow it down a little, will you?" Becker replied. "I was just an average kid and pretty much behaved myself. My parents were quite strict."

"Oh, that's right, your father was a general," she remembered.

"He became a general later on," Becker corrected her. "That's enough about me. I would rather hear about your childhood. I'm sure you were a spoiled brat. For that matter, you still are. Everybody is always fawning over you. No wonder."

"They are not," she shot back. "I guess maybe I was spoiled as a child because I was rebellious as a teenager. But one thing for sure, Konrad Becker, is that you sure as hell don't spoil me."

"Yeah, well, if you had been mine, I would have spanked that little ass of yours," he said.

"Okay, now I'm yours, so what are you waiting for?" Sara teased.

"Okay, you get the last word. Get me another beer and quit tempting me. I'm trying to be the kind of man that you would take home to mother."

"Hey, now that's a good reason for me to go home and see my dear, sweet mother," she joked.

"If you don't mind," he replied, "let's not go to your mother's tonight. I am too tired."

"I had better not answer that," she said in a sexy voice.

"Maybe you really are a nice girl. It is getting late," Becker said, "so I think I'll call it a night before I decide that I am not as tired as I thought I was. Goodnight, and don't forget to call Richter in the morning."

"It's not that late. Can't you stay just a little longer? For me," she begged.

"No, I really need to go. I don't like that look in those pretty eyes of yours. You are a very provocative and dangerous woman," he said as he opened the door and gave her a goodnight kiss lingered a little longer than it should have.

The next day, Berta informed Colonel Becker that Colonel Richter was in the outer office to see him. "Thank you, Berta, show him in," Becker said. "Good morning, Leon," he said as

Richter entered the room. "Thanks for coming by, and please have a seat."

"Good morning, Konrad. It's good to see you. What can I do for you today?"

"Leon, I have been doing some soul searching for a while about a problem that seems to be getting out of hand. I'm talking about all the back and forth between the SS and the SA," Becker said. What he really wanted to say was the violence against the Jews, but he knew he could not. "The violence that has permeated the SA and the SS against the civilian population has reached the point that I have received orders from above to step in and see if we can't do something about it," Becker said.

"Konrad," Richter said, "I am well aware of the problem and was wondering when someone was going to bring some of the violence under control. They are out there rounding up law-abiding citizens along with the undesirables and committing all kind of atrocities against them. Ever since your boss, Goring, brought in thousands of the SA and SS people and made them auxiliary police officers and left them under the command of Himmler and Rohm, all hell has broken loose."

"Apparently Goring feels like that was a huge mistake," Becker said, "and now that the violence has spread, the powers that be have had enough and want some of it quelled. Unfortunately, they don't want all of it stopped. They are mainly concerned about their own people rather than the civilians."

"Yeah right, so what is it that you want from me, Konrad?" Richter asked.

"Leon, I need to set up a special unit to deal with this problem. This is where you come in. I don't need any more plainclothes operatives. I need some soldiers. I am going to start off with twenty-five. I want well-trained, commando soldiers that ask no questions and are willing to carry out whatever orders that they are given. This is going to be an elite unit and must be carefully selected. They must also pledge absolute secrecy regarding their special assignments. Can you supply me with such men?" Becker asked.

"I think so," Richter said. "You will have to give me a little time. I have a special unit that I use on occasion, but it consists of only fifteen men. It is a crack outfit. They are tough and, in my opinion, have no reservations about whatever assignments are given them. I have another pool of men that I can draw from, but like I said, I need some time."

"Take whatever time you need because it is essential that the men picked are the absolute cream of the crop," Becker said. "Meanwhile, Captain Schwarz can talk to the leader of the fifteen that are now available and work out logistics. The other ten can be added to the unit as they become available. Who is the leader of the unit?"

"That would be Sergeant Derrick Mauch," Richter replied. "He's an outstanding soldier, and he will do a good job for you. I would recommend that you and Captain Schwarz bring him in for an interview before signing off on him."

"I agree, Leon. We are also going to have to provide housing for this group. I want them close by so that, when we have to take action, it can be swift. Another requirement, of course, is that they be heavily armed, and we will probably need at least two armored vehicles and a troop carrier."

"Konrad, don't worry, Sergeant Mauch will take care of that if he is selected for the operation."

"Good. I knew I could count on you, Leon. I will have Captain Schwarz report to you this afternoon or tomorrow to get the program underway. Again, thank you for the cooperation."

"No problem, Konrad," Richter said. "I'm always glad to help you, you know that. I wish you well with this new unit. In case you need to expand the unit or set up another one, just let me know, and we will get right on it. If you have nothing else, I have a meeting that I must attend." Richter stood up. "Heil Hitler."

"Thanks again, Leon, and I'll call you next week for a drink. Heil Hitler."

After the colonel left, Becker called Captain Schwarz in. "Captain, I just got through meeting with Colonel Richter about the new unit we are setting up. We are going to have a twenty-five-man strike force unit to start going after these criminals in the SS and SA who have been victimizing the general public. Goring says their activity may pose a threat to law and order. The bastards are not really concerned about law and order or general population abuses.

"In a nutshell, the new unit is going to be a crack, well-trained group of soldiers that will be charged with the elimination of rogue members of both the SA and SS that are suspected of unauthorized activity," Becker continued. "You can read whatever you want into that, but it gives us wide discretion in how we take care of the problem. I think the biggest concern is the looting where the loot is not filtering up to the state or into the right hands. How would you like to lead this new unit?"

"Colonel, I am on board. We need something like that, and I would be honored to be a part of it."

"Good, captain. I'm glad to hear you say that because we need you on this project. But I must warn you, it is a dangerous undertaking and under normal circumstances would be unlawful. Our cover for this operation is the enabling act, which pretty much gives the Gestapo a blank check in dealing with so-called enemies of the state. The definition of enemies of the state rests in the infinite wisdom of the Gestapo. The punishment for suspects that are targeted or apprehended is to be decided by this office. The unit will be authorized to use deadly force when warranted. Are you still in?"

"Colonel, I am in 100 percent. What is our next step?" Schwarz asked.

"All right, then you should report to Colonel Richter at once to work out the details and arrange for the transfer of manpower and support materials. He knows what you need. Report back to me after you have met with Richter. If there are any problems, then I want to know about them immediately. I know I need not emphasize to you the importance of secrecy in this operation. This will be covert. If the true nature of it were to be revealed, the entire operation would be compromised, and it could result in the termination of the program."

"I understand perfectly, sir," Schwarz replied.

After Captain Schwarz left the office, Becker's thoughts went back to the plan. This would, he thought, provide some salvation to what he had thought to be a lack of real production on his part in his mission. First, he was outraged at the treatment Jews were receiving. Innocent men, women and children were being taken from their homes, in some cases with only the clothes on their backs. Their possessions were being taken away. They were physically abused, and while some were allowed to migrate, the authorities were beginning to round others up and place them under arrest. The jails were overfilled, and therefore work camps or concentration camps were being established to handle the overflow.

Obviously Becker could not stop it, but in his mind he believed that he could cause serious problems for some of the officials who were the worst offenders in carrying out the orders. They were the ones he could strike back at. That is where the new unit could be of use. In Becker's mind, the unit's main purpose would be to execute as many of those officials as they could. His thoughts were that these officials were the real enemies of the state and therefore had signed their own death warrants. Only he, Konrad Becker, would know the true purpose of the operation. For everyone else, the purpose would be to protect the Third Reich from enemies of the state, a laudable purpose that should not be questioned by any loyal followers of the *fuhrer* and the Third Reich. He knew in his own mind that the unit that he was creating was mainly a death squad and that he possessed the power to impose the death penalty on those individuals who incurred his wrath.

It finally dawned on Becker that Goring must be informed that day. That was imperative. In case something went wrong, Becker would have the cover of authority behind him, even though Goring might not know all the intimate details. After having Berta check to see if Goring was in his office and available, Becker went over to meet with him.

After being ushered into the minister's office and exchanging greetings, Becker proceeded to discuss the new program. He gave a full explanation of the purpose of the program and emphasized to Goring that there would be plenty of room on the list for undesirables or enemies of the minister. That made the minister's interest in the plan perk up.

"Colonel, I like the plan," Goring said. "In fact, we should have already had something like this in place. Rohm and Himmler are fully aware of what their people are doing, although I know Himmler is becoming concerned because he fears he and some of his henchman may be targets themselves."

"Right you are, Herr Minister," Becker agreed. "It appears that most of the violence directed toward their respective agencies is random and not organized. We do know from our surveillance program that some of Himmler's top people are guilty of targeting us. When I say 'us,' I am of course referring to you and the Gestapo," Becker pointed.

"Yes, colonel, I am well aware of that. There is no question that Himmler has his beady eyes on taking over the Gestapo, and the little four-eyed bastard would stop at nothing to make that happen. As for Rohm, we know that he is a danger to all of us, including the *fuhrer*. After Rohm signed that agreement to quit stockpiling arms, he made several nasty comments about the *fuhrer*. The *fuhrer* was informed of those comments by one of Rohm's inner circle, and yet the *fuhrer* refused to act. Maybe if your people can pick up something similar to those remarks, it just might move him," Goring suggested.

"Herr Minister, we are working on getting some equipment in his office, but we have not had much luck in finding someone over there that we feel would be amenable to such activity. He has tight security, but we will continue to try to get something over there."

"Good. When do you expect your new unit to go into operation, colonel?" Goring asked.

"I expect to get it going within the next week or two," Becker answered. "Colonel Leon Richter of the army is supplying us with the manpower, and he already has a commando unit of fifteen men in place. We are going to add an additional ten men to the unit, which should give us a sizeable force in dealing with our potential targets."

"Colonel, this is just between you and me, but for all practical purposes, this new unit must act with the utmost secrecy," Goring cautioned.

"We have gone over all of that and more, Herr Minister," Becker said. "The men in this unit have been and will be thoroughly scrutinized and indoctrinated before they are accepted into the program. Captain Schwarz is in charge of the program and is at this very moment working on putting it all together. There will be no aspects of the program left to chance."

"Fine colonel, I heartily approve, and if Rohm or some of those other bastards wind up disappearing, I will not lose any sleep over it. And thank you for filling me in on the plan. I wish I could reveal it to the *fuhrer*, but I think at this time we will keep it under wraps," Goring said.

"Thank you, sir, and if you have nothing further, I will return to duty. Heil Hitler."

Becker left the building and returned to his office. Upon returning, he sent for Sara. "Sara, I have something I want to talk to you about. Have a seat."

"What have I done now? This sounds serious," she said with a worried look.

"It is serious, but it is nothing that you have done, so just relax and listen up," he replied.

"Yes sir."

"What I am about to tell you is not to be discussed with anyone. And when I say anyone, I mean just that. It stays in your head, understand?" Becker said.

"Yes, sir, I understand."

"As we were talking last night, I believe I mentioned that I was thinking of doing something to counteract the violent tactics of Donst and others. Well, getting to the point, we are establishing a special unit to combat threats or perceived threats against the state. Those threats against me and the Gestapo come under that same category as threats against the state. This new unit will operate in complete secrecy. Nobody outside of this office will have any knowledge of what the unit will be doing. In fact, only three people *in* this office will have any knowledge of what the unit really does, and those three people are you, me and Captain Schwarz. Outside of the three of us, everyone else will only know that the unit has routine duties, such as protection and occasional assistance in making arrests where there are more than two individuals involved. The real reason for forming this unit is to take out enemies of the state," Becker said. "I know that is a broad term, but the fact of the matter is we are going to be taking out individuals or groups that we deem to be a threat or guilty of unlawful acts. When I use the word taking out, what I mean is that they are going to be executed. You may be a little sensitive to this. In fact, you may be a little shocked, but I felt you should know about it. You will not be asked to take any active part in the operation. I will leave it up to you as to whether you are willing to go any further with this particular program. We can leave you out of it, and you can always maintain that you had no knowledge of what this unit was doing. I don't want to put you in harm's way or put you in a situation where you might sometime in the future be implicated in something that some might call nefarious. I have told you basically all you need to know for now, and I will let you decide if you want to go any further," he concluded.

"Wow, this is scary. It makes me happy that you trust me this much," she said. "I would like to be as involved as you want me to be. I know what you are doing is right, and I would be hurt and disappointed if you had not included me. I have my Luger," Sara said, "and I know how to use it. So just give me the order, Konrad, and I'll take out the Pope if you say so."

"That will not be necessary, my dear. I don't want you to shoot anybody unless you have to in order to protect yourself. I don't contemplate calling on you to do anything other than be a confidant and be aware of what we are doing.

"There are too many innocent people out there that are being hurt for no other reason than their religious beliefs," Becker continued. "You've seen it yourself. Women and children hauled off to never be seen again. Others being sent to concentration camps to live and die like dogs. At this point, it's not men like Donst or even that worthless piece of shit husband of yours that we are talking about. They are merely a nuisance to be dealt with at the proper time in a proper manner. I'm really talking about those officials who are carrying out orders to commit the vicious acts against innocent people, and who do so with such cruelty. What I just said should never be repeated to anyone, not even the captain," Becker ordered.

"I know now why I am so proud of you, colonel," she said.

"My instincts were right all along, from the first time I laid eyes on you. You are truly a good man, and I will follow you to the bitter end, even if that means death."

"All right, Sara, let's not get melodramatic. I have told you this because I do trust you, and I had to tell you, mainly because of our personal relationship. Someday I will tell you more about my life, the real story, but for now you know enough."

"So you do have secrets from me," she teased. "It had better not be another woman or I will put that Luger to good use."

"No, nothing like that so don't get your panties twisted in a knot," Becker said.

Sara reached over and gave Becker a hug and a light kiss and asked him to call her that night. Then she left the office.

Later in the afternoon, Captain Schwarz returned to the office. "Colonel, I just left Colonel Richter's office, and we had a productive meeting. The paperwork is underway, and we are trying to find a convenient location to house the troops. We decided that, for security purposes, they should be located in a separate facility, away from the barracks that they are presently living in. We have located a building only a couple of blocks from here that may suffice," Schwarz said.

"I am going to meet Sergeant Mauch tomorrow, and we will inspect the place to see if it meets our needs," Schwarz continued. "It has been used as a rooming house in the past, and there are still a few people living there. If the place meets our requirements, we will have those people vacate the premises. I drove by it on the way back, and it looks perfect. We can have general services take care of whatever cleaning up or remodeling we may want done. That would include kitchen and dining facilities for the troops. I also plan to have a talk with Sergeant Mauch to go over his duties and instruct him as to what his role will be."

"Captain, looks like you are right on top of this thing," Becker replied. "I also had Sara in here and basically told her what we were doing. Like you, she had no problem and says she is anxious to be a part of the program. Of course, she will play a more limited role, but I wanted her to be fully aware of what we are going to be doing. I made it clear to her that I did not want to put her into harm's way. She indicated that she really didn't mind being put in that position. But we can use her skills in many ways, so she is on board. What about the support equipment, captain?"

"That, too, is in the works, sir," Schwarz said. "There will be two armored personnel carriers initially, along with two regular troop carriers. The men will be issued the latest version of submachine guns, MP38s, a prototype that hasn't been put into service with the regular army yet but has been thoroughly tested and will afford us the best in that regard. Ammunition, including grenades, will also be supplied and readily available for additional supplies as needed. There is no question but that this unit will be the most combat-ready force in the Third Reich."

"Very good," Becker said. "It will only be a matter of time before the SS and SA get this news. They will be left to wonder what the real purpose of the new unit will be, but I am sure that the leaders over there will have some grave concerns. As well they should. Minister Goring has been thoroughly briefed and has expressed his approval," Becker said as the meeting ended.

The next day Captain Schwarz, and Sergeant Mauch, dropped by the office to update Colonel Becker and introduce the sergeant. "Colonel, I would like for you to meet Sergeant Derrick Mauch. Sergeant Mauch, as you know, will be the squad leader for the new unit that we are bringing into service with the Gestapo."

"Hello sergeant. Welcome aboard," Becker said. "I'm sure Captain Schwarz has discussed the role you will play in this venture. I want to reemphasize the importance of secrecy in this operation. We will not tolerate loose talk or any other lapse of responsibility on the part of the personnel assigned to this unit.

To ensure that we have total compliance, you should make clear to everyone involved that there will be swift and harsh punishment for anyone who violates the requirements. Without drawing a picture, when I say harsh, I mean harsh. Do you fully understand that, sergeant?"

"Yes sir, Colonel Becker. The captain has fully explained that to me and I will pass it on to all those assigned to my unit."

"Also, Sergeant Mauch, you and your men will be treated quite well, befitting your status as part of an elite group," Becker said. "In return, we expect total devotion and loyalty. With that, you are dismissed, and you may wait outside while I confer further with Captain Schwarz."

"Yes, sir," Mauch responded. "Heil Hitler."

The colonel returned the salute. After Mauch had left the office, he resumed his conversation with Captain Schwarz. "Captain, what do you think about the sergeant?"

"I am impressed with him, colonel. I looked over his personnel jacket, and he has an excellent record, but more importantly, he is sharp and has pledged his full loyalty to ensuring the success of this new unit. He's a personable young man, and Colonel Richter said he is fearless," Schwarz said.

"Good. Did you look at the building you are considering for housing the unit?" Becker asked.

"Yes, sir, we did. With modifications, it will suit us just fine," Schwarz replied. "I have contacted general services, and they are making all the necessary arrangements to rent the building and modify it as we have requested. Everybody seems to be busting their asses to accommodate us, and of course we can thank you for that, colonel. I should also point out that there is more than enough vacant space outside to accommodate our equipment."

"It sounds like you have everything under control, captain," Becker said. "By the way, have you heard anything lately from our surveillance operatives?"

"Yes, colonel, I have, but I have been tied up on this new unit for the last two days. I will get back to that and work up a report for you," Schwarz answered. "I should have it on your desk first thing in the morning. Also, I think we have something on Donst and Hartman. We still have not had any success bugging Rohm. Without an insider, it is extremely difficult to get access to his office. We may be able to get a bug in his residence with a break in when he is absent, though. I think he lives alone, but he does have caretakers at the place. The problem with that is, we just don't know how much business he conducts at home or whether he does any entertaining there that might involve conversations that would be of interest to us."

The next morning, the captain brought the new transcript into the office. "Colonel, here is a copy of the transcript of a conversation between Donst and Hartman."

Donst: Colonel, I have received a message from Hawes, and he has agreed to work with us on Becker. Hawes is the captain from Hammelburg that attended the military academy with Becker.

Hartman: Oh, yes. How are we going to work this?

Donst: We thought about trying to have a chance meeting between the two of them, but the more I thought about it, the less I thought it feasible. I finally figured that maybe we should have some kind of meeting or reception that we could invite Becker to attend. Maybe it would be better if someone of your rank did the inviting. Becker would be more likely to accept an invitation from you than me. If it came from me, he would likely trash it.

Hartman: That's okay by me. What do you have in mind?

Donst: It needs to be a rather large gathering so it won't look like we set it up. The meeting needs to appear to be a coincidence, in which Hawes just happens to be there. Becker is not stupid. If he suspects some chicanery, he could cause us a problem. The bastard is pretty mean, and he has developed a reputation for being a headhunter. In fact, some have nicknamed him that, the headhunter.

Hartman: Yes, I see what you mean. Go ahead and set it up. As far as I know, he doesn't know me, so maybe it will work."

Donst: Right. I was thinking that maybe the *Reichswher* Officers' Club would be good, if we can swing it.

Hartman: Wait a minute. That is an excellent idea. Only members and their guests are permitted to enjoy the services of the club. The problem is, though, that I am not a member. Only high-ranking officers of the army are eligible for membership. But Becker is eligible, and I would be willing to bet that he is a member. If so, my guess is that he probably lunches at the club on a regular basis, and that may be our best bet—to have Hawes accidentally bump into him there. It shouldn't raise any red flags if Hawes is a guest of one of the members. We must find a member willing to have us as their guests. In fact, we will need two members, one to host Hawes as a guest and the other one to host us.

Donst: Of course we would also need someone to invite us to avoid suspicion. Brilliant, colonel, I must say. There might be someone at the Ministry of Defense that would be willing to extend us that courtesy.

Hartman: Isn't that where Becker worked before he was knighted?

Donst: Yes. I didn't think about that.

Hartman: No problem. There are plenty of generals around town who would love to do us a favor. And check with the club manager and inquire as to the frequency of Becker's visits. Discreetly of course.

Donst: Yes, sir. I'll do better than that. I have a contact who works over there, and I'll ring him up right now. [A couple of minutes of silence.] Yes, I would like to speak to Bruno Drachenberg. Bruno, this is Major Donst with the SS. I am doing just fine. Listen up. I was wondering if, by chance, you are familiar with Colonel Konrad Becker of the Gestapo. Oh, you do. And you say he and his lady companion are frequent visitors for lunch and sometimes for dinner in the evening? No, Bruno, that is all I need to know. I expect you to keep this conversation to yourself, do you understand? That is all and thank you." He turned to Hartman. "Sir, you heard my conversation. He said everybody is familiar with the colonel. Becker and that bitch of his are regulars. We are in luck. I will bring Hawes in at once.

Hartman: Good work, major. Meanwhile, I will hasten to locate a couple of members who are willing to host us for lunch. We may have to make arrangements for several days in a row in order to make sure that our Colonel Becker makes an appearance.

"Captain, I find that quite interesting," Becker commented after he read the transcript. "It just might be fun to go along with those scheming bastards. They have gone to a lot of trouble, so maybe I shouldn't disappoint them. Donst was informed by Drachenberg that I do have lunch at the club regularly. Make a note of that name. Perhaps we should make plans to have lunch at the *Reichswehr* Club for the next few days. What do you think?" Becker asked.

"I would like to see the looks on their faces when their grand scheme is played out. Besides, they have damn good food" Schwarz said.

"And captain, let's not forget to bring my bitch along," Becker joked. "We don't want to disappoint our friends at the SS."

"Yes colonel, by all means. Meantime, I have to get with Sergeant Mauch to work on the transition of the new unit," Schwarz said as saluted and left the office.

Sara came into Becker's office. "Sara, here is our latest

transcript between Donst and Hartman," Becker said. "Take a look at it."

"Good morning, my dear sir," she said, beaming. "I would be delighted to look at it."

"Aren't you in a good mood this morning?" he noted. "You didn't get laid last night, did you?"

"Oh, now stop it, colonel. That is not funny," Sara said as she started to read the transcript while Becker chuckled. "Besides, if I ever do get laid again, you will see a smile on my face as big as the Brandenberg Gate.

"Why, that asshole!" she almost shouted after a moment of reading. "Did you see what he said about me?"

"Yes, I did, and so as not to disappoint them, I decided that I would make sure the bitch is with me when I go to lunch at the *Reichswehr* Club, starting tomorrow. Is that all right with the bitch?" Becker said, laughing.

"Yes, it's okay with the bitch," she said. "I guess nobody loves me, since they call me such vile names. But that's okay. I'll get even one of these days, just wait and see, Colonel Becker."

"Oh, poor Sara," he teased. "You know we all love you. It's just a price you pay for being put on a pedestal."

"A pedestal, you say? Are you kidding me? I think being put on a shit list, oops, pardon my language, would be more appropriate."

"Sara is that a nice thing to say? Maybe I should start taking Berta with me on some of these outings," Becker suggested. "No doubt she would draw less attention."

"Konrad, let's face it. You love having me around to show off. And when you get right down to it, I love it, too," she said.

"All right, you win. Now get back to work," he said as he started reading some of the paperwork on his desk.

The next day Becker, Schwarz and the effervescent Sara

showed up at the *Reichswehr* Club for lunch. "Where are our distinguished friends from the SS?" asked Schwarz.

"Maybe they couldn't find anyone that would be willing to be seen with them in public," replied Becker. "I would guess, however, that they have not had enough time to bring in their mystery man. We must be patient with them. After all, they have gone to a lot of trouble to surprise me with a gift from the past."

"Colonel," Sara said, "when they do show up, please don't introduce me as the bitch."

"Oh, no, Sara, I wouldn't do that. I'll let the captain do it." They all laughed and got up from the table and left the club.

The next day Sara popped her head in the door. "Colonel, are we going to lunch today?" she asked.

"Is it lunch time already?" Becker answered. "Alert the captain and have Heinz bring the car around, and we will be on our way. By the way, you look fetching today. Are you auditioning for a film role?"

"Maybe, do you think I will get the part?" she answered before going to get Schwarz and Heinz.

"Good afternoon, Colonel Becker," said the hostess. "It is a pleasure to have you and your guests with us again today. If you will follow me, I will show you to your table. Will this one do, sir?"

"Yes, this will do. Bring us a glass of wine while we decide what to order," Becker said.

"We just received a shipment of a new French wine called Pinot Noch. Will that be okay, sir?"

"Yes, I think so. We will give it a try," replied Becker as they took their seats.

"Uh oh, don't look now colonel, but I see some old friends headed this way," Captain Schwarz whispered.

"What an unpleasant surprise," Becker answered. "Has this club no standards?"

"Colonel Becker, what a surprise to see you," remarked Major Donst.

"It shouldn't be, major," Becker replied. "I am a member of this club and visit here quite frequently. You remember Sara Klein and Captain Schwarz?"

"Yes, of course. Good afternoon to both of you. Colonel Becker. Have you met Colonel Hartman? He is a deputy to *Reichsfuhrer* Himmler."

"Colonel," Becker said, "it's nice to meet you. Hartman, hmm, that name sounds familiar. Were you in the army, Colonel?"

"Uh, no, I have been with the SA and the SS for ten years," Hartman replied. "It is a great pleasure to meet you, sir, and I am also pleased to meet your staff. Captain Schwarz and Frau, or is it Fraulein?"

"It is frau, but you may address me as Sara, Colonel Hartman."

"Thank you, Sara. I have heard a great deal about you and your work, Colonel Becker," Hartman said. "And that of your excellent staff as well."

"Thank you very much, Colonel Hartman. You are too kind. Since you are not and have not been in the *Reichswehr*, may I inquire as to whom you are a guest of today?" Becker asked. "The gentleman standing behind you there, I presume," he added.

"Oh, excuse me, Colonel Becker," Hartman responded. "May I introduce our host for today, Colonel Curt Blum?"

"At your service, sir," Blum said as he kicked his heels together and saluted.

"How do you do, Colonel Blum?" Becker answered. "I would ask you gentleman to join us, but as you can see our table is not large enough to accommodate all of us."

"That is quite all right, Colonel Becker. We are going to be seated at the table next to yours. It was generous of you anyway," Donst managed to get out.

Hartman seemed to be getting more nervous as the three

of them seated themselves at a nearby table. The table was close enough, Becker thought, that they could listen in on conversations in a normal speaking voice. That meant that any conversation among Becker's party would have to be conducted quietly. This posed no problem, as all they had to do was to keep it down.

A few minutes later, two men were escorted in and seated at the table on the other side of Becker's. One of them was a colonel, and the other a captain.

"Colonel, it looks like this place is getting crowded today, and everyone wants to sit close to us," Schwarz said.

"So I have noticed, captain. Signal for the waiter to come over and take our order. I am sure Sara is getting hungry after all of this attention."

"Now that you mention it, I am ready to eat something," she said. "I didn't have any breakfast."

After Becker and his guests had ordered, one of the men at the other table approached them. "I am sorry to bother you, colonel but you look familiar. You look like my roommate at the military academy during the war. My name is Captain Dieter Hawes."

"Captain Hawes, I am Captain Kurt Schwarz. You are addressing Colonel Konrad Becker of the Gestapo. A lot of people think they know the colonel, and we are about to have lunch," Schwarz reprimanded.

"That's okay, captain. Let's hear what the gentleman has to say," Becker intervened.

"Thank you, sir. Then you are my ex-roommate," Hawes said. "I will never forget the name. You were quite well known back then, Colonel Becker."

"What did you say your name was again, captain?" asked Becker.

"Dieter Hawes, sir," he answered.

Out of the corner of his eyes, Becker observed the motley crew that was seated at the next table watching his reaction. They seemed to be getting quite excited at what they were hearing. "Captain, I don't seem to recall the name Hawes. You wouldn't be Pootie, would you? I seem to recall that I had a roommate that we called Pootie."

"Actually, you were the only one that called me Pootie, sir," replied Hawes.

"Well, hello, Pootie. What brings you to Berlin?" Becker asked.

"How did you know that I was not from Berlin, sir?" Hawes asked.

"Pootie, I am with the Gestapo, you know, and also I note that you have the Second Infantry Division insignia on your sleeve. Since that division is stationed in Hammelburg, I assume that you are stationed there. Am I not correct?" Becker asked.

"Yes sir. You are quite observant, sir," Hawes nervously replied.

"Tell me, Pootie, what are you doing in Berlin?" Becker asked.

"Well, sir, I am ... uh, well, I ... uh, am visiting some friends," Hawes stammered.

"And who are these friends, Pootie?" asked Becker.

"Well, uh, sir, you wouldn't know them," he said weakly.

"Pootie—do you mind if I call you Pootie?" asked Becker.

"No, sir, it's okay if you prefer to call me that. I am just not used to being called that name."

"I see," Becker replied. "May I ask who the officer is that you are sitting with who is acting as your host?"

"Oh ... uh, his name is, uh ... I'm sorry, colonel, I am a little nervous today. I just never expected to meet somebody I used to know, and particularly someone who is in such a high position," Hawes said as the sweat rolled down his face.

"That's all right, Pootie. Just relax, and maybe you can think of the gentleman's name."

"Yes sir. It's, uh, Colonel Tabor. Yes, that's it, Colonel Tabor," he finally answered.

"That wasn't so bad, Pootie, now was it?"

"No, sir," Hawes answered.

"Pootie, how long have you known Colonel Tabor?" Becker asked.

By then, Donst and Hartman were beside themselves. Becker knew that they had to be thinking, what the hell is this fellow doing asking all of these questions? Sheer panic seemed to be setting in, and it was quite obvious to Captain Schwarz and Becker. Schwarz was thinking that he had never had so much pleasure watching a screw up as he was watching the reaction of those two bozos sitting at the next table.

After what seemed like a long time, Becker said, "Pootie, or Captain Hawes, I should say, I see that our food is being brought out, so I think we should continue this reunion at a later time. After we are through here, I would like for you to speak with Captain Schwarz to schedule another meeting tomorrow morning at Gestapo headquarters."

"Yes, sir, colonel," Hawes nervously replied. He saluted and returned to his table. The poor chap, red-faced from embarrassment, was obviously in great pain and more than likely had lost his appetite. As for the two military geniuses with their host at the next table, it looked as if they were in need of emergency medical attention. For Captain Schwarz and Sara Klein, it was truly a day to remember. Before they finished eating their lunch, both Donst and Hartman scurried out, with their host in hot pursuit. Shortly thereafter, a bedraggled Captain Hawes and his host, Colonel Tabor, meekly departed the club without looking back.

"Colonel, for a while there I thought I would wet my pants. It looks like your adversaries have greatly underestimated you," Sara said as she finished her salad.

"I didn't wet my pants," Schwarz chimed in, "but I was quite impressed with the way you totally buried all three of those bastards. It was unbelievable. No wonder Goring put you in the position you are in."

"Captain, I didn't say I wet my pants," Sara said indignantly. "I said I thought I would. It is just a saying."

"Okay, Sara, I didn't say you did," Schwarz answered. "Relax."

"Both of you relax and finish up, and let's get back to the office," Becker ordered. "I can't wait to hear what they have to say when they get back to the office. And captain, your men are standing by, are they not?"

"Yes, sir, colonel, they are on the job and have been alerted for a possible conversation to take place this afternoon."

Becker signed the tab, and they returned to the office with a feeling of satisfaction and accomplishment. Well deserved, no less.

The next morning, the first thing Becker asked for was the transcript. "I have it right here, colonel. Shall I call Sara in so she can sit in?" Schwarz asked.

"Yes get her in here, and let's see what we have," Becker replied.

As soon as Sara came in, they started to go over the transcript.

Hartman: God damn it, Donst, what the hell are you trying to do to me? This whole damn thing was a disaster. Couldn't you have better prepared that god damn Hawes? That man couldn't even remember the name of his host. I am totally embarrassed. How the hell can I face Colonel Tabor and Colonel Blum? If the *Reichsfuhrer* hears of this, and I am sure he will, he will have my head. I am at my wit's end.

Donst: Sir, things didn't exactly go the way I had planned.

Hartman: Planned, my ass. You dumb son of a bitch, don't you see it was a total disaster? That hayseed Hawes you brought down here should be working behind a plow rather than being an officer in the *Reichswehr*. I'll be lucky if I don't wind up at Dachau after this episode. By the way, where is Hawes? Is he going to come by this office?

Donst: Yes, sir, I instructed him to report back here as soon as he left the club.

Hartman: He damn sure better, and this time I hope you can better prepare him for tomorrow. That Becker is ruthless, I'm telling you. It may be better if you send him back home and forget about that meeting tomorrow.

Unidentified person: Major, sorry to interrupt you, but a Captain Hawes is waiting to see you.

Donst: Send him in here.

Hawes: Sirs, I am back, at least what is left of me. There is nothing left of my ass. That Becker hasn't changed a bit. I'm telling you, that man is ruthless.

Donst: Yeah, we were just talking about what happened. I hope you can compose yourself and perform better when you go to the Gestapo headquarters tomorrow.

Hartman: Look here, Hawes. I will not mince words with you like the major has. Your performance at the club was a total disaster. There is just no other way to put it. If you can't do any better tomorrow, then I suggest you hightail it out of here and get back to Hammelburg. That man has absolutely no compassion, and there has been talk that he would as soon put a bullet through your head as he would swat a fly.

Hawes: Obviously, sir, he has no sentiment for the past. He made me feel like I had just committed a serious crime, and he was ready to do me in. My God, what have you people done to me?

Donst: To be honest Hawes, you really did not perform well. You are going to have to do better tomorrow, or we may be shipping your ass back to Hammelburg in a pine box.

Hawes: With all due respect sir, what do you mean I didn't perform very well? I didn't come to Berlin to be roasted like a boar.

Hartman: Now look, Hawes, don't get smart with us. The major is right. You are an officer in the *Reichswehr*. How about acting like one? In case you don't realize it, you have put Major Donst and me in a precarious position. This whole thing looked like an ambush from the start. Did you talk to anyone about this?

Hawes: No, sir, I didn't discuss this with anybody. Not even my wife knew what I was coming here for. Thank God for that.

Hartman: Something looks awfully fishy here to me. Donst, you didn't discuss this with anyone, did you?

Donst: Of course not, sir. But I told you before that Becker was no fool. I see now why Goring put him where he is. He is a real danger to all of us.

Hartman: I expect you to take care of this mess. That is, if you know what's good for you. If you don't, all of us may well wind up in the Rhine. I have to leave now, so I am holding both of you responsible. Is that clear?

Donst: Yes, sir. Heil Hitler.

Hawes: Major, you didn't tell me the whole story. I didn't know that man was running the Gestapo. I am well aware of how they operate. Look at the mess you got me into.

Donst: Shut up and listen to me, Hawes. If you think back, I told you that he was with the Gestapo. You had better prepare yourself for tomorrow, or your ass is going to be hung out to dry. I'm tired of making excuses for people like you. After your meeting tomorrow with Becker, you are to report back here to me. Is that clear?

Hawes: Yes sir.

"There it is," Becker said. "It would appear that our friends at the SS are in disarray over their management skills. Based on my reading of this transcript, I would say that Hartman may be disenchanted with the performance of his underlings in this clown show. Does anybody disagree with that assessment?"

The verdict was unanimous agreement with the colonel's assessment.

"Captain, what time is Hawes coming in?" Becker asked.

"He is sitting in the outer office now, sir. Berta says he was waiting outside when she got here this morning. I guess he is anxious to pick up where he left off yesterday in looking back at the good old days," Schwarz said.

"Bring him in, captain, and let's get this over with," Becker said. "I have a busy day ahead of me."

"Yes sir." The Captain went to the door and motioned for Hawes to come in.

"Heil Hitler," Hawes said as he saluted.

"Heil Hitler. Good morning, Hawes," Becker said. "Have a seat. I trust you are enjoying the nightlife of Berlin?"

"No, sir, I retired early last evening, so I didn't experience the night life," Hawes replied. It was obvious that the poor man was suffering from sleep deprivation. He looked very tired.

"Captain Hawes, as you may have guessed by now, things are different in Berlin than they are in Hammelburg. This city is full of intrigue. There is frenzy among government officials to rush to the top, with little concern of how they get there. Here at the Gestapo, we are very inquisitive about everything. That is why we exist. Our meeting yesterday somehow seemed more than a mere coincidence," Becker went on. "A young captain accompanied by a retired senior army officer raises questions. While renewing old acquaintances are relevant and sometimes enjoyable, they are less relevant in the real scheme of things, as it relates to the Gestapo. But I am not going to dwell on that. Let me ask you a few more questions, and then we will reminisce about the past.

"Hawes, that colonel that you were the guest of yesterday, how long have you known that gentleman?" Becker asked. "Now, Hawes, I want straight answers. Making a false statement to the Gestapo is a criminal offense. I want to be clear on that."

"Yes sir. I met him yesterday," Hawes answered.

"Who introduced you to him?" Becker asked.

"Colonel, I don't want to get into trouble," Hawes answered. "I am between a rock and a hard place."

"Cut the shit, Hawes, and answer my questions, or you will be between a wall and a firing squad," Becker demanded.

"Yes sir. Major Wilhelm Donst, sir," Hawes nervously responded.

"Major Donst, was he one of the gentlemen seated at the table next to mine?"

"I believe so, yes, sir," Hawes answered.

"How long have you known Major Donst?" Becker asked.

"Not very long sir, just a few weeks."

"Did you know the other two gentlemen seated at the table with Major Donst?"

"I knew one of them. Colonel Hartman was his name sir," Hawes answered.

"And how long have you known Hartman?" Becker asked.

"I just met him, sir."

"Hawes. Why don't you tell me how you became involved with Hartman and Donst and what the hell you are doing here in Berlin?" Becker asked.

"Yes, sir, Colonel Becker," Hawes said. "To start with, I was contacted by some SS people several weeks ago. They asked me about the military academy and wanted to know if I knew you. After I told them I remembered you, they asked me—or, I should say, told me—to come to Berlin and meet with Major Donst. I did come to Berlin and met with Major Donst and another man. At that time, they asked me if I would be willing to come back again and accidentally run into you somewhere. I guess they mainly wanted to know if you would remember me. I didn't want to do it, but I felt I would have some trouble if I didn't, so I agreed, and here I am. I'm really sorry about this whole thing, sir."

"Well, Hawes, what did your SS officers think about your performance yesterday?" Becker asked.

"They were quite disappointed, Colonel Becker, sir. Colonel Hartman was displeased with both Major Donst and me. Major Donst was furious and placed all of the blame on me. He also threatened me about this meeting today and ordered me to report back to him after I am finished."

"Hawes, by being honest with me you have made a wise decision. After we are through today, I suggest you catch the first train out of here and get back to Hammelburg and leave playing conspiracy games to professionals. It is clear that Donst and Hartman were using you for their own personal gain. That and the fact that we were once roommates is why I am willing to overlook the part you played in this farce. I am not a sentimental man, but I to try to be fair-minded. Returning to report to Donst will only get you into deeper trouble.

"If you are contacted by him after you leave," Becker continued, "then I suggest that you tell him what you told me and that I told you to leave town without reporting back to him. You may tell him that failure to comply with my order would result in your arrest for plotting against the Gestapo. Before you leave the building, I want you to give a statement to an inspector outlining what you have just told me. Captain Schwarz will review it, and then you will be free to go."

"Thank you so much, Colonel Becker. You are being very generous, and I will never forget this act of kindness."

"Before you go, Hawes, there is one more thing I would like to ask you about. What happened to Pauletta?" Becker asked.

"I really don't know, sir. She went off to have her baby, and then I was shipped out to the frontlines, and I never heard from her again. I think that Major Donst is trying to locate her. I gave them the name of her father. I have no idea what they plan to do with her or even what they might want her for. She was just a seventeen-year-old girl and would have little or no knowledge about what we did at the academy. Those vicious rumors about you knocking her up were just not credible, and I am sorry I believed them," Hawes said.

"She was a nice young lady," Becker said, "and I hope she is doing well. I guess her child would be around sixteen now. As for what Donst wants with her, it has to be that they are desperate to find out something negative about me. Let them waste their time. They will find nothing there. Hawes, I know that you and I were never really friends, but we did cross paths at one time earlier in our lives, and I harbor no ill feelings toward you.

"Sara, will you take Captain Hawes to one of the inspectors so that he can give them his statement?" Becker ordered. "And Pootie, I wish you well with this parting advice. Concentrate on raising your family and leave the meddling in the lives of others to people who are professionals at it. Good luck."

As Sara led Captain Hawes out, Becker felt that it would be the last time he would see or hear from Dieter Hawes.

"Colonel, I fully expected to see you rip that fellow a new ass," Schwarz said, "but you got the information out of him that you wanted and let him off the hook."

"I guess I'm getting soft in my old age," Becker said. "But the poor man came clean, and there is no doubt that they intimidated and used him. There was no reason for me to treat him any other way. He has a family in Hammelburg, and that is where he should be."

Sara came back into the office. "Colonel, you never cease to amaze me" she said. "I thought for sure when that man came in here and left that he would never see another sunrise. You really do have a heart."

"Now, let's not overdo it here," Becker remarked. "He's a decent man and made a mistake, and he deserved another chance. That's all. He will think twice before he ever let's someone use him again, you can bet on it. Captain, go down and make sure the statement satisfies our requirements. Donst and Hartman already have a record on file with us, so this will add to it. I am sure the next meeting between Hartman and Donst will be interesting, so when you get another transcript, bring it in."

"I am sorry to interrupt you, colonel, but the minister's office just called, and Goring would like to see you," Berta announced.

"I better take care of this, Sara. I'll catch up with you later," Becker said before he put his hat on and left the office.

Chapter Seventeen

Upon arriving at the ministry, Becker was immediately ushered into Goring's office.

"Hello, colonel. Have a seat," Goring offered. "I have been thinking about that new unit of yours, and I have an assignment for you. As you know, when I was named minister, most of the police forces in Germany came under my command. Some of the police chiefs have loyalties elsewhere. Some are SA and some are SS, and there are a few that are causing me problems. They have had ample opportunity to come around and have failed to do so. It is essential that, in order to exercise complete control over police operations throughout the country, we must have total loyalty. What I am saying is that the ones who have not come around are trying to undermine me. They need to be taken out. That is where your new unit comes in. This must be done with precision, and it must be covert. Do you think your new unit can do it?"

"No problem, Herr Minister," Becker said. "We are not on

line yet, but we should be at least partially operational in the next week or so. Certainly we have enough to do what you are talking about. In fact, we have in-house people who can do that very thing."

"Good, colonel. I knew I could count on you. I will give you a list of names, and you can take them in whatever order that is convenient."

"I understand, Herr Minister. Incidentally, we just caught Donst and Hartman in a scam aimed at the Gestapo, and we have a statement implicating both of them on file."

"It may be time to close the books on those two," Goring said. "They have become more than a nuisance and should be dealt with."

"Yes, Herr Minister, they will be dealt with when the time is appropriate. After this last failure, they may decide it's time to pull in their horns, at least for the time being, but we know that it won't affect their ultimate goal of taking over the Gestapo."

"By the way, how is that sweetie of yours, Sara Klein?" Goring asked.

"That sweetie is doing fine, sir, but I still haven't consummated the relationship with her."

"Ha, I find that hard to believe, colonel. Don't wait too long. There are limits on how long a lady is willing to wait, you know, and that is especially true of a beautiful woman like that one."

"I understand," Becker replied. "Her divorce is pending, so I prefer to wait it out to avoid any unpleasantness. I know she is not going anywhere. A little wait is not going to hurt either one of us, although I must admit sometimes it can be quite frustrating."

"Colonel, give her my best, and I will contact you if I think of something else."

With that, the meeting ended and Becker returned to Gestapo headquarters. Becker had Goring's hit list, and it dawned on him again how ruthless the fat man was. Too bad Goring himself was not on the list, Becker thought. He would have the lecherous bastard right up there at the top if he didn't need him.

Things were fairly quiet around the office for a while after the luncheon incident, until Captain Schwarz brought in another transcript of Donst and Hartman. Sara was called in and, along with Becker, they read the transcript.

Hartman: Major, did you straighten out that mess that you and that *dumbkoph* Hawes created at the *Reichswehr* Club?

Donst: Not exactly, sir. I think we may have a problem.

Hartman: What do you mean, we have a problem? I hope you don't try to drag me into this mess.

Donst: Oh, no, sir, I wouldn't do anything like that, but that son of a bitch Hawes may have. He disobeyed my orders to report back to me after his interrogation by the Gestapo and hauled ass out of town. I contacted him by phone, and he told me that they broke him down. He confessed to his part in the plan. He implicated both you and me. I meant to call you sooner and tell you about it, but quite frankly, I was too upset to explain it. I have had the runs now for two days over this thing, and I just don't know what to do.

Hartman: Now look here, you asshole. This was all your idea. Pull yourself together and tell me just what happened with the Gestapo.

Donst: According to Hawes, he was forced to tell the whole story as to how he got involved. Becker also told him that he was to return to duty and expressly forbade him to report back to me under the threat of being arrested and charged with plotting against the Gestapo. Sir, what is going to happen to us?

Hartman: Us? Us? What the hell do you mean by us? What a fool you are. Do you realize what you have done, man? You have put my career in jeopardy. Under the circumstances, I may have to press court martial charges against you, Donst. We at the SS do not tolerate failure.

Donst: But, sir, you signed off on this operation.

Hartman: Enough of this nonsense. I suggest you think this over and come up with a solution. You might want to consider leaving a note exonerating me in this dastardly scheme and taking your life. It would be the honorable thing to do, and of course I would see that your family is cared for.

Donst: Oh, shit. Surely you are not serious, sir?

Hartman: You're damn right, I'm serious. I'm late for another meeting, so think about what I just said. Heil Hitler.

"Sir, can you believe this?" said Schwarz. "They are falling apart over there."

"It does appear that way, captain. Evidently things have not gone according to plan. Maybe those clowns are rehearsing for a role in one of Leni Riefenstahl's propaganda films. Sara, maybe you should contact Leni and give her these scripts for consideration," Becker said as they all burst out laughing.

"Colonel, let's hope that Donst can get over the runs before there is a casting call," chimed in Sara.

The door opened, and Berta stuck her head in. "What's going on in here?" she asked. "They can hear you laughing all the way down the hall."

"It's okay, Berta. Sara was just telling us one of her dirty jokes, and finally this one was funny," Becker said while trying to contain his laughter and as he turned to Sara and Schwarz "Hey, I have an idea" Becker said. "Why don't we go to the *Reichswehr* Club for lunch? Who knows who we might run into over there." They were all still laughing.

"That's the best idea I have heard today," Sara said. "This calls for a celebration. Maybe this time we can just relax and enjoy our lunch."

Later in the day, Captain Schwarz received a call from Lenore. "Captain Schwarz?"

"This is Captain Schwarz."

"Hello Kurt. This is Lenore. How are you?"

"Hello, Lenore. What a pleasant surprise. I'm doing fine. I have been meaning to call you, but I have been very busy."

"I have been patiently waiting, Kurt," she said. "I was afraid you had forgotten me."

"You know better than that, Lenore. Maybe we can get together one night this week."

"You promise, Kurt?"

"Yes, I promise," he said.

"I'll be waiting," she said. "But listen, the reason I called is that Willy is acting real strange."

"Who is Willy?" Kurt asked.

"Oh, I'm sorry, I mean Wilhelm. You know, Major Donst."

"Oh yeah, that asshole, what the hell's wrong with him?"

"Kurt, he has been acting crazy for the last couple of days. He keeps talking about killing himself, and when he is over here, he spends most of his time on the toilet. I'm beginning to get scared of him. What should I do?"

"Lenore, you should get away from there for a few days. If you don't have a place to go, I can put you up at my place," Schwarz said.

"Oh, Kurt, would you? I would feel so much safer if I was with someone like you. Willy keeps that pistol with him all the time. He won't tell me what's wrong. He just keeps mumbling about everything going sour and that everybody has turned against him."

"Okay, Lenore, here is what I'll do. I will pick you up at work, and we'll go by your place. You can pick up some things, and I'll take you home with me. Or if you like, I will pick you up at your place. In fact, that may be better for me, as I am not sure what time I will be through here today, okay?" Schwarz said.

"Kurt, that would be wonderful," she said. "I usually get home about six, and I can be ready by seven. Is that okay?"

"Seven works for me. I'll see you then. In the meantime, if he shows up, just don't answer the door and pretend that you are gone. Goodbye."

"Colonel, are you busy?" Schwarz said as he stuck his head into the office, "And. guess who I just got a call from?" Schwarz said.

"I don't know, captain, who? The *fuhrer*?" Becker asked.

"No, it was Lenore. You know, the woman that was with Donst."

"Oh, yeah, what did she want?" Becker asked.

"She was quite upset," Schwarz answered. "She said her friend Donst has been acting crazy and talking about killing himself. I think she is afraid that he might want to take someone with him, and she isn't that committed. I told her she could stay with me a few days until things cool down. She was really upset."

"That is a hell of a note," Becker said. "I knew that son of a bitch was crazy, but I didn't think he was *that* loony. Why don't you bring Lenore to the club at the hotel this evening captain. That might comfort her some, and maybe she can shed more light on what that nutty bastard is thinking. I'll tell Sara to meet us there. Maybe that will help calm the poor woman down."

"Thanks, colonel. We will be there around eight."

One thing about this job, and that is, there is never a dull moment, Becker thought.

Later that evening at the club, Captain Schwarz made introductions. "Colonel, I don't think you have met Lenore," he said. "Lenore, this is Colonel Konrad Becker. I think you have already met Sara Klein. Colonel Becker, this is Lenore Gutzman."

"My pleasure, Lenore," the colonel said as he reached out to shake her hand. *Damn,* he thought, *how about that name? She almost could have been a cousin, the way names are spelled and misspelled.* "Lenore, has your family always spelled your name Guttman? That name sounds Jewish."

"It is not Guttman, sir. It is Gutzman, and that is the way we have always spelled our name. Certainly we are not Jewish" she added.

"Oh, I see. Well, I meant no disrespect. It is a pleasure to meet you," Becker replied.

"Thank you, sir. I have heard so much about you that I feel like I know you," Lenore said. "And hello, Sara, it is nice to see you again. We talked in the ladies room, but we were never formally introduced."

This was the first time the colonel had seen Lenore up close, and he was impressed with her good looks. She was not as pretty as Sara, nor did she have as good a figure, but nevertheless, she was quite a good-looking woman. He wondered how she could have been attracted to the likes of Wilhelm Donst.

"It is nice to see you again, Lenore. I love that dress you are wearing. May I ask where you bought it?" Sara inquired.

"Thank you, Sara, it's a Francois, and I got it at a boutique on Leopoldstrasse."

"Lenore, the captain tells me that your friend Major Donst is experiencing some health problems. Perhaps you can tell us in more detail what seems to be troubling the poor chap," Becker inquired.

"Colonel, I am terribly upset at the way he has been acting for the last several days," Lenore answered.

"Yes, the captain told me about his frequent visits to the toilet and that he had intimated that he might take his own life," Becker replied. "Do you think maybe that he has contracted some kind of a bug or virus that is causing him discomfort?"

"Yes, sir, that is possible. I'm sorry, but this is such a delicate subject, I am afraid I am becoming embarrassed," she said tearfully.

"Oh, Lenore, I understand, dear. Now colonel, can't we change the subject to something more interesting?" Sara pleaded.

"By all means Sara, I didn't realize how sensitive this subject would be for you ladies. My apologies Lenore, I didn't mean to dwell on such an unpleasant topic," Becker said. "Perhaps my curiosity was a tad too much. Let's leave the toilet question, and maybe you can tell us about some of the mental symptoms that Donst has exhibited."

"Thank you so much, colonel. I really appreciate your concern, particularly in light of Willy's wish that you were dead."

"My dear lady, Willy, as you call him is not the only person wishing me dead. There are quite a few people out there that fit that description, and rightly so, because of their fears of being brought to justice for their crimes against the state. The major's wish for my demise is of no concern to me. From what I have heard, he should devote more of his time and energy to his own survival," Becker said.

"But enough talk about Donst," Becker quipped. "I suggest that we waste no more time discussing that pathetic person, unless you can tell us something that might be of some significance. I feel, however, that you should be warned that fraternization with the likes of Donst could be detrimental to your own well-being."

"Colonel, I very much wish that I could break off my relations with him, but I fear he may retaliate against me," Lenore answered. "He is responsible for my job, you know, and I am sure he could have me fired with the snap of his fingers."

"Captain, I think maybe you should pay a visit to Lenore's place of employment and make it clear to those in authority that the Gestapo would find it unacceptable if Ms. Gutzman were to lose her job without proper cause," Becker said. "Get the name of the person who has the authority to discharge her, and notify that person he would be brought in to justify his decision."

"Yes, sir," Schwarz replied. "I'll take care of that tomorrow."

"Oh, colonel, how can I ever thank you enough?" Lenore asked.

"Just say thank you, and that will be quite enough," Sara said. She gave Lenore a look that left no doubt that she meant business. There would be no quid-pro-quo arrangement, as had been the case with Lenore's recent benefactor.

After some nervous laughter, Lenore thanked the colonel in a more formal manner, and from there, they all enjoyed the rest of the evening discussing more social topics. Becker decided that he would let Captain Schwarz deal with Lenore, as he was in a better position to get information on Major Donst from her.

The next morning Captain Schwarz reported to the colonel. "Captain, how did it go after we parted last night?" Becker asked.

"Fine, sir, I had a great time. I think Lenore is going to be okay. She wants to work with us and says she will do anything that we want her to. Sara may have taken it the wrong way last night when Lenore asked how she could ever thank you enough."

"Don't worry about Sara," said Becker. "She is possessive. You should know her enough by now not to pay her any attention. That is enough about Sara. There are some other things I need to go over with you. How are things coming along on the new unit?"

"Everything is coming along fine, sir," Schwarz said. "The first fifteen troops are already in place. I have had a couple of meetings with them, and I have had several more with Mauch. They have their equipment, so right now we are waiting on general services to complete the renovations on the building. They have put a rush on the project and are working two shifts to get it done. We should be able to occupy the building in the next two or three days. The fence around the compound has been completed, and the vehicles are on site."

"As soon as they get moved in, I will make an inspection and speak to the group as a whole," said Becker. "Captain, I have something else for you to do. We need ten inspectors to do some undercover work. We are looking for the same requirement that we have in place for our other people. Check with Diels and see who we presently have in house, and then go outside the agency and find the rest. But I want the best men that you can find."

"Yes, sir, what they will be doing?" Schwarz asked.

"As we discussed before, the problem of random violence must be addressed. There is fear that the violence is getting out of hand and could be detrimental to law and order," the colonel said. Of course, Becker knew that he was really looking for a way to strike back at the thugs that were praying on innocent people, notably Jews. This new initiative would be the shield he needed to carry out his plan. He would eliminate as many Nazi thugs as possible without arousing undue suspicion.

"Captain, you ask what the undercover agents will be doing," Becker said. "The answer is that they will compile a list of the names of the leaders of those roving thugs. That list of names will be used in taking corrective action. In other words, the men on the list will be eliminated. Do you follow me, captain?"

"Yes sir, I do. But how are we going to get much done with only ten inspectors covering the whole country?" Schwarz asked.

"The ten inspectors are only a start and limited to Berlin. We just can't rush into this program without first making sure we have the right people."

"I understand, sir," Schwarz answered. "I suppose the corrective action will come from the new unit?"

"For the most part that is true, captain," replied Becker. "Each case will be handled on an individual basis. In some cases, the problem can be handled with one or two men, and in such cases, our agents can do the job. In others it may require the unit. I have just laid out the plan in general. We will have to fine tune the program as we go forward. Do you have any more questions?"

"No, sir, I think I understand the plan. I like it, and I'm eager to get started."

"Then go out and get us those ten agents so we can get started."

"I'm on my way," Schwarz said as he left the office.

The next day Becker called Captain Schwarz and Sara Klein to a staff meeting. "Captain, is there any progress on our new agents?" Becker asked.

"Yes sir, we have five men that I have talked to that I feel qualified to do the job. They meet the strict requirements that you have laid out. I still have about forty more to interview after I review their records. If Sara can help me, we should be able to finish in a couple more days. We just need five more for now. Diels has done a good job of bringing in good people. They all have a lot of police experience, so you don't have to draw them a picture of what is expected from them."

"Good. Sara, drop what you are doing and help Kurt with this," Becker ordered. "I am assuming he has talked to you about what we are doing. Am I right?"

"Yes, he explained it to me yesterday," she replied.

"All right, is there anything else we need to discuss?" asked Becker.

"I talked to Lenore, and she is doing much better," said the captain. "I had that little chat with her supervisor, and he was very cooperative. He doesn't want any trouble with us. Lenore said that Donst has been calling her and sounds desperate. He wants to see her, but she has managed to hold him off with excuses. He thinks his world is falling apart. She doesn't want to have any more to do with him, but I told her not to make a final decision until we give her the okay."

"Captain, tell her to dump him and stay away from him. He's crazy, and we don't need to collect any more information on him other than what we'll get with our bug," Becker said.

"Thank you, colonel. I'm sure she will be pleased to hear that," Schwarz replied. "She is still staying at my place and is not in a hurry to go back home except to pick up some clothes and other necessities. I am fine with it. She is no trouble, and frankly, she has been a big help to me in cleaning up the place."

"Sara, what are you grinning about?" asked Becker.

"Nothing, colonel, I was just thinking about what I told Kurt about Lenore."

"And what was that?" Becker inquired. "I told him that as long as Lenore played by the rules, she would be most welcome in our group. The main rule is not to come on to the big boss. I was kidding, of course."

"So it is our group now, is it?" asked Becker. "Captain, I hope you can keep these women in line."

"I can, colonel. Sara is crazy, but she means well. Lenore knows her place, and she is desperate to please me, so we'll all be fine," Schwarz answered.

"What about the unit?" Becker asked.

"It looks like they will be moving into the new quarters the day after tomorrow if we don't hit a snag. I will arrange for an inspection sometime during the day, whenever it's convenient for you, sir."

"Check with me Thursday morning, and I'll let you know," Becker replied. "Sara, do you have anything else?"

"Yes, sir, when are we going back to the *Reichswehr* Club?" asked Sara. "I just love the food there, and they are so friendly."

"Sara, all you think about now is food," the captain said. "If she gets fat on us, colonel, I think we should send her packing."

"Oh! shut up, Kurt?" Sara blurted out. "I only weigh 110 pounds. And I do think of other things. You don't think I'm getting fat, do you, colonel?"

"What a silly question," Becker shot back. "Let's cut the nonsense and get back to the business at hand. We have a lot of work to do, so unless there is something else to discuss, the meeting is over. Let's get back to work."

Later that day, Sara bumped into the captain in the hall. "Say Kurt, what's wrong with the boss today? Did you see the way he chewed me out after I asked him if I was getting fat?"

"Sara, it was a silly question," the captain replied. "You float around here like a butterfly with that skinny ass of yours and then you ask a question like that. You had just got through saying you only weighed 110 pounds."

"Oh, screw you, Kurt," she said. "You always take up for him. In case you didn't know it, you really hurt my feelings."

"Well, excuse me, Sara," he replied. "Get over it. Maybe deep down the colonel hates you now."

On Thursday at the morning staff meeting, Captain Schwarz informed Becker that the unit had moved into its new barracks and was standing by for inspection. "That's good. We will do it at eleven," Becker said. "When we finish with the inspection, we will go by the *Reichswehr* Club for lunch. Captain, did you get through with your interviews with the agents?"

"Yes sir, we did, and we have our full complement of agents and are awaiting further instructions. We also are happy to report that, after making our selections, we still have another twenty agents available that we feel are qualified and ready for use as soon as we are ready for them."

"Then let's set up a meeting with those that were selected for tomorrow morning at ten," Becker said.

Shortly after eleven, Becker and his aides arrived at the unit compound. They were greeted by Sergeant Mauch and ushered into the building. After making a quick tour of the facilities, Becker instructed Mauch to assemble the troops in the large room intended to be used as a recreation area. Once the troops were assembled, the colonel entered the room as Mauch barked out an order. "Attention. Colonel Konrad Becker is here for the inspection."

The colonel walked past the men standing at attention, looked them over, and said, "Stand at ease. I would like to welcome you to your new home as well as your new assignment. You have been carefully selected for this duty because of your past service and superior performance record as soldiers in the *Reichswehr(German army)*. Your new assignment is unique in that you will be part of an elite group. You are going to receive special privileges, but I must make it clear that with those special privileges come special responsibilities. You are expected to conduct yourselves at all times in the highest tradition of a German soldier. You are now members of the Gestapo Combat Unit, or GCU. Your group leader, of course, is Sergeant Mauch, and your field commander is Captain Kurt Schwarz. Captain Schwarz is standing here with me today, along with my special assistant Sara Klein. You are the first fifteen soldiers to be selected for service in this unit. Ten more will join you shortly, and others will be added as needed.

"All right, men, now that we have that out of the way, we can proceed," Becker continued. "First of all, as I pointed out earlier, this group will be extended special privileges in addition to what has been granted and is now available to regular army personnel. At the present time, there will be at least twelve men on duty at all times. This number will increase as new recruits come into the program. You all have been issued a sidearm and a submachine gun. This equipment should be readily available when you are on duty. You have been given special living accommodations, and we will see to it that the food you are served will be of high quality. You will be granted leave when appropriate and when circumstances permit. If you encounter personal problems, then you should bring those to the attention of your superior officers, and you will receive the assistance, if possible, that is needed. I have no further comments to make at this time, other than, welcome to the Gestapo. I will now turn this meeting over to the captain and Sergeant Mauch. Heil Hitler."

A chorus of heels clicking and heil Hitlers followed. Becker was feeling good about his new unit. Now he could spend some time on target selections.

After lunch, Becker, Schwarz and Sara returned to the office to discuss the first assignment of the GCU.

"Captain, I have this list of Goring's," Becker said. "Now is a good time to get started on the names."

"How many names do you have, colonel?" Schwarz asked.

"Looks like about a dozen. We will start with the Berlin area first. Looks like only two in Berlin. The rest are scattered all over the country. Let's take this one first, Bernard Weiss with the SA. He is one of Rohm's cohorts. It says here that he hangs out at a beer hall called Shultz's on Bremenstrasse. Where the hell is Bremenstrasse?" Becker asked.

"I know where that is, colonel," Schwarz replied. "I have been there a few times myself. We could pick him up or have someone waylay him when he comes out."

"Kurt, I am a little dubious about this whole thing. The idea of killing people without some justification is not very appealing to me. I am not suggesting that the names on Goring's list don't deserve it. I'm just not comfortable with it. I certainly am not going to use the GCU to conduct such an operation. No, I think we should proceed cautiously in this matter. You go ahead and assign an inspector to check Weiss out. Find out what he is doing, and let's come up with some kind of justification before we have him killed. I will have to tell Goring that, at least for the time being, we should not use our new unit for assassinations."

"Yes, sir, I will have one of the inspectors take care of it. We will need a description or a photo for identification," Schwarz said.

"Have an inspector get on it," Becker said. "He can dig up a photo and then check inside Shultz's until he locates our target. Leave the details up to our agent and let him take care of it. I think we will do the same for the others on that list. It may well turn out that every one of the bastards might deserve to die, but let's handle the thing in a prudent manner." "Yes, sir," Schwarz replied.

Chapter Eighteen

The next morning at the staff meeting, Captain Schwarz had a couple of surprise announcements. "Colonel, Lenore told me last night that she has not heard from Donst for several days. She thinks it is strange because up until now he was constantly calling and wanting to see her. And that's not all, either. Our surveillance crew has a new transcript, but Donst is missing from the conversation. Here it is."

Unknown: Good morning, Dirk.

Hartman: Good morning, colonel. Are you getting settled in okay?

Unknown: Yes, thank you. I still have a few things to do. We boxed up the major's stuff, and one of the girls took it down to the storeroom.

Hartman: Good. If you need anything, just let me know. I'll try to bring you up to speed on our main project. I'm sure you have heard of Colonel Becker at the Gestapo. From what we can tell, Diels is just a figurehead there, and Becker pretty much is the number one man. He is the fair-haired boy for Hermann Goring, and as mentioned to you earlier, Becker is a pain in the ass. We are going to have to deal with him. This is where you come in.

Unknown: Yeah, I have heard of him. He seems to have struck fear into a lot of people. Maybe we can cut him down a notch or two. I have had dealings with upstarts like him before.

Hartman: I must warn you, colonel, not to take him lightly. We tried that and got burned pretty bad. I made the mistake of putting Major Donst in charge of our operation, and that turned out to be a disaster. We don't want to make the same mistake twice.

Unknown: Don't worry, Hartman. The bigger they come, the harder they fall. Is Donst available? I would like to debrief him, if I may.

Hartman: Not exactly. Let's say he is temporarily indisposed. The last encounter he had with Becker turned ugly, to put it mildly. The little bastard almost implicated me in his failure. Fortunately for me, I don't think Becker is aware of me being involved with this venture, other than what some bozo army captain that Donst brought into the picture might have told him. I can always claim my involvement was incidental.

Unknown: I see. I take it that you prefer to remain in the background. Is that correct?

Hartman: That is correct. You understand. I have a close association with Herr Himmler, and we don't want any of this to be traced back to him. It might prove to be somewhat of a problem due to Himmler's relationship with Herr Goring.

Unknown: Yes, of course, colonel, I understand. I would never do anything to the detriment of Herr Himmler. I do feel it necessary to review the work and the actions taken by Donst in this matter.

Hartman: Maybe it's best if I locate Donst and have him come in so that you may meet with him. However, his present mental condition may pose a problem. His behavior has been erratic since he failed in an attempt to expose Becker as a fraud. Donst, of course, was acting on his own and his actions were a total train wreck. I felt sorry for the man, but he was just in over his head.

Unknown: Colonel Hartman, I have had experience with people like that, and I understand what you must have gone through in dealing with such an incompetent."

Hartman: You are very understanding, colonel, and let me say again how fortunate we are to have you join us. Herr Himmler has spoken highly of you and says you are one of his best men.

Unknown: Indeed. I am very pleased to hear that, and you and the *Reichsfuhrer* may rest assured that we will be successful in dealing with this Becker fellow.

"What the hell is going on over there, captain?" Becker asked. "Get in touch with Major Koenig at the SS and find out who this new officer is. He sounds like a pompous ass to me."

"Yes, sir," Schwarz replied. "He certainly is not without confidence in himself, that's for sure. Poor Donst. I wonder what they have done with him, colonel."

"Your guess is as good as mine, but it sounds to me like they may have him stashed away somewhere in a padded cell. You say that Lenore hasn't heard from him, so I guess he has become dispensable."

"It all points in that direction, sir. And I was just beginning to like the little bastard. His incompetence is going to be missed." Schwarz laughed. "Can you believe that Hartman? What a phony. He treated poor old Donst like a dog and now professes to have compassion for him. That fool thinks we are not on to him."

"Little does he know," Becker replied.

"Colonel, while you and Sara are talking, I'll try to get Koenig on the phone to see what he knows about our mystery colonel at the SS."

"Yeah, okay, captain. I had already removed Donst from my personal hit list because he had become quite the entertainer. That brings up another question, and that is, where is Karl Klein? Have you heard from him lately, Sara?"

"No, sir, I have not, but he knows that I don't want to hear from him and that may be the main reason. I can try to find him and see what he has to say, if you like," she said.

"Good idea," Becker said. "Why don't you do that? He may know something about Donst."

"Colonel, are you still mad at me?" she asked.

"Mad at you about what?" Becker replied.

"You know the other day when I asked that silly question about whether you thought I was getting too fat."

"Sara, are you still in high school? Let's get real here. Why would you come up with something like that, anyway?" Becker asked.

"You haven't talked to me since then, and you act as if I am not even here."

"Okay, Sara, you are here. How are you? Now how is that?" Becker asked sarcastically.

"Now you are making fun of me," she whined.

"Okay, I give up. If I was mad at you. I am not mad anymore, and if I acted like you weren't here, then I am now acting like you are here now. Are you satisfied?" he asked.

"Yes, sir, I guess so," she meekly replied.

Captain Schwarz knocked on the door and entered. "Colonel, I just got off the phone with Koenig, and he doesn't know anything about Donst or the new colonel. He is going to look into it and get back to us as soon as possible."

"Thanks, captain. Let me know when you hear back from him. That's about it, staff."

Later in the day, the captain came in to Becker's office almost out of breath. "Colonel, I just heard back from Major Koenig. He has some information on our mystery colonel. His name is Horst Heitman. He is one of Himmler's cronies from Munich. He is supposed to be tough. He started out with the SA, and after he hooked up with Himmler, he got into the SS. He definitely has taken Donst's old office. That makes it convenient for us, since we already have a bug in there. He looks like he might be more of a challenge for us, though."

"You may be right, captain," Becker replied. "Contact our Munich headquarters and see what they can tell us about Colonel Heitman. We will have to take this fellow more seriously than those clowns we have been dealing with. Sara, how are you doing on the plan to start attending some of those general staff meetings?"

"There is one tomorrow afternoon at three at the chancellery, sir. There is always a reception afterward. Shall I schedule it?"

"Who is chairing?" Becker asked.

"General von Beck, sir" she replied.

"Yeah, go ahead. I know it's going to be boring, but maybe things will pick up a bit at the reception."

The next morning started with more revelations. "Colonel, I talked to our station manager in Munich, and he gave me a pretty good run down on Heitman," Schwarz said.

"Okay, captain, let's hear it," Becker said.

"Heitman has a reputation for ruthlessness. He even looks ruthless. He has a dark, ruddy complexion, stands about six feet tall and weighs 190 or 200 pounds. He is forty-one years old and married with three children. He has been arrested seven times since 1925. Three of the arrests were for anti-government activities, two for assault, one for a weapons violation and one for spousal abuse."

"Not exactly what you would call a sterling reputation, but I guess its good enough for the SS," the colonel said with obvious amusement.

"I also have a report from some of our new field agents that Edmund Papen, one of Rohm's cronies, has taken a more active role in the SA's war on the people. He has set up several special units that have increased their attacks not only on Jews, but other groups as well. They have been observed seizing and burning books at various locations in Berlin. There also has been an increase in random beatings and arson attacks on synagogues and churches, mostly attributed to Papen' bands of hoodlums."

"Isn't that the same man that we had run-ins with over those thugs that were abusing the old professor and that ill-fated raid at the Weimar Center?" asked Becker.

"Yes, sir, I believe that is correct. Evidently he has decided to play a more prominent role in the SA's field operations."

"That being the case, I want your agents to increase their surveillance of him. He and his unit may very well qualify for attention from the GCU." Becker turned to Sara. "Were you able to make contact with Karl?"

"Yes, sir, I was. He is still his old nasty self, but I did get him to tell me about Donst. He said that Donst had been admitted to a psychiatric facility for observation and is also suffering from a bad case of diarrhea. Karl said that he had talked to Donst's wife, who said they were concerned about the threats he was making about taking his own life."

"Thank you. Is there anything new on the divorce?" Becker asked.

"Not really. Karl says he is going to contest it, but I think he is just bluffing. He says he is going to name you as a correspondent. Just kidding, he didn't say that," she quickly added.

"I wouldn't think so," Becker replied. "He would rather see

you become a divorcee than a widow. Let's wrap it up, and we will leave here at 2:30 for the general staff meeting."

When they arrived at the chancellery, Becker told Heinz, "Sergeant, you can come in with us, but you will have to leave your weapon outside. No weapons inside the chancellery except for the guards on duty."

"Yes sir, colonel."

"I see there is a lot of the big brass here, colonel," said Sara.

"Yeah, that's right, Sara. This is a military briefing, and there will be quite a few generals in attendance. In fact here comes one of them to greet us."

"Good afternoon, Colonel Becker. We are honored by your presence, General von Schleicher said as he approached the colonel."Hello, General von Schleicher," Becker replied. "It's good to see you again."

"Is this the first military staff meeting that you have attended?" Schleicher asked.

"Why, yes, general, I believe it is. I have been quite busy tracking down enemies of the state, you know. Perhaps I have been neglecting some of my social duties. You remember Captain Schwarz and Sara Klein, of course."

"Yes, I remember the captain, and how could I ever forget that lovely young lady? It was I that hired her, you know," the general replied.

After spending a few more minutes with the general, the colonel excused himself, and his group moved on to mingle with the other attendees. Becker was well-received by the others in attendance. His reputation had preceded him, and it was obvious that his position as a leader of the Gestapo was both respected and feared. This did not go unnoticed by Sara, who continued to marvel at her boss's appeal.

The meeting was finally called to order, and General Beck

was introduced and gave a thirty-minute presentation. After that, the gathering moved into the next large room, where beverages and snacks were being served. While Becker, Sara and Captain Schwarz were talking to each other, Becker felt a tap on the shoulder.

"Excuse me, Colonel Becker," a voice said. Becker turned around to find Hartman. "Colonel Becker, I have someone I would like to introduce to you."

"Colonel Heitman, I presume," Becker said as he faced the startled man. Becker recognized him from the description he had been given by the Munich office.

"Have you met Colonel Heitman before?" said a shocked Colonel Hartman.

"Actually, no, but the Gestapo would be derelict in its duties if we failed to recognize such distinguished officers of the SS. Welcome to Berlin, Colonel Heitman. Are you on business in our great city, or just paying us a visit?" Becker inquired.

"It is my pleasure to meet you, Colonel Becker," a somewhat shaken Heitman said. "I have heard a great deal about you, but I did not know that your talents included clairvoyance. Very impressive, sir," Heitman said.

"Thank you, colonel, but you are too kind. We at the Gestapo try to stay on top of everything happening in the Third Reich," Becker replied. "May I introduce some of my staff that is with me today? Captain Kurt Schwarz, one of my senior aides and commander of the GCU, and my administrative assistant, Sara Klein."

"A pleasure, captain" said Heitman. "So this is that beautiful assistant of yours that I have heard so much about. I am delighted to meet you, Sara. May I say that what I have heard does not measure up to what I am seeing in person?"

"Thank you, sir, and welcome to Berlin," she said with an orchestrated blush. "And hello to you, as well, Colonel Hartman.

Heitman and Hartman," she repeated. "That sounds like a team. You are not in show business, are you?"

Everyone burst out laughing.

"Hardly, Ms Klein," retorted Hartman. "Not only are you a beautiful woman, but you have a charming sense of humor. It is nice to see you again, as well as the captain.

"The GCU, I don't think I am familiar with that term. Is that a part of the Gestapo, Captain Schwarz?" Hartman asked.

"Yes, it is, colonel. GCU stands for Gestapo Combat Unit."

"And what does the GCU do, captain?" asked Hartman.

"Sir, I cannot tell you that due to the nature of our business. I am sure you understand." Schwarz replied.

"Of course, captain, my apology for asking," Hartman said. "Colonel Becker, if the rest of your staff is as impressive as these two, then you and Diels are to be commended on your selection process."

"Thank you, Colonel Hartman. We strive to recruit the best," Becker said. He turned to Colonel Heitman. "It was a pleasure to meet you, colonel, and I hope we will be seeing more of you in the future. Heil Hitler."

"Oh, I'm sure you will, Colonel Becker, and may I say the same for the lady and the Captain. Heil Hitler?"

That was the first encounter with Colonel Heitman, but it would not be the last.

"Colonel, I think you set both of them on their heels when you feigned recognition of Heitman," the captain said after Hartman and Heitman had left. "It completely threw them off their game, no doubt about it."

"I think Sara trumped me when she asked if they were a team," said Becker. "Sara, what possessed you to come out with that zinger?"

"I guess it must be from hanging out with you two, sir, but

their names do sound like a stage act," she said. "You know, like Fritz and Schitz, the famous comedy team."

"With that zinger, I think we will leave here and call it a day," said the colonel.

The next morning, as Schwarz entered the office, Becker asked, "Captain, what is on the agenda for today?"

"I am to meet with some of our field agents and our electronic listening device supervisor. I also have a meeting with Mauch and the GCU team. One of our agents has brought to my attention that there is a big push on at SS to promote their new star over there, who just happens to be Heitman. Can you believe that?" Schwarz said.

"That explains their opening act yesterday," said Becker. "Wonder who is going to wind up with top billing in their act? At least we are one step ahead of them. We just need to keep it that way. They are probably over there plotting their next move right now."

"That Heitman gives me the creeps," said Sara. "I caught him staring at my behind a couple of times."

"Oh, Sara, everybody stares at your behind," quipped the captain. "So what's new? You would be in here complaining if you thought they weren't."

"Now, hold on you two," Becker intervened. "Let's not start anything this morning. Captain, go and check to see if we have anything from the surveillance crew."

As the captain left the room, Sara looked at Becker. "Konrad, why do you let Captain Schwarz treat me with such disrespect?" she asked.

"Look, Sara, he is just pulling your chain. Lighten up a bit, will you? Maybe he has a secret yearning for you and is frustrated over it. But I'll tell him to drop the personal remarks. It's not very professional, anyway. Now pull yourself together and be a man."

"Yes, sir," she replied as the captain returned.

"Colonel, there is a meeting going on now at Heitman's office between Donst and Heitman. There was an earlier meeting between Heitman and Hartman, and we should have that transcript shortly. Berta will bring it in as soon as it arrives," Schwarz said.

"Good, and Sara thinks those catty remarks that you have been making to her are a sign of your frustration over a failed love life," Becker said.

"Actually, colonel my love life is alive and well. Since I met Lenore, it is heating up to a boiling point. Sara, we all love you, and that is why we like to tease you," Schwarz said. "I didn't mean to imply that you had a good-looking behind, even though everybody seems to think so."

"I know that, Kurt. The colonel and I were just teasing to see how you like it. I know I have a pretty behind, so I guess I'll just have to live with it. What is that saying? 'If you have it flaunt it,'" she said with a laugh.

"No, Sara, I think the saying is, 'If you don't use it, you lose it,'" said the captain.

"Kurt, it's not my fault that I am not using it. I'm more than ready to use it. I am just waiting on you-know-who."

"All right, Sara," Becker said. "You get the last word." There was a knock on the door. "See what Berta wants," Becker said. "Maybe she has that transcript."

Berta had the new transcript.

Heitman: Good morning, Dirk, come on in.

Hartman: Good morning, Horst. They are going to bring Major Donst in this morning, so I thought I would give you a heads up.

Heitman: Very good. I need to talk to him. Is he rational?

Hartman: Hell, I don't know. If he starts acting up, have him returned to the facility. From what I hear, he is doing much better, but we will see. What did you think about Becker?

Heitman: He was impressive. I was taken aback when he knew who I was. They must have one hell of an operation over there. My God, I couldn't believe it.

Hartman: I told you he was no lightweight. Now you know why we want to bring his ass down.

Heitman: Yeah. I guess we do have our work cut out for us. How the hell did he get that SS designation? And how about that assistant of his? Did you get a load of that ass? I could hardly keep my eyes off of her. Man. How does he get away with something like that? Why, hell, the *fuhrer* himself doesn't have anything like that, or if he does, nobody has seen it.

Hartman: That is a good question, colonel. The *fuhrer* himself awarded him the SS designation. Of course, that's Goring again. As for that woman, he takes her everywhere he goes, along with his bodyguards. And they are equipped with the latest prototype submachine gun. He shows that woman off like she's some kind of a trophy. I am surprised that Goring hasn't snatched her up for himself.

Heitman: If it wasn't for Goring, Becker would never get away with something like that. Why can't the *Reichsfuhrer* furnish us with someone like her?

Hartman: Probably because there is not another one like her, or Himmler would have her himself. [Laughter.] You should complain, though. That woman that Donst left here is not all that bad herself. Maybe you should give her a shot.

Heitman: You mean that secretary? I might just have to do that. I have been sizing her up, but she is married, you know.

Hartman: Now, colonel, don't get too picky. Donst didn't let that stop him.

Heitman: Are you sure about that? On second thought, I may have to do that. I am not sure how long it will be before the wife moves up here, and you know a man has to be taken care of.

Hartman: Yeah, by the way, Donst said he had some young thing that he was doodling. He said he had her stashed in an apartment somewhere on the west side of town. He didn't admit to it, but I am sure he was keeping her up. He claimed that she was wild in bed. Maybe he will be willing to share. [Laughter.]

Heitman: Colonel, how about you? Got anything on the string?

Hartman: Oh, I'm doing all right. It's almost time for Donst to be here, so I am going to get back to my office. Let me know how your meeting turns out. Heil Hitler.

Heitman: Heil Hitler. End of transcript.

"Colonel, there you have it," Schwarz said. "Those two devoted public servants of the state are right on top of their jobs protecting the fatherland."

"Yeah, captain. I guess about all we can learn from that conversation is that Sara has a good-looking rear end. If I am not mistaken, we already covered that subject today. What about that, Sara?"

"Is my butt the only thing people are talking about in this country?" Sara said indignantly. "God, give me a break. Is that all men think about? Never mind, don't answer that."

"They did mention my name once or twice, and I believe they were rather complimentary," Becker said with a big smile.

"They didn't mention Kurt," said Sara, "but they did bring up his newfound love. I am sure they were talking about our dear sweet Lenore. Is she really wild in bed, Kurt? Or was she just that way with that stud Donst?"

"Sara, I think you really enjoyed that little piece of gossip, and we don't know for sure that they were talking about Lenore," the captain responded. "If Donst was talking about Lenore, I think he was lying. She is affectionate, but she is a nice girl. That little bastard had the gall to talk about her like that. She is just an innocent young girl that has been taken advantage of."

"Yeah sure, Kurt," Sara said sarcastically. "She is probably still a virgin."

"Sara, is that anyway to talk to the captain?" Becker said. "Where is your compassion?"

"My compassion, that's a good one. Where is his compassion?" she blurted out.

"Now, now, staff. Let's stick to analyzing these transcripts and not get into personalities. This business is not about your ass, Sara, or your new girlfriend Captain. So if you two don't mind, let's get back to the basics here. I guess we can expect the next chapter of this play to begin shortly when the major comes on stage," Becker said with a chuckle. "It's time for lunch. We should have the other transcript when we return."

When they returned from lunch, the transcript of Major Donst and Colonel Heitman had been delivered and was waiting on Becker's desk. As they began to read the transcripts, the colonel remarked, "I know we have gotten a great deal of amusement from reading some of these transcripts, but we should not lose sight of the fact that we are dealing with evil thugs who would not hesitate for one minute to have all of us killed. Just remember that. I have a sense of humor just like the next man, but I never stop thinking of what these people are capable of doing."

Becker had been thinking about that for some time. He felt it was time to remind his associates of that fact. He did not want them to be lulled into thinking that this was like a chess game, and there were not consequences. He made sure that they were fully aware of his position.

They turned to the transcript.

Donst: Heil Hitler. I am Major Wilhelm Donst, sir.

Heitman: Good morning, major. Please be seated, and I'll be with you in just a moment.

Donst: Thank you, sir.

Female voice: Hello, major, we've missed you. How are you doing?

Donst: I'm doing quite well, Gertrude, thank you. I am just getting over the flu.

Heitman: That will be all for now, Gertrude, and hold all my calls unless they are from Colonel Hartman.

Female voice: Yes, sir. Thank you. Nice to have seen you, Major Donst, I hope you feel better.

Heitman: She is rather attractive, wouldn't you say, major?"

Donst: Yes, sir, I suppose you could say that. I always kept my distance from the employees, sir. For security purposes, you know.

Heitman: Yes, of course. Now, tell me about Colonel Becker of the Gestapo. I would like for you to fill me in on what all you have done regarding him.

Donst: Sir, I was assigned by Colonel Hartman to assist him in an investigation of Colonel Becker. This was part of our efforts to destabilize Gestapo activities in preparation for the SS to take over the agency.

For the next thirty minutes, Donst went into more detail about what he had been doing, including the participation of Karl Klein and Captain Hawes.

Heitman: So it would appear the culmination of your efforts resulted in that fiasco at the *Reichswehrr* Club, am I correct?

Donst: I'll admit that things didn't go as we had hoped, but in all fairness, the plan was approved by Colonel Hartman himself. In fact, he was the one who suggested the whole thing and set everything up at the club. But don't get me wrong, sir, I am not putting the blame on Colonel Hartman.

Heitman: Then who are you putting the blame on? From what you have just told me, you are certainly not putting the blame on yourself.

Donst: Sir, I was just following orders.

Heitman: Stop right there, major. I am in no mood for bullshit. You were given an assignment, and you failed to carry it out in a successful manner. Major, we don't tolerate failure around here, so don't come in here and try to give me some lame excuse for your performance in a critical assignment.

Donst: Yes, sir.

Heitman: Where are these people that were working on this project with you? I am talking specifically about Klein and Hawes and any others that were involved, with the exception of Colonel Hartman, of course.

Donst: Captain Hawes returned to his division in Hammelburg, and Klein is here in Berlin. I haven't seen him since I was hospitalized. I can reach him if need be.

Heitman: Leave the information where we can reach him with that woman that was just in here. By the way, what can you tell me about her?

Donst: Yes, sir. You mean Gertrude? She is very efficient and dependable, and that is about all I know about her, sir. What is to become of me? Will I be reporting back here for duty when I am released?

Heitman: I don't know anything about that, major. You will be notified of future assignments in due time. It certainly will not be in this office. Now, let's get back to that secretary. Are you telling me that you have not had any social contact with her?

Donst: Come to think of it, we might have gone out for a

drink a couple of times. Heitman: Let's quit dancing around here. Were you bagging her?

Donst: Yes, sir, maybe a couple of times, but we were off duty.

Heitman: Why didn't you tell me that in the first place? You may go now, and if I need any further information, you will be contacted. Heil Hitler.

Donst: Heil Hitler. End of transcript.

"There you have it, staff. What do you think?" asked Becker.

"That conversation was not very informative, colonel. My main observation would be that Donst is on the fast track to oblivion, if not worse. I kind of feel sorry for him," Schwarz remarked.

"What do you think, Sara?" Becker asked.

"I share the captain's take, sir. Donst mentioned not having seen Karl, but I seem to recall Karl giving me something on him after he had been admitted to that mental facility. Maybe Karl had talked to his wife or someone else."

"I noticed that Heitman rejected Donst's attempt to put some of the blame for his failure on Hartman," Schwarz said.

"No big surprise there. We know that Hartman was up to his ass in everything that went on with their little project," Becker interjected. "There certainly was no entertainment value to this particular meeting. Heitman seems to be all business, except maybe for that secretary. He tried to pry something out of Donst on her, but Donst tried to dodge it. He didn't help himself when he finally confessed. He obviously didn't want to add to his problems, although it would appear that Heitman was more interested in pursuing a possible lead for a liaison than building a case against Donst. There also seemed to be a little resentment expressed about me having the SS designation."

"Sir, they did seem to be resentful about that," Schwarz said. "If I may be excused now, I have those field agents waiting for me. Unless you have something else, I will ask your permission to leave."

"Sure, captain, and let me know what they have been doing when you get through," Becker said. As the captain left the office, Becker turned to Sara. "Sara, I guess that about winds it down, unless you have something else."

"I don't have any more to say about the transcripts, but I do have a question. Why is everybody in Berlin getting laid but me?" she asked, apparently thinking back to Donst's secretary.

"Look, you naughty girl, you are not the only one in Berlin that is not getting laid, so have a little patience," replied Becker. "By the way, what is the status on your divorce?"

"Barring any last-minute glitches, it should be granted the week after next. I'll be a free woman. Isn't that marvelous? I can't wait. Aren't you excited for me?" she asked.

"Congratulations. Yes, I am happy for you, but let's not get ahead of ourselves. It hasn't happened yet, so hold off on the celebrations," Becker said.

"Will you take me somewhere, Konrad? Anywhere will be fine with me."

"I will think about it," Becker replied. "I could use a few days away myself, but let's wait and see what we have going at that time. Meanwhile, you had better get back to your office. I have some calls I have to make, and I'm sure you have plenty to do yourself."

She left the office, and Becker was left to figure out how he was going to handle Sara now that she would soon be single and more than available. He decided that he would think about it later. He knew she had her mind set, and there may not be any way to change it.

A couple of hours later, the captain came in to discuss his

meeting with the field agents. "Colonel, I have something for you on Bernard Weiss," Schwarz said. "The inspector tells me that he has checked him out pretty thoroughly, and he has also been observing him at the beer hall. Weiss is a typical Rohm goon. He has a rap sheet dating way back, but more recently he has been involved in robbing prominent Jewish families. Instead of turning in the proceeds to the state, he has been converting them to his own use. He hangs out at Shultz's quite a bit and stays half-tanked, bullying anyone that comes into contact with him."

"That is interesting. Have your inspector take him out, but make it look like a mugging or a random attack. Can the agent handle it by himself, or does he need some help?" Becker said.

"Sir, I think he should have some help. He has been working with another agent on this, and they are both capable. But to play it safe, I am going to have both of them carry out the assignment."

"Then it's done. What else did they have to say, captain?"

"They tell me that there is quite a bit of this going on, mostly involving the SA, but some SS thugs are doing the same thing."

"What about that other name on Goring's list here in Berlin?" Becker asked.

"Yes sir. That would be Vaughn Weddle, a police captain. He's tight with some SS people. That's probably why Goring wants him taken out."

"What do you have on him?" Becker asked.

"Has a bad reputation of being on the take and is also doing the same as Weiss. Just maybe on a smaller scale, as he serves as a police captain, and that makes it a little harder for him to find helpers on the force."

"Okay, take his ass out, too. This is a twofer. Goring will be pleased, and we get rid of a couple of rats," Becker said. "In other cases, where they are operating in gangs, then you can use the

GCU. In those cases, we need to catch them in the act and be able to show that they were acting for themselves and not the state."

"Yes sir, according to our agents, most of these incidents involve more than just two individuals and we will need the GCU," Schwarz said.

"Okay, we have done a day's work, so let's pack it in," Becker said. "See you tomorrow."

Two days later, a newspaper headline read, "Police Captain Found Slain." The story reported, "Berlin Police Captain Vaughn Weddle was found dead early this morning in an automobile in West Berlin, an apparent victim of foul play. Sources revealed the captain was under investigation for unspecified criminal conduct." Another headline read, "Prominent SA Official Shot Dead." The article went on to read, "Bernard Weiss, a high-ranking official with the SA, was found shot to death outside Shultz's Beer Hall early today by an unknown assailant. Weiss was a regular visitor at the beer hall. Robbery may have been a motive. Reached at his office on *Wilhelmstrasse*, Colonel Konrad Becker said that both cases were under investigation by the Gestapo. Becker stated that this was the second high-profile death of a loyal and devoted servant of the Third Reich in the last twenty-four hours, and suicide had not been ruled out. He expressed sympathy for the families of the victims."

"Colonel, you have a phone call from Minister Goring," Berta announced.

"Thank you, Berta. Hello, Herr Minister. How are you today?" Becker asked.

"I'm doing fine, colonel. What about the killings yesterday?" Goring asked.

"Yes, Herr Minister, it was quite a shock to have two fine public officials taken away from us. From the evidence, it appears that both of these were execution-style killings. The men may have been victims of colleagues. Both of the individuals were reported to be under considerable stress."

"It's too bad, but shit happens," the minister replied. "Good work, colonel."

"Thank you. Herr Minister, we are just doing our job. We have arrested close associates of both victims and should have confessions before the day is out."

"Thank you, sir, and you have a good day," Goring said.

Captain Schwarz came in, and Becker asked if the suspects had confessed. "Yes, they have, colonel. They both succumbed to some of our new, enhanced interrogation techniques and have been shot. The case is now closed. And to think the killers were close friends of the two men."

"Yeah, captain, you just never know who you can trust these days. Was there a motive for the slayings?" Becker asked.

"We believe it was a disagreement over money in one case, and the other was a lovers' quarrel," Schwarz replied.

"I am sure the families of the victims will be relieved to know that suicide has been ruled out," Becker noted. "There should be no complications with their insurance policies. My compliments, captain, to you and your men on quickly solving this case."

"Thank you, colonel. That's our job. The two accused were actually accomplices of the victims, so it was a good opportunity to rid the world of a couple more thugs," Schwarz said.

Becker believed taking out the latter was more or less a bonus for his real mission.

Chapter Nineteen

A few days later, a call came in from a Gestapo agent in the field that about a dozen Storm Troopers were roaming through a Jewish neighborhood, robbing and beating residents. The GCU was immediately dispatched to the scene, and a battle broke out upon the unit's arrival. Eleven Storm Troopers were killed and three more taken into custody. The GCU suffered no casualties. Those arrested were brought back to headquarters and taken down to the basement for questioning. By the next morning, they had all confessed to robbing and stealing valuable paintings and jewelry and keeping the treasure for themselves. They were taken out and shot. The stolen property was left on the scene and apparently retrieved by the owners. The event was reported to the media as looting by thieves impersonating Storm Troopers.

At SA headquarters, Rohm and his deputies were in a rage. Rohm called Goring, ranting about how the Gestapo was out of control and trying to get him. "Herr Minister, we are outraged over here about our men being ambushed and killed by that renegade bunch at the Gestapo," Rohm said. "If you don't reign in that son of a bitch Becker, then we will."

"Calm down, Ernst. I will check into it, meanwhile, if I were you, I would stay as far away from Becker as you can. He doesn't like you anyway," Goring warned.

"I'll just take it up with the *fuhrer*," Rohm shouted before hanging up the phone.

When Becker met with Minister Goring the next day, Goring shared an incomplete plan for eliminating Rohm and other prominent enemies of the *fuhrer*.

"Looks like a good plan to me. Herr Minister. Are you sure you don't want us to take care of it?" Becker asked.

"No, colonel, the *fuhrer* is going to lead the attack. You just have your unit remain on standby in case they are needed. No definite time has been set yet for the operation, so I'll let you know when I get the word," Goring said.

The next day at Gestapo headquarters, Becker called Captain Schwarz into the office to discuss the Rohm plan. "Have a seat, captain. I met with the minister yesterday, and they are finally ready to move on Rohm. The plan has not been finalized, so at this point I can't say for sure what our role will in the purge. So far our participation may be limited to a standby role. Hitler has signed off on the program, and at this point it comes down to a time and place for the event to take place. That's all I can tell you now."

"I was wondering if they were ever going to do it, colonel," Schwarz commented. "I'll still believe it when I see it. I do have some other things I need to talk to you about. Our GCU has been busy the last few days. We are up to full complement of twenty-five now, and the way things are going, we are going to have to bring on some new men. We have room for another fifty men at the GCU headquarters."

"Talk to Richter about that, captain," Becker instructed. "What else do you have today?"

"We have another transcript of Hartman and Heitman, and it looks like big trouble for us. Do you have time to look at it?" Schwarz asked.

"Yes, let's see what they are up to," Becker answered.

Hartman: Horst, how did your session go with Major Donst?

Heitman: It was more or less a waste of time. He told me basically the same thing you did, except he tried to put his slant on it, like he was just following your orders. I caught him in a couple of lies. He acted like he didn't even know the secretary. He at first denied doing her and then admitted it when I pressed him on it. I think it's time to cut him loose. He is of no further use to us. I'll leave it up to you to decide what you want to do with him. I don't want him back here.

Hartman: I'll take care of it, but we have something more important to discuss. Colonel Becker has to be taken out one way or the other, and knowing Becker, my guess is it's going to be elimination. The order comes down from the top. From last count, the Gestapo has taken out more than thirty-five of our SS troops in the last ten days. We don't even have a count on the number of SA Becker has had killed. The son of a bitch has been clever about it. He is making it look like he is just doing his duty to protect the *fuhrer* and the state. We know better. They are on a killing spree over there, and who knows who is going to be next.

Heitman: Yeah, I see. He is too dangerous. It could be you or me next, for that matter. They are going after senior-level officers. Remember, I told you when I was first brought in here that the only way to deal with a man like Becker was to kill him. You can't reason with him. I agree that he has to go; we just need to decide on how we are going to do it. I'm told he never goes anywhere alone. We are going to have enough men to swing it.

Hartman: You are right. We are going to have to lure him to a place he feels safe, where he leaves that guard of his outside. Offhand, I can't think of any public place that is feasible. That rules out hotels and restaurants, too many people around. Say, I just thought of something. There is a lodge just outside of Berlin that may be the place. It is widely used by the SS and other agencies for social events. I am sure the Gestapo has used the place. If we can get him out there, we could easily have about six or eight of our trusted SS guards stationed inside. They could take him out without too much of a fight. He wouldn't stand a chance.

Heitman: Sounds logical to me. I would like to go to the lodge and check it out for myself. We are going to have to plan this carefully. If something goes wrong, you and I both may never see another sunrise.

Hartman: I'll take you out there this afternoon. The more I think about it, the more I think it's perfect. We may want to do it when the purge takes place. The *reichsfuhrer* told me yesterday that the *fuhrer* had given the go-ahead to get rid of Rohm and a bunch of other traitors.

Heitman: Excellent. I knew it was coming, and yes, it may be perfect timing to take Becker out. The question is, how do we get Becker out there when we don't know the exact time of the purge? Or maybe I should ask, how do we get Becker out there period?

Hartman: You raise a good question. It doesn't necessarily have to be at the exact time of the purge. That may be impossible. Possibly we could stage an event that necessitated his presence. I could issue him an invitation to meet regarding the purge. It would be hard for him to turn it down since the Gestapo will be playing such a prominent role in the purge.

Heitman: Colonel, I like the idea. What's the name of this lodge, anyway?

Hartman: Von Turpin Lodge. After the war, the Weimar Republic took it over, and it has been used for government purposes ever since. There is only a lone guard out there, but that should pose no problem. There is never anything happening out there that would require heavy security unless someone like the *fuhrer* or another high-ranking official was using the place, and he would have his own security force.

Heitman: Let's pay a visit to the von Turpin Lodge, and then we can sit down and finalize our plan. End of transcript.

"Captain, you are right, these bastards mean business. I really didn't think Hartman had the guts, but Heitman's participation apparently has juiced him up a bit. I want a floor plan of the lodge, and we of course will pay a visit out there ourselves. Are you familiar with the lodge?" Becker asked.

"Yes, I am colonel. I have been there a number of times, and Hartman is right, it would be a good location for an ambush. There is a large, wooded area adjacent to the main building," Schwarz said. "There are probably guards there only when the building is in use. As Hartman said, the only time any real security is needed is when a high-ranking official is present. Of course they would not expect us to have any security other than Heinz. They are probably counting on just you and me and maybe Sara, along with Heinz. It would be easy."

"Captain, I am going to go through with the meeting. I wouldn't want to disappoint our distinguished hosts after they have gone to all that trouble to have a reception for me. They are going to be in for one hell of a surprise," Becker said. "After we take a tour of the place and study the layout, we will station our forces accordingly. In addition to our GCU, I want you to ask Richter to furnish us with 100 additional troops. They can be stationed just inside the wooded area, out of sight. They will mainly be there for shock value, but they'll be good insurance if we need them. I want a show of force so that any other plotters will think twice. And I damn sure don't want to be caught short. I don't want anyone to see the troops when they arrive at the lodge. They'll have to be dropped off several hours in advance and the trucks and other vehicles parked at some other location. We will make sure that we arrive after our hosts do. They will have their security force on the inside, and apparently they figure that they only need eight or ten men. After we inspect the lodge, we will determine the placement of the GCU. Hartman and Heitman also may decide to beef up their security force a bit, but it will make little or no difference. They will be no match for us," Becker said with confidence.

"Yes, sir. Will there be anything else, sir?" asked Schwarz.

"After we inspect the place, captain, I want you to have your surveillance crew place listening devices in the building. There should be space in there where we can position the GCU. That way, at the proper time your unit can appear. You will respond to a signal from me, or when you think it necessary. Call general services and tell them to have a representative with a key out there to meet us in one hour. Then have Heinz bring the car around. I want to check that building out before we go any further with our plans."

"Yes, sir," Schwarz replied.

At the lodge, the representative met Becker, the captain, and Sergeant Heinz and admitted them to the building. There were two architect's drawings of the exterior and interior of the building in the main office of the lodge.

"Captain, pick up a set of those drawings, and we will take them with us. Also, instruct the general service representatives that they are not to divulge news of our visit to anyone."

After spending two hours carefully examining the building

and the grounds, the men returned to Gestapo headquarters. There Becker and Schwarz studied the drawings of the building and began laying out a plan for the confrontation with the SS officers. They anticipated that the meeting would take place in the main entrance room on the first floor. The ceiling in the main entrance room extended to the top of the second floor. On the second floor, a balcony surrounded the main floor except for the front wall. The first floor main entrance room provided access to the other parts of the lodge with rest room facilities, a ballroom, a kitchen, a large storage room and nine guest rooms. The second-floor balcony led to another large storage room and ten guest rooms. Both storage rooms contained cleaning equipment and supplies and were kept locked. They were only used by custodians. There was also a loft that had enough space to easily accommodate twenty-five men.

"Captain, they are going to expect you, Sara and Sergeant Heinz to accompany me when we go out there. I am reluctant to take Sara along because something could go wrong. As for you, I want you with the GCU. This operation leaves no room for chance. I can get that lieutenant that worked the Weimar Center incident to go along as my aide. I can't think of his name ... oh, yeah, I believe it was Mench. See if Richter can have him on standby to assist us," Becker ordered.

"Yes, sir," Schwarz answered. "Most likely we will get his unit anyway, but they will have to have someone else outside in charge of the soldiers. How soon do you think it will be before they set up their ambush?"

"From what Hartman and Heitman said in the last transcript, they are in a hurry to do it," Becker said. "Alert your surveillance detail and instruct them to get their next transcript over here as soon as possible. My hunch is that they will discuss this in the morning."

The colonel's hunch proved to be right on the button. The

next morning, Captain Schwarz came in with the fresh transcript. "We've got one, and it's a good one," he said.

Hartman: Good morning, Colonel Heitman. Now that we have taken a look at the lodge, I think it will be perfect.

Heitman: Let's finalize our plan.

Hartman: We are pretty sure that Becker will bring that captain, the woman and his bodyguard driver. We might as well conduct our business in that large lounge area where you enter the building. I think we should get it over as soon as possible.

Heitman: I quite agree. Strike quickly before he can catch on. All we have to do is neutralize the bodyguard, and from there it should be easy. We discussed earlier that we would have about eight SS officers there. Do you think that eight will be enough? I mean, why take a chance?

Hartman: Yes, you are right. Let's bump it up to fifteen. As you say, why take a chance? Becker will only have his sidearm. The aide and the woman may also be armed, but they will pose no danger with the bodyguard out of the way. As soon as they enter the building, our men will disarm the guard and take him into custody.

Heitman: I agree. We should do this in the afternoon so we will have enough time to get in there, inspect the premises and go through the plan with our people. We need to carry out the operation with precision.

Hartman: Right. This is going to be easy picking. I can't wait to see the look on that son of a bitch's face. Maybe you should make the call to Becker and issue the invitation. He obviously doesn't care for me, and since he just met you, he will probably be more likely to accept an invitation from you.

Heitman: All right. Let's set it up, say, for two in the afternoon. We can get in there about twelve, which will give us a couple of hours to be ready.

Hartman: Good. I'll get a key to the building from general services. We don't need any outside witnesses, as we will dispose of all four of them. I think it would be proper to allow Becker the opportunity to take his own life. His military record demands such treatment. If he refuses, then we have to take him outside and have the firing squad do the job.

Hartman: Excellent, colonel. Now we need to select a day. We need to give him a little flexibility but impress upon him the urgency of the meeting and let him name the day.

Heitman: Will do. I will put in a call for him today. I think this is going to turn out well for us and our careers, colonel. *Reichsfuhrer* Himmler is going to pleased.

Hartman: No doubt about it. It's going to be like shooting fish in a barrel. I will leave you so you can get right on it. Call me when you have everything set up.

Heitman: I will give them some time to get into the office, and I will make the call. Heil Hitler.

"Captain, I like the plan," Becker said. "They are right that it's a good one, but unfortunately for them, it's not going to turn out the way they want it."

"Yes, sir, it's perfect—for us, that is. Heitman is going to call you today, so what day are we going to do it?" Schwarz asked.

"That depends how quickly we can mobilize our forces. What did Richter say?" asked Becker.

"He said the 100-man unit has been put on alert and will be ready on thirty minutes notice. Also, Lieutenant Mench will accompany you as your aide. Another lieutenant will command the 100-man task force stationed in the adjacent wooded area. So I would say that we are ready anytime after today."

"The sooner the better, I'll tell Heitman that the day after tomorrow will work for me," Becker said. "That should give us plenty of time to make preparations. Hartman says they are going to get there by twelve. I want our people there by eight. We need plenty of time to get that large a contingency force in place. You should spend the rest of the day with the GCU soldiers going over their role in this thing," Becker went on. "I suggest that you split the group into two units. Have one unit on the second floor in that storage area or the loft, and the other unit downstairs in the storage room. The building key will not get the SS into the storage rooms, so hopefully they won't make an effort to check them out. The loft is not locked, so maybe we should stick to the storage areas. And captain, you also need to have some of your field agents track the movements of the SS officers and radio ahead to you and the lieutenant when they leave the city so you can prepare for their arrival. After they get there, your men are going to be cooped up in those storage rooms for a couple of hours before we arrive. Will that be a problem?" Becker asked.

"No colonel, it will not be a problem for us. We had an extra set of keys made after we went to the lodge, and our surveillance crew will install listening devices in the main entrance and adjoining rooms and a monitor in both storage rooms. There will also be a monitor in the armored vehicles so that those crews will be alerted when to move in. We will wait for your signal before deploying the unit unless something happens that would trigger a quicker response. Incidentally, what will the signal be?" Schwarz asked.

"I will give the order, 'Captain Schwarz, deploy your forces.' That should fit right in. Now what kind of signal do we use for the outside force, captain?"

"Colonel, we have a portable blast horn, but we are also installing a horn on the side of the building facing the wooded area. You can hear those things in Stuttgart, they are so loud. A switch will be installed on the front wall on the left side of the big window. All you have to do is push the button, so it might be wise to locate yourself close to that area."

"Captain, it sounds like you have everything covered. Good job," Becker said.

"Thank you, sir. What about Sara? Does she know anything?" Schwarz asked. "She has been acting really curious about what we have been doing the last couple of days."

"No, she doesn't, and I want to keep it that way," Becker replied. "It's too dangerous, and there really is not much she can do."

"Do you think that her not being there will raise any suspicion?" Schwarz asked.

"No, it shouldn't. As long as I show up, they couldn't care less about who I'm with," Becker said.

Their conversation was interrupted by Berta. "Colonel," she said, "there is a Colonel Heitman on the phone. Shall I put him through?"

"Yes, Berta. Hold on a minute, captain, while I take this call. This is probably the one.

"Hello, Colonel Heitman, what can I do for you?" Becker asked. He paused while Heitman spoke, then said, "Yes, I am pretty much up to date on Rohm. ... I agree, we do need to coordinate our efforts, and I am willing to meet with you. ... No, I can't meet today. Hold a minute and let me check the schedule." After a brief pause, Becker said, "Okay, it looks like the day after tomorrow will work for me. How about two o'clock Thursday afternoon? ... Where shall we meet? ... I have heard of the von Turpin Lodge, but I'm not that familiar with it. No problem, my driver will know how to get there. Thank you and I look forward to our meeting. Goodbye" Becker added.

"Captain, guess what" Becker said. "I have just been invited to attend a meeting with our good friends at the SS, and out of sheer gratitude, I accepted."

"Yes sir. I think you made a good decision," Schwarz answered.

"Captain, we have a lot of work to do between now and Thursday, so let's get to it."

The next day was fairly uneventful. Sara popped in several times to ask Becker what was going on. She did the same with Schwarz, but all to no avail. She learned nothing.

Chapter Twenty

Thursday morning rolled around, and the captain and the GCU departed at 7:30 AM for the lodge. Later that morning, Sara asked the colonel about the daily agenda.

"If you must know, miss nosy, I have a meeting with Colonel Heitman and the SS at two this afternoon. I would take you with me, but it is supposed to be confidential and limited only to senior officials."

"I thought something was going on behind my back," she said. "Do you think it is safe for you to be meeting with those people?"

"No, Sara, it probably is not safe without you being with me to take a bullet, but the reality is that it is a meeting that I have to attend, so I am going to leave you in charge of the office."

"Oh, big deal, does that mean I can order Berta around? And where is the captain?" she asked.

"The captain has already gone and is making the necessary

preparations for the meeting. And I know your next question is going to be, 'Where is the meeting?' The meeting is going to take place at the von Turpin Lodge."

"I know where that is, but why go way out there for a meeting?" she asked.

"The fresh air will be good for us. I will fill you in on the meeting when we get back."

"I thought it was highly confidential and only senior officials," she said.

"At the SS, they think it is highly confidential. I guess they don't know that I tell you everything, so let's just keep it that way, okay? Sergeant Heinz has already been briefed on where we are going and is to pick me up at one fifteen, so you can make sure he is reminded."

"Yes sir. Please be careful, will you?" Sara said.

"As always, and pray for me while I'm gone."

She nodded and blew him a kiss as she left the room.

Sergeant Heinz was on time and had Lieutenant Mench with him, and they departed for the lodge. Becker discussed the operation with the two men on the way over, even though they had already been thoroughly briefed by Captain Schwarz. The forty-five-minute drive would put them there right at two. Any other time, Becker would deliberately arrive late for such a meeting, but today was different. He wanted to be on time so as not to disrupt any part of the plan.

When they arrived, Heinz turned the Mercedes into the drive leading up to the lodge and parked in front of the main entrance. Becker noted that one other automobile was parked, which was expected. That car belonged to the hosts, no doubt.

Becker was met at the entrance by both Colonel Heitman and Colonel Hartman. "Good afternoon, Colonel Becker. It was gracious of you to accept our invitation on such short notice. I don't see Captain Schwarz," Heitman said with a questioning look, "or that lovely assistant of yours."

"No, the captain is on another assignment, and Mrs. Klein is in charge of the office. I would like for you to meet my new aide, Lieutenant Albert Mench."

Suddenly the double doors leading further into the lodge opened, and about a dozen SS troops entered the room with guns drawn. Sergeant Heinz was seized and disarmed.

"What the hell is going on here?" Colonel Becker demanded.

"Relax, Colonel Becker," Hartman ordered. "We are placing you under arrest, colonel, for treason and plotting against the state. You and the lieutenant need to hand over your weapons."

"Are you serious?" exclaimed Becker.

"I am very serious Colonel Becker, the charade is over. Out of respect for your previous service to Germany, we are going to allow you to do the honorable thing for an officer of your rank and take your own life. Here is your pistol, but please don't try to do something foolish, or your aide and the sergeant will be shot," advised Heitman.

"Then you leave me no choice," the colonel said as he took his luger and pointed it at his temple and pulled the trigger. There was a click, and then another click, and the colonel lowered the gun to his side and said, "Well, assholes, I guess it's just not my time." He walked over to the window and said to Hartman and Heitman, "Look outside." He pushed the button for the outside horn, and it went off with an ear-splitting sound. Suddenly the armed troops came out of the wooded area and flooded the parking lot in formation.

The look on the faces of the two SS colonels said it all. Their knees buckled at the sight of the large complement of combat troops assembled outside. "Oh, my God, what have we done?" muttered Heitman. A couple of moments later, machine gun fire erupted from outside the back room's double doors, and the balcony filled with heavily armed troops from the GCU.

"Drop your weapons and place your hands in the air," ordered Captain Schwarz as he descended the stairs from the balcony.

The SS troops dropped their weapons and raised their hands.

"All of you SS people move against the wall and keep your hands where we can see them," ordered Captain Schwarz.

"Colonel Heitman and Colonel Hartman, step forward," Becker's voiced boomed. "Now it is you two traitors that I am placing under arrest for attempting the assassination of a senior Gestapo official."

The SS colonels, obviously in shock, stepped forward.

"Gentlemen, since neither of you are senior officers of the *Reichswehr*, I am unable to offer you the same option that you offered me, and that is to allow you to take your own lives. You are not entitled to that honor, and therefore it is my duty to order you outside, where you will face a firing squad. Do you have any last words?" Becker asked the two men.

Hartman started sobbing. "Colonel Becker, this is a big misunderstanding. This was just a prank that Heitman thought up. I plead with you not to take it seriously. I ask for your forgiveness, sir. Please do not make my wife a widow and my children fatherless."

Heitman was stoic. He shed a tear or two but otherwise just stood erect. He knew that he had gambled and lost, and mercy would not be forthcoming.

"Hartman, get up off your knees and act like a man," Becker ordered. "Sergeant Mauch, escort these two traitors out to the courtyard and carry out the sentence that I have imposed on them under the military rules of war."

Sergeant Mauch and ten of his troops marched the two outside to face their fate.

"Captain Schwarz, do you have any casualties?" asked Becker.

"No, sir, we did not suffer any casualties. There are four SS men dead in the hall outside of this room and one SS officer gravely wounded."

"Thank you, captain. Now listen up, SS troops. You are witnesses to an insurrection as well as an attempt on the life of a senior Gestapo official. Those of you who are willing to testify to those facts, raise your hands. Those who are not, step forward so that you can join your commanding officers outside to face a firing squad." All of the hands in the room shot up at once. "I see all hands raised and no one stepping forward, therefore, you will all be taken to Gestapo headquarters to make a sworn statement. If there are no further incidents, you will be released to return to your unit. Are there any questions?" Becker asked. "If not, then Lieutenant Mench, have these men escorted out and loaded on a truck for transport to headquarters."

"Yes sir, you gave me quite a scare back there when you raised the pistol to your head and pulled the trigger. I thought for sure that you were a goner," said Mench.

"Mench, as you may have guessed, I unloaded the weapon before I left headquarters."

From outside the command, they heard the order, "Ready, aim, fire," and a burst of gunfire erupted. A few minutes later, the same process was repeated. Hartman's operation had failed, and so ended the careers and lives of Dirk Hartman and Horst Heitman.

"Captain, as soon as the medics arrive, have your men assist them in getting the wounded and deceased out of here, and have all the units report back to their base," ordered Becker. "Notify the appropriate officials of the action that took place here today and report back to headquarters."

"Yes, sir," Schwarz replied with a salute.

"I will speak to the *Reichswehr* troops outside and then report to the minister. I will then head back to headquarters," Said Becker. He then went out to address the assembled troops.

As he approached the assembly, the lieutenant shouted, "Attention. Colonel Becker will make a brief statement." The group stood at attention.

"I would like to compliment you men on the exemplary manner in which you performed your duty here today," the colonel said. "You are a credit to the fatherland. You are hereby ordered to return to regular duty. Heil Hitler."

Becker thanked his GCU for an outstanding performance and then got into the Mercedes and instructed Heinz to drive to Minister Goring's office. He arrived there at four o'clock; just two hours after the failed ambush attempt had started.

The colonel was admitted to the minister's office as soon as the office could be cleared of guests.

"Mr. Minister, I have some grave news to report. This afternoon at approximately two o'clock I arrived at the von Turpin Lodge, where I had been invited to attend a meeting with two senior SS officers to supposedly discuss the Rohm plan. After entering the building, I was placed under arrest by SS Colonels Hartman and Heitman and falsely accused of committing crimes against the state. Fortunately, I had been warned that such treachery was waiting for me, and I had made adequate preparation, the details of which I will supply in a written report. Our GCU had been secreted in a storage area of the building, and one hundred *Reichswehr* combat troops were outside, hidden in the wooded area adjacent to the main building. When an alarm was sounded, our unit overpowered the SS troops that were there to carry out my arrest. There was an outbreak of gunfire, and as a result, four SS troops were killed and one wounded. Our forces suffered no casualties. After we took control of the situation, the two commanders and perpetrators of the ambush were taken outside and shot as war criminals. As soon as the insurrection ended, I came directly here to give you this report. There are about ten SS troops that have been taken to Gestapo headquarters to give statements confirming what I have just reported to you. That is my report to you, Herr Minister," Becker concluded.

"Thank you, colonel. This is, of course, a very serious matter and I will have to deal with it. Himmler is going to be furious and will take the matter straight to the *fuhrer*. Under the circumstances, you acted appropriately, and I will stand behind you on this. I know Himmler was behind the ambush, but I can't prove that so I will not bring it up. The news media will no doubt make this a big story, so I would suggest that you refrain from making any statements other than a generic explanation that an insurrection was put down. I will have Herr Goebbels handle the press. You have probably put yourself at the top of Himmler's hit list, but evidently you were already on there, so moving up to the top will not change much. Then again, he may have more respect for you now, and the opposite could happen. I will try to get to the *fuhrer* before Himmler does and have the *fuhrer* prepared. Thank you for coming by. You handled that situation just as I thought you would under the circumstances."

"Thank you, sir. If you will excuse me, I must get back to headquarters," Becker said as he saluted. "Heil Hitler."

Becker returned to Gestapo headquarters to talk to his staff. "It is getting a little late, and I am extremely tired, so I think we should wait until tomorrow morning to review today's actions" he told his staff. "We will also have a better understanding of what the fallout is going to be. There may be repercussions."

Sara stayed behind to console the colonel and express her feelings about what had happened. She was upset, and Becker told her to go home and get some rest and that they would discuss the whole thing the next morning.

The next morning the newspaper headline was, "Two Senior

SS Officers Dead After Dispute With Gestapo." The story went on to say, "A deadly skirmish that was believed to be an attempt to eliminate a powerful Gestapo officer resulted in the execution of two SS officers at the von Turpin Lodge yesterday afternoon. The two dead officers, executed by firing squad, were identified as SS Colonel Dirk Hartman and SS Colonel Horst Heitman.

"Their intended victim was Senior Colonel Konrad Becker of the Gestapo. Sources say that Colonel Becker was lured to the Lodge on the pretense of a meeting to discuss a joint SS-Gestapo venture. The plot unraveled because Gestapo agents discovered it and positioned necessary security forces at the lodge without the knowledge of the SS. Four SS support troops also died in the fray, and one was seriously wounded. The SS force was no match for the special GCU of the Gestapo and the 100-man force of a *Reichswehr* combat unit. The *Reich* minister of Propaganda further stated that, although the incident was highly regrettable, Colonel Becker and Gestapo personnel acted properly, and there would be no further investigation into the matter. When reached by reporters, Colonel Becker praised the brave and courageous efforts of his men and stated that he would have no further comment. SS officers who survived the battle confirmed the Gestapo's version of the incident. SS *Reichsfuhrer* Himmler was unavailable for comment but was said to be unhappy over the turn of events."

Chapter Twenty-One

At Gestapo headquarters, Becker called in his staff. "I assume you all know by now what happened out at the lodge yesterday. Captain, I want to thank you again for the way you and your men performed under combat-like conditions. The operation was carried out with precision, and I would be hard put to find any flaws in its execution. And Sara, I know you are disappointed because we conducted this operation without you. I just felt that it would be too dangerous, and I did not want to take a chance that you might get hurt."

"Thank you, sir. I am thankful that you were not injured and everything turned out like it did," Sara said.

"Thank you, colonel, for the compliments," Schwarz remarked. "Our men did a splendid job, and I think we showed the SS and the SA that they can't mess with the Gestapo."

"Yeah, that's true, but this thing is not over by a long shot," Becker said. "We stepped on some powerful toes, and they are going to come after us. Maybe not now, since they have to deal with Rohm, but after that, well, look out. I need to call Richter and thank him. He has been a big help to us."

"Oh, and guess who called me this morning?" Sara asked. Without waiting for a reply, she continued, "My soon to be ex-husband. He is scared silly and, for a change, was acting very nice. He was shook up over Hartman, and he said that Donst is losing it. He thinks that he is next and doesn't know what to do. Karl said both he and Donst regret what they did and would like to apologize."

"Neither of those nitwits are worth the lead it would take to kill them, but maybe they will decide to stay out of my way," Becker said. "I do regret that we had to take the lives of those four SS men. They were just following orders, but we had no choice. Someone, maybe you Sara, should contact their families and reassure them that it was in the line of duty, and that their loved ones bear no stigma for taking part in the operation."

"Yes sir, I will, but I think it would help the families if Captain Schwarz went with me," Sara said.

"All right, captain, you go with her."

After the meeting ended, Becker thought about his future with the Gestapo and his mission. It was time to start thinking about an exit plan, something he had given very little attention to up until now. He would have to give it some serious thought because the situation was now a ticking time bomb. He had just had a close call, and if not for the listening devices that had been planted, he most likely would be a dead man.

And what should he do about Sara? This really was a tough question because he now realized how attached he had become to her. He could get on a train and pretend to take a vacation to many cities outside Germany, and return to the United States without any problem. At least, that was the case for the time being. That could change without warning if the authorities were to step in and stop him for whatever reason they decided on. Staying in Germany, he was more or less in the hands of Goring, up to a certain point. The more Becker thought about it, the more he could see a pattern that did not bode well for him. Hitler's dictatorial powers were growing by the day. And so was the march to war. The Versailles Treaty was being ignored, and the military buildup was going into full swing. All of these things would be factors in making a decision about what course of action he should take. He would sleep on it, he thought.

To get his mind off of the problem, he told Sara that he would pick her up at seven and take her out to dinner. That suited her just fine, after all she was feeling a little neglected—or maybe a whole lot neglected—lately.

"Don't you look nice tonight," he said as he picked her up at a little after seven that evening.

"I have to look nice for my hero, especially since you have not been paying me enough attention these days," she answered.

"How about we go to the *Kaiserhoff* for dinner and dancing? Would you like that?" he asked.

"That would be wonderful. I am all yours," she said.

Heinz dropped them off in front of the hotel. As he was leaving to park the car, Becker gave him an unusual order. "Sergeant Heinz, why don't you just wait outside for us this time? I don't think I will need any protection here, especially in light of what happened at the lodge."

"Yes, sir, I will be here if you need me," Heinz replied.

The doorman signaled for the bell captain to escort the colonel and his lady to the restaurant, where they were seated. The *Kaiserhoff* was a favorite hangout for Nazi notables, and so it was no surprise that the colonel was recognized as he was being seated. All prominent Nazi officials now knew of Colonel Konrad Becker. Recent events had catapulted him to something of a national celebrity, something he did not want. He remarked to Sara that he guessed he was going to have to get used to the admiring glances he was getting from the important patrons having dinner. Quite a few of them got up and came over to say hello, in some cases introducing themselves. They were all complimentary and expressed their support for him after his recent ordeal.

When everything settled down, Becker leaned over to Sara and said, "Maybe we should have gone to some quiet little place where we could have more privacy."

"This is fine and you deserve all of the tributes you are getting," Sara replied. "I love it, and I am so proud of you. We can have plenty of privacy when we get home. For now, let's enjoy the moment."

When they finished their dinner, Becker signaled the waiter for the check. A few minutes later, the head waiter appeared and told Becker that there would be no charge, compliments of the hotel. After thanking the waiter, Becker and Sara went up to the club for some dancing. After dancing a few numbers, the pair left the hotel and returned to the *Tiergarten*.

Things seemed to settle down for the next few days, and then the word came down that the Rohm purge was set. The *fuhrer* himself would lead the charge, called "Operation Hummingbird," and better known as the "Night of the Long Knives." The purge was not limited to the elimination of Rohm. It would include a number of prominent officials and former officials.

The *fuhrer* and his party flew into Munich early one morning in late June. They assembled a large force of SS and police officers there and drove to *Bad Wiessee*, a town on Lake Tegernsee, south of Munich, where Rohm and some of his associates were having a holiday at a hotel. After arriving, the *fuhrer* placed Rohm and other high-ranking SA officials under arrest. Rohm was taken to Munich, where he would later be shot after turning down the opportunity to take his own life. When the purge finally ended, almost 100 people had been killed. Hitler would later proclaim that he had acted to protect the German people from treasonous acts, and that the ringleaders had been executed. Colonel Becker played no role in the operation, and after it was over, he was relieved that he hadn't been involved. He also was aware that his lack of participation could be an ominous sign for his future.

Chapter Twenty-Two

About a week after the purge, Becker received a call from Goring's office requesting that he report to the minister. He complied with the request and was promptly ushered into Goring's office.

"Good morning, colonel," Goring said. "How are things going at headquarters?"

"Good morning, sir. Everything is going well with us. We have been busy cracking a few heads of some of the roaming thugs from the SS and SA."

"Colonel, that is what I want to talk to you about this morning. As you know, Himmler and his henchman have been working tirelessly to take over the Gestapo. I fought them off as long as I could, but Himmler has convinced the *fuhrer* that the Gestapo and all police should be under one umbrella, and that Himmler should be over all police activities. I am sorry to have to tell you this, but the *fuhrer* has made his decision. I have discussed your situation with Himmler, and he has agreed for you to stay on. He will, however, be bringing in his own people, and quite frankly, I am repulsed by some of them."

"Yes, I have met some of them," Becker replied. "They do have a ruthless reputation, and there is no doubt that I am not held in very high esteem by Himmler."

"Well, colonel, I would like for you to stay where you are because I need a presence over there. I have been assured that you will be protected. I have also been chosen by the *fuhrer* to take over the *Luftwaffe(German air force)*. I would be also happy if you chose to join me there."

"I don't know about that, Herr Minister," Becker answered. "I know nothing of flying, and I would be placing myself in a position of not knowing my job. I have spent almost my entire military career in the intelligence field. I prefer to stay there, but let me think about it."

"Of course colonel, by all means think about it. If you like, I can find a place for you in some other agency, or you can go back to the *Reichswehr*. Again, I would ask you to consider staying where you are."

"I will give it some thought, Herr Minister, and get back to you. How much time do we have before this takes place?" Becker asked.

"Colonel, I would say we are looking at maybe a couple of months, a month at least, before there can be an orderly transition. So we have some time. There is no urgency. Just let me know what you want to do," Goring said.

"Yes Herr Minister. I'm sure we can come up with something suitable. I will call you as soon as possible. Meantime, I want to thank you for giving me this opportunity to serve the fatherland, and also for the magnificent support that you have given me in carrying out my duties. Heil Hitler."

On the way back to Gestapo headquarters, Becker felt a sense of urgency. This was all happening too soon. Yes, he had thought about contingency plans for the end of his spy mission recently, but now it was a reality. Then it dawned on him. Why not return to the Foreign Service as a military attaché? Goring could arrange it. And why not throw in the idea of being sent back to America, where he could work as an espionage agent for Germany? Why hadn't he thought of that sooner? His superiors would be stupid not to buy into the idea. He spoke fluent English. He was already familiar with the country. The *fuhrer* fully expected that the United States would become an enemy of Nazi Germany. This would be the perfect way out. Also, it still would leave him in an important position to provide valuable information to the United States about German espionage activities.

Should he talk to Sara about it? No, not yet, anyway. Maybe it would be best to get it set up and approved before he discussed it with anyone, even Sara. By the time he got back to the office, his mind was made up. He was going to do it. He would run it by Goring the next day. He did feel obligated to tell Sara and the captain about the upcoming changes since they would be directly affected. As he went into his office, he told Berta to ask Captain Schwarz and Sara to report to his office. A few minutes later, Sara and the captain came into the office.

"Have a seat. I have something I need to tell both of you," Becker said. "I have news, and unfortunately, it is not good. This is confidential, and you are not to discuss it with anyone. The Gestapo is going to be placed under the direction of Heinrich Himmler. We don't know exactly when the actual transfer will take place, but it should be within the next two months," Becker said.

"Oh, God, no," Sara said with tears streaming down her cheeks. "What is going to happen to us?"

"I don't know yet for sure," Becker answered. "I just left Goring's office, and he informed me about the move. He also assured me that he had discussed my status with Himmler, and Himmler agreed that I could stay on if I so desired. Goring is going to become head of the *Luftwaffe*, and he offered me a position there, which I quickly rejected. I can arrange for both of you to stay on, but I can't promise anything after that," Becker went on. "As for myself, I would find it very difficult to work for Himmler and his henchmen. I will meet with Goring again tomorrow and explore some other options. Meanwhile, you are to keep this information to yourselves. Not even Berta can know. I'm sure Diels has been informed, and he will be replaced for sure."

"Colonel, I want to say what an honor it has been for me to work for you. If you leave, then I want to leave also," said Captain Schwarz. "I would prefer to return to the *Reichswehr*, if that is possible."

"I am sure that I can arrange that, Kurt," Becker assured him.

"What about me?" Sara asked. "What is going to happen to me? I can't stay here."

"Sara, don't worry. I will see to it that you are taken care of, I promise." He could see that Sara was taking it hard. She excused herself and left the room in tears.

"Colonel, I'm worried about Sara," Schwarz said. "You and this job are her life now."

"Yeah, why don't you go and talk to her, captain? See if you can calm her down and tell her not to worry, that everything will work out. And tell Berta that everything is okay, that I just had to get on to Sara for something, and that she will get over it. I don't want the whole damn office to be wondering what the hell is going on."

"Yes, sir," the captain replied as he left the office.

Later that evening, Becker stopped by Sara's apartment to check on her. When she opened the door, she grabbed him around the neck and started crying.

"Look, Sara, will you please cut it out and pull yourself together? I told you that things are going to be all right. Did the captain talk to you?" he asked.

"Yes, he did. He told me that everything was going to be okay, but I know it's not. I know he just told me that to console me. Konrad, I am in total shock. I am not worried about that damn job. It's you that I am worried about. I can't stand the thought of not being with you every day, or worse, not being with you at all. I'm sorry if I am being a baby, but I can't help it."

"Sara, nobody said anything about you not being with me. I told you that I was going to work it out. Now stop that bawling and get me a beer."

Becker stayed with Sara for about an hour and finally got her to calm down. He gave her something that would make her sleep and put her to bed.

The next day Becker called Goring's office to make an appointment to see the minister. He was told that he could come right over.

"Good morning, Herr Minister. I have something that I need to talk to you about," Becker said.

"Good morning, colonel. I hope you have made a decision to remain with the Gestapo."

"No, Herr Minister, but I do have a solution that would satisfy all concerned and also best serve the interest of the fatherland. I would like to serve my country as an espionage agent. As you may remember, I was once the military attaché for our embassy in America. I would like to return as military attaché and be assigned the same duties at the embassy in Washington. I speak fluent English, and this would afford us an excellent opportunity to gather information on the United States that would be advantageous to Germany."

"You mean become a spy?" Goring said with a look of

astonishment. "Colonel, you may have something there," he said, his tone changing. "I hate to lose you at the Gestapo, but we are in desperate need of sources in the United States that can provide us with information. There is no doubt that the *fuhrer* will embrace the idea. If that is what you want, it can easily be arranged. You know we expect someday to be at war with the United States, and we can use all of the secret information that we can get. At present we have some agents in America, but none on such a high level. I can make this happen. All we need do is to move you over to Ausland SD, our sister agency of the Gestapo. At present, they are still under my command but will no doubt be taken over by Himmler when he assumes command of the Gestapo. Another option we have is to move you to Abwehr. Abwehr, as you know, is the intelligence division of the Ministry of Defense and reports to the army *Oberkommando der Wehrmacht* (Commander of the Army). We can exercise that option at a later date, however. For the time being, it will be much simpler for me to just assign you to Ausland SD (security service of the SS) and notify the Foreign Ministry that you are being assigned to the embassy in Washington.

"Later we can move you to the Abwehr," Goring continued. "Meantime, you should speak to General Schellenberg to consult with him on the move to Ausland SD. Also, I want to remind you that anytime you want to return to Germany, we will have a place for you. How soon can you be ready to make this move, colonel?"

"There is nothing holding me back, so I can be ready to go as soon as I can tie up some loose ends," Becker answered. "We can go ahead with the transfer immediately. One more request, Herr Minister. I would like to take Sara Klein with me as my assistant at the embassy."

"Colonel, I knew you had a yen for that pretty young woman. Yes, I think she would be a big help to you. Does she like the idea of being a Mata Hari?" Goring said with a chuckle. "I will be happy to arrange for her transfer as well."

"Thank you, Herr Minister," Becker said.

"Good. It's done, and I wish you and that beautiful young lady well in your new assignment. Is there anything else I can do for you?" Goring asked.

"Yes, there is one more thing. My aide, Captain Kurt Schwarz, would like to return to duty with the *Reichswehr*. He is an outstanding officer and has performed his duties with the Gestapo brilliantly."

"Of course that can be arranged. I am familiar with his work with you. Quite frankly, I wouldn't mind having him serve on my staff at the *Luftwaffe*. And colonel, don't tell me he knows nothing about airplanes, because he won't be flying planes as a member of my staff. If he is interested, have him contact my secretary, and she can make arrangements for him to meet with one of my senior aides."

"Thank you, Herr Minister. Heil Hitler."

On the way back to the office, euphoria swept over Becker. He couldn't believe his good fortune. What more could he want? Everything was falling into place. He had definitely made up his mind about Sara. He was going to have her at last. There was no doubt in his mind that when he broke the news to her, she would be the happiest woman in the world.

When he arrived at the office, he decided speak to Sara and the captain separately. He called for the captain first. Needless to say, the captain was almost speechless when Becker told him that he might become a member of Goring's staff at *Luftwaffe*. This was an opportunity of a lifetime, and Schwarz quickly embraced the idea. Becker told him to call Goring's secretary to make an appointment. Schwarz profusely thanked the colonel and expressed his undying loyalty.

Next the colonel sent for Sara. "Come in and sit down, Sara, I have some news for you."

"I hope it's as good as what Kurt must have gotten. He left your office with a grin on his face a mile wide," she said.

"We will see. As for me, I am being transferred to the Ausland SD and will be assigned to the German Embassy in the United States," Becker said.

"Oh, no," Sara said as her shoulders slumped over. "You have just placed a dagger in my heart."

"Just hold it for a minute. What if I told you that you can go with me?"

"Ohhhhhh," she screamed. "Do you really mean it? Yes, yes, oh, yes, I will go."

"I mean it," he said. "Everything has been approved by the minister, and the paperwork is being done this very minute."

"Oh, Konrad," she said as she jumped into Becker's lap and flung her arms around his neck. "Pinch me to make sure I am not dreaming."

"I guess I'll let you sit here for a minute since office protocol is no longer a factor. This thing is going to happen immediately, so how long will it take for you to wrap up your business and be ready to go?"

"My divorce will be granted next week, and I can be packed and ready to go before that."

"What about you parents?" he asked "What will they think?"

"I don't know, and I don't care. I will take care of it, so don't worry about them. What should I take with me?" Sara asked.

"Take your clothes and personal effects. You should pack most of your belongings in trunks and take a suitcase with things you will need in transit," Becker said. "I would make you get off of me, but what the hell; we are going to be leaving here soon. What day next week is the divorce hearing?"

"Oh, so you are finally showing some interest in my marital status," she answered. "My hearing is set for Monday, and then I will be a free woman. Konrad, you have made me so happy. I am ready to go anywhere in the world with you. I am so excited. Can I tell anybody?"

"Only your parents until I make an announcement at the office. Now you can get off my lap and get back to work before you lose your job."

She gave him a kiss and floated out of the office on a cloud.

The appearance would be that Becker would be working for the foreign minister, but in truth, he would be reporting back to the Ausland-SD, headed up by General Schellenberg.

Later that evening, he asked Sara again about her parents. "What about your folks? When are you going to tell them?" he asked.

"I need to talk to you about that, but I will do it later," she said. "Right now all I can think about is going to America. Tell me what it's like."

"I'll tell you on the way over there," he said. He had some other things to tell her, but not before they had landed in the United States. He felt guilty about not telling her who he really was, but it would have to wait until they were safely in the United States. And even then he wondered how much she needed to know and how would she react when she found out that he was Jewish. That really worried him because he knew how much the Nazis hated the Jews and wondered how deep those feelings were among the general population. He would have to wait and see. Tonight would be time for a celebration. He suggested that they call Captain Schwarz to come over and join them at his apartment and bring his new girlfriend. He knew that the captain and Lenore were growing closer.

That evening, the captain and Lenore showed up at Becker's apartment and were greeted by Sara, who was riding high.

Becker revealed the new plan, and they all joined in a toast to the future.

The next morning Becker called all of the staff together and told them that he would be leaving for a new post and wished them all well.

On Monday, a delirious Sara called Becker and told him that the divorce had been granted and that she was a free woman. She also made it plain that the two of them would celebrate her new status that evening at her place.

"What can I say?" said Becker.

"You don't have to say anything, just be there," she said.

The time for talking had passed. Becker knew that he was in for an evening of pleasure and braced himself for the explosion of pent-up emotions that had built up for both of them. It turned out to be a night to remember and reinforced his belief that he had finally found the love of his life.

Chapter Twenty-Three

A week later, Colonel Konrad Becker and the recently divorced Sara Klein traveled to Bremenhaven, where they boarded the passenger liner TS Bremen and set sail for America. Although the couple had adjoining state rooms, they spent most of their time in Becker's room when not availing themselves of the many services provided first-class travelers on a luxury liner. Needless to say, it was a trip that would be the envy of most honeymooners. They arrived in New York City five days later, and from there, they traveled by train to Washington, where they were met and given a royal welcome by the German consulate.

It had been more than two years since Becker first landed in Freidrichshafen, Germany, in 1931 and began his life as a secret agent of the United States. Now the Nazis thought that he was a secret agent for Germany.

The first order of business upon returning to Washington was to report to the State Department officials to apprise them of his new status. The next step would be to secure living accommodations. The embassy provided the military attaché living quarters, but there would be no such living quarters for Sara Klein, who would be an employee of the Foreign Service. She would, however, be entitled to an allowance for living expenses. Becker decided that for the first few days they would stay at the Mayflower while looking for a permanent place for Sara to stay. Since Becker would be spending most of his off-duty time with Sara, they decided to rent a more upscale residence for her that would meet both of their needs.

State Department officials were delighted with the new assignment of their spy, and they arranged for the secret communications necessary to carry out the program.

Later that evening Becker could tell that something was bothering Sara, and she finally said she needed to talk about something. "Konrad, there has been something bothering me for some time. I have been afraid to tell you because I am afraid after I tell you, you won't love me anymore."

"Nonsense, what are you talking about?" he asked.

"Do you remember that I told you that I left home when I was very young to get away from my parents?" she asked.

"Yes, I remember, why?"

"That was not really true. My parents were wonderful people, and I loved them very much. The real reason I left home was to get away from the taunts and the mean treatment we were getting both at home and my school."

"Wait a minute, Sara. I don't care why you left home," he replied.

"Let me finish," she said. "I have got to get this off of my chest. Do you see this beautiful blond hair? Well, I am not a true blonde. I changed the color of my hair to hide who I was. My maiden name was Goldstein. Do you know what that means? My father was Jewish.

"Both of my parents advised me to leave home and change my name so that I would not be a victim of the verbal abuse that I was receiving at school and possible future physical abuse. They were convinced that things would only get worse for me as the Nazi party continued to grow. I was told that not even my looks would protect me from the hatred," she went on. "My father gave me some money, and, with one suitcase filled with everything I owned, I took the train to Berlin and changed my name to Sara Engel. I was only seventeen years old at the time. I got a job as a waitress at a beer hall and did quite well with my tips and salary. It was there that I met Karl Klein. He was charming and had a good job with the government. He asked me to marry him, and I decided that this was my best chance to become somebody, so I said yes.

"Then you came along," she said, and now you know my life story. You are the only man that I have ever loved, and I had to tell you the truth about my life. I could never lie to or deceive you."

"Sara, I have always dreamed of finding and falling in love with a girl with a Jewish father. You have made my dream come true."

She burst into tears as she put her arms around his neck. He still had a story to tell her, but it could wait. Nothing could spoil this moment that they shared together.